On Wings of an Avalanche

By
C.D. Gill

C.D. Gill

Cover Design: Seedlings Design Studio, LLC

www.cdgill.com

To my British pilot and best adventure partner:

May the wind be smooth beneath your wings,
May the sun warm your face wherever you roam,
May the sky make all of your dreams come true,
And may your heart always lead you home.

Chapter 1

Mali, Africa
August 2008

Her moral and ethical compass pointed in two directions—life or death. Dr. Madison Cote counted life as success and death as failure. Both earned her equal respect. But when it came to sustaining life, she did whatever was required. Already during her surgeries today, she'd used unconventional methods to avert several potential crises, methods that would raise a hospital board's eyebrows. But the red tape didn't extend to her Malian bush hospital. And she liked it that way.

For the third time in one minute, Madison wiped the sweat droplets trickling down her clenched jaw. A solar-powered fan teased her with a hint of a breeze, offering more relief than sitting uphill from the Niger did. The fan's effectiveness tripled when the mosquito net encircling her operating table wasn't in the way. But she didn't have time to cool off, since the generator would turn off at dusk and she had several more patients to get through before then.

She couldn't begrudge the simplicity of it all— not when so much need found its way through the heavy wooden doors each day. The average age of her patients was twelve. She diagnosed everything from rabies to typhoid fever and performed general operations when there was an anesthetist on hand. Every case fell to her. These kids would lead the country and their homes and her job was to make sure they lived long enough to change their world. She'd grown to love the contented exhaustion and the satisfaction of knowing she made a difference.

This patient, a ten-year-old boy, had carried a five-pound mass in his abdomen for the better part of three years. Locals thought perhaps he was a girl with male anatomy and his swollen abdomen was actually a pregnancy. Those theories proved untrue when he didn't deliver after nine months. By some small miracle, word had spread to his village of a western doctor performing surgeries to rescue people from death's eager clutches.

Despite March's blistering heat, the brave little boy walked for four days in shredded shoes and collapsed a half mile from the hospital's door. Today's procedure was the boy's reward for his patience and endurance. And not a moment too

4

soon. The putrid smell of infection had assaulted her nose as soon as she cut him open. She held her breath to keep from gagging.

The lamp humming overhead spotlighted her work and soothed her nerves with its steady confidence. With every trusting face that relaxed under the anesthesia, the reality that no one was around to fix her mistakes sunk a little deeper in her psyche. Her surgical execution needed to be flawless every time or children died and there was no one to blame but herself. After one last swipe of her scalpel, she handed her tool to her hovering surgical assistant Konji and lifted the mass out with a grunt.

The door burst open, slamming against the brick wall. The thud jolted Madison's brain. Her body jerked, causing her fingers to squeeze the mass in response. She glanced over as Ina rushed in, her eyes wide over her mask.

"Ina, you know better than to endanger our patient like that."

"Doctor, General Abdou Karim is outside demanding you give his son Amadou a kidney transplant." Ina's heaving chest betrayed the steadiness of her voice.

Kidney transplant? Not in this country. Madison set the mass on the tray and dropped it in a bag marked for disposal. General Karim wasn't the first person to demand immediate medical attention. The line of patients waiting for her every day included at least two or three who insisted their minor cases were emergencies.

"I'll have to get to him in a little bit. Our OR schedule is packed."

"Doctor, he surrounded our building with armed men. You do it now or we all die." Ina's tone left no question she'd been threatened.

That was a first. Her stomach dropped to her knees. Another few months left until she fulfilled Dr. Cavine's will stipulations and she'd be free of such threats on her life.

Madison shook her head. "We're going to have to dissuade him. We don't have the ability to do a transplant in our little hospital, Ina." The outdated donated equipment surrounding them was proof enough of that.

"He already found a match for his son, Doctor. He brought a donor with him that he says is a tissue and blood type match."

Madison blinked as the jaw of her mind clattered to the floor. Had Ina said what she thought she said?

"I don't want to know how that happened." The tissue-match process was more advanced than the most of the hospitals in Bamako could do. "Who told him it was a kidney problem? Who made him believe we could perform a surgery of that significance in our facilities?"

Ina shrugged her slight shoulders. "He said a western doctor told him."

Her thanks to that weasel of a doctor would be a punch in the nose. Or worse. The nerve of him to get a warlord's hopes up and potentially get her killed.

Madison shook her head again. The sweat-soaked end of her ponytail slapped her neck like a whip. "Symptoms?"

"Pain in his abdomen, nausea, loss of appetite, and fever."

The symptoms were consistent with kidney failure but could also be any number of things. Like food poisoning. Or General Karim testing her.

With her bloodied gloves held at chest level, Madison ducked under the mosquito net and strode to the glass-slated window and peered out. Ina hadn't lied. In both directions mean-looking men held large guns, probably waiting for a signal to charge the hospital. She leaned away from the window and let her head rest against the wall. How would she dig her way out of this one?

Tell him what he wants to hear.

The sigh that escaped her lips started from the bottom of her soul. "Let me stitch this boy up and move him into recovery first. Tell General it will cost him fifty thousand francs per hour of surgery and to plan for eight hours. He and his men aren't allowed anywhere near this operating room. Move Amadou in here and prep him for surgery."

"They are both prepped, Doctor." Ina's kind eyes crinkled. "We had to make it look like we were doing something to buy time. I didn't want to interrupt you before you extracted the mass."

"Smart thinking, Ina. Well done."

Ina's intuition always managed to surprise Madison. She was the best nurse in the hospital. As she disappeared, Madison stood over her patient while Konji finished stitching him together.

"Roger, do we have enough lightweight juice to keep two kids asleep for eight hours or so?"

Roger's rigid posture eased at her question. Her responses had alarmed him though he didn't speak a word of French. The clanking of glass muffled his muttering as he dug through a box nearby. He emerged with a couple of bottles that he flicked, drawing a satisfied smile. That seemed to be how anesthetists worked. A flick and a smile meant the drugs were right on point.

"Should do. I've got a fine lot of gas here that'll do the trick without leaving their brains in a hash."

She summarized the situation to Roger, leaving out the sudden-death part. "Obviously, we can't do a kidney transplant here even if Amadou did need one so let's make sure they stay asleep while I find out what's really wrong."

Roger nodded. The wiry-haired middle-aged man was a godsend from Wales who had known Madison's mentor Dr. Cavine, the hospital's deceased founder. Roger's hospital granted him two months out of each year to do charity medical work around the world, so Roger came in July each year—war, pest, or famine. The more serious operations waited until he arrived. No one expected anything different. It was how things worked.

And, obviously, General Karim knew Roger was here. How closely was he watching?

Amadou and his donor shuffled in, their yellow paper robes gaping in the back. Their wide eyes took in her patient's limp form on the metal table and Konji mopping the blood and pus from the floor. Walk 'em in. Wheel 'em out. It was the Malian method.

With any luck the sight would discourage Amadou from fabricating symptoms or illnesses.

Madison cleared her throat and used her doctor voice. "Amadou, please tell me what is wrong."

"My side. My kidney." His moans didn't sound manufactured.

"Point to where it hurts."

Amadou rubbed his hand across his midriff. Incredibly vague.

"Is it very sharp or a dull pain?"

"Dull, but then very sharp." The boy flinched again, his face twisted in agony. A tear slipped down his cheek.

Madison nodded at Roger. "Put them both in deep."

The donor's lip quivered but he made no sound when the needle pierced his skin. A pat on the arm was the best she could do to reassure him as he fell asleep. Her stomach churned. To stay alive and keep everyone around her alive, General needed to believe that she had performed a successful transplant. At the least, she would do exploratory surgery so Amadou would have the stitches for appearance's sake.

Two hours passed in labored silence with a barked command to Konji and Ina every now and then. Thank God Ina spoke fluent French or they'd both be in trouble.

Madison took a deep breath. "Ina, please tell General Karim his son is still in surgery and it is going well. Then start on your rounds. Konji and I have this under control."

Ina slipped out the door.

Five more hours ticked by before she sent both boys to the recovery room, wrapped in bandages. As two nurses wheeled the boys out, Madison pulled off her apron, surgery cap, and gloves. Time would tell how well Amadou's body recovered from his appendectomy. The procedure had been routine once she found the problem. Roger and Konji had chatted away their tension as she dropped the offending organ onto a tray. Sometimes the most inconspicuous member produced unexpected agony.

The nightly dinner for the hospital staff had been served and cleaned up by now, leaving her to succumb to her exhaustion on an empty stomach. She dropped into the wooden chair in her office and rubbed her eyes. Night started to pull its cloak over the sky. Darkness ushered in a refreshing temperature drop. The sweet scent of cool air mingled with the songs of the night bugs drained the tension from her muscles.

Rest.

She rolled her head from side to side, working the kinks from their hiding places. Hours hunched over the operating table took their toll on her body. What she wouldn't give to have someone willing to massage her shoulders and rub her feet at the end of a long day.

A soft knock sounded on her door. She whimpered, tempted to tell them to return in the morning. The knock came again. Heaving a groan, she pushed from her chair and cracked the door open.

"Doctor, may I come in?" The low voice sent her stomach into her throat.

She blinked. The man who had threatened to kill her eight hours earlier stood a foot from her. No one else was nearby. Letting him in was a terrible idea, but he wasn't accustomed to being told no.

"Come in, General. Looks like you called off your guard dogs." Likely because he was the fiercest of the pack and needed no protection. "Are you armed?"

"I am always armed."

General stepped into the office, his eyes narrowed. Her heart pulsed in her ears as she came face to face with the man who defied everything she stood for. He appeared about thirty, an old man in some countries, his features unmarred by war or disease. He was different than she'd expected.

He clasped his hands behind his back and peered down his nose at her. "I am sorry I had to do that. I had no choice."

"No choice," she whispered.

Like all the kids who had been pushed to the back of the line today because he demanded surgery for his son.

"Doctor, I am prepared to pay you as you asked for doing the surgery. I also promise you my protection provided Amadou lives."

Where was the class in med school on how to deal with a distraught warlord father? This was way over her pay grade.

"General, it is no one's fault if his body rejects the kidney. These things happen. In fact, the rate of acceptance is—"

"I don't care about the rate of acceptance, Doctor." His white teeth clacked as he hissed from behind them. "I care about your success with my son." General angled his body toward her. His fingers traced the length of her arm. "You are mesmerizing with your pale skin and womanly form. I'd hate to see any harm come to you because you are left uncared for so far away from your family."

What family? She held her tongue as fire zipped through her veins.

Why did it always come to a test of wills? One of these days, someone would follow through on their threats when they didn't get what they wanted. No one would miss her but the needy children who were the closest thing to family she had. She needed them as much as they needed her.

"General, I would hate to see harm come to me as well. I am in the business of saving lives, like your son's. This area would suffer immensely if they no longer had the benefit of my medical attention."

Her bold words called his bluff. General moved closer, his body inches from hers. Her quick breaths made her head light.

She wouldn't back down.

Not to him.

He lifted his hand. She squeezed her eyes shut waiting for the strike to come. Instead, a finger ran along her jaw. She eased her eyes open. General's expression softened, his brown eyes staring into hers. He'd have to be deaf not to hear the pounding of her heart. No man had been this close to her in a long time.

"I admire your confidence." With a light touch, he pressed against her lower back bringing her into full contact with his hard body. "You don't have to be alone if you don't want to be."

His whispers sent chills across her skin and his gentleness caught her off guard. She swallowed hard. "I appreciate the offer, but my contract does not allow me to establish romantic relationships with Malian citizens."

General tilted his head, his lips too close to hers. "Your contract with who?"

"The Malian government, of course." Her words came out as a squeak. Eager for distance between them, she seized a stack of visa renewal paperwork on her desk and waved them at him. "Can't let mesmerizing foreign doctors try to stay in the country unauthorized."

General smirked. "Then they see what I see."

Where had the oxygen in the room gone? Her fingers straightened the stack. "Perhaps they do." Her heartbeat slowed to an even pace. "General, I do not mean to be rude, but Amadou will fare better under the care of a well-rested doctor. I really should get some sleep."

General lifted his chin as if to analyze her sincerity then walked to the door. With his hand on the knob he turned and pinned her with one last look.

"Think on my offer, Doctor. The government would never have to know."

A smile of relief played on her lips. "It's one I won't soon forget."

The door clicked shut. Adrenaline fled from her body on an exhale. The surgery had earned her his favor. Heavens knew she needed an ally in this country, although she hadn't counted on it being the most feared criminal south of Bamako. Her little hospital on the Niger had been untouched by violence thus far, and until today, she assumed it had flown under General's radar as well. Her stomach churned with force as she picked her way downhill to the river to bathe. Could she have been any more naïve? No white doctor in the Mali bush could go unnoticed.

Back inside after a quick dip in the river, she dropped onto her rickety cot tucked in her office closet. The memory of his touch drew a hard shiver from her. As if she were his to claim. Her shorts' pocket crinkled as she tugged a sheet over her aching limbs. A flattened peanut butter granola bar was going to be as good as dinner would get tonight. It distracted her stomach enough to let her fall into a haze of sleep.

"Doctor." A voice called to her in her dream. "Doctor. We need you. Doctor, wake up."

Was she awake or was she dreaming? Strong hands gripped her arm and shook her body.

"Doctor, wake up. Something is wrong with my son."

She bolted to a sitting position, her chest tight. General's voice yanked the remnants of sleep from her mind. An orange glow from the office outlined General and nurse Hawa crouched next to her bed.

This wasn't ideal. Her hands smoothed her hair into the ponytail as she focused on Hawa. "What's going on?"

General arrested her hand in his. The warmth surprised her. "Something is wrong with Amadou, Doctor."

His earlier threats propelled her from her cot. She tugged a clean set of scrubs over her tank top and shorts and slid on watery sandals. Hawa's flashlight illuminated the panic in General's eyes. In the recovery room, Hawa handed her a chart.

"Hawa, what is the time?"

"One in the morning, Doctor."

She shouldn't have asked.

With one look at the chart, she set the clipboard down. Annoyance wrestled with humor. Only part of the staff could read and write in French. The other nurses and a majority of her patients either spoke it or they hovered in no man's land between literacy and illiteracy. Drawn stick figures would be more helpful than trying to read words spelled out phonetically. At the next staff meeting, she might recommend it.

"Explain to me what you've written on the chart," Madison said as she tapped the clipboard. She checked Amadou's eyes for dilation and exposed the bandaging wrapped around his abdomen. No signs of seeping.

Hawa shifted on her feet next to the bed. "Very high blood pressure and the patient complained of pain in his arm. I noted signs of swelling and tenderness."

"Possible blood clot. Keep warm compresses on his arm. I'm giving him aspirin. Add that to his regiment every few hours."

"Doctor, is it something to do with his new kidney?" General asked.

"No, General. It's not to do with his kidney. Please let me focus on your son."

"Remember our earlier conversation, Doctor. You help him. I help you." General's voice was dull and void of heat.

She popped two tablets onto Amadou's tongue and handed him a glass of water. "Swallow."

He swallowed them with no problem. She glanced over at General sitting in a chair beside the bed, worry etched into his face. His vulnerability infused a kind of human quality to him. Maybe deep down he was like any father who would give the world for his son to be happy. Did he have anyone who actually loved him?

Perhaps they had that in common.

Madison strode across the room to where Hawa prepared the warm compresses. She tapped her on the shoulder.

"I'm going to bed. Come wake me if you don't see any changes in the next hour or so."

"Yes, Doctor."

"Please keep General in the recovery room. I don't need him wandering the halls. And I don't ever want to wake up to him in my room again."

She slipped out and checked over her shoulder several times to be sure General didn't follow her. It was bad enough that he knew where she slept. She might need to start keeping her office door locked.

A problem for another day. She needed to make it through Amadou's recovery and she'd be home free as long as General didn't create any more problems for her.

Chapter 2

Alps, France
August 2008

If there was any place for a misstep, a couple thousand feet up a mountain cliff was not it.

Chip Chapman lowered himself onto the rock beside his twin Pax, as Opa, a thinner version of Father Christmas, stretched out an arm's length away. Nestled into the sky, white and gray peaks of all sizes filled the landscape in every direction. The cold air didn't bite as badly as it had during England's winters when Father covered the windows with plastic bags instead of turning on the heat. Chip's lungs couldn't expand to capacity for a full breath at this altitude, but breathlessness was the lifeblood of adventure.

"Are you ready for next week, Chip?" Opa asked.

The familiar tingle of anticipation swept through Chip's chest. The sky felt more like home than England. At twenty-thousand feet limits disappeared and Chip felt untouchable. Flying at the speed of sound was his drug of choice.

"Sixteen-year-old me thought he was ready." Chip snorted. "With six more years of training behind me, I'd like to think the Royal Air Force might not be ready for me."

Pax and Opa touched their fingers to their forehead in a high-altitude laugh.

"Hold on to that enthusiasm. Once the honeymoon is over, reality hits like a pub brawl." Pax swigged his water and sent a stream through his front teeth.

Pax had always presented a cynical front, but pursuing a doctorate in psychology lodged his tent stakes deep in that camp. He hailed cynicism as a personality pillar. Chip blamed Father.

Opa pointed to the tallest peak in the range which had its own cloud collection around the base. "When you return from boot camp, that's our next challenge. Mont Blanc has more people die on it in a year than most peaks see in a century."

"How many deaths are we talking? Hundreds?" Pax asked.

"Thousands. Last week almost thirty people died from an avalanche. And last month, a novice fell, dragged his friend down, and the guide couldn't hold them. They all dropped to their deaths. Guides can't save everyone." Opa stood and swung his pack over his shoulders. "Can't be too careful on a climb, boys. Never underestimate the value of training."

Opa dropped nuggets of golden advice like Father spewed criticism. How Father turned out so vastly different from Opa was beyond Chip's realm of comprehension. Where years of sun exposure on the ranch had leathered Opa's wrinkles, Father's pale skin only saw the light of day that filtered uninvited through the office curtains. Where Opa showered physical and verbal affection freely, Father offered abuse of the same. Where Opa valued nothing more than family, Father filled his shot glass and time with whatever booze he had on hand to "fork at."

Chip stepped into the footprints Opa left behind. Man, he'd miss this. Adventures with Opa never got old. The snow crunching under his feet sang harmony with the tune the wind whistled. In years past, he'd have taken up the rear so he could stop and catch his breath when he wanted. But hiring a drill sergeant fitness coach paid off. This year, his body was in top form for good reason. The military offered him a chance to create a life worth living. To be selfless and courageous. To be a man of honor. To do something for himself and everyone else at the same time.

When the lack of Pax's steady footsteps behind him registered, Chip whirled around. Pax crouched behind the lens of his fancy camera, letting his trigger finger rapid-fire. The day Pax boxed his camera into storage would be the day Chip wrestled him to the ground and forced him to see whoever made money off of shrinking shrinks. For now, capturing moments of beauty released Pax from the hell that was their past.

Chip opened his mouth to toss a sarcastic comment Pax's way but seized the words when Pax's forefinger poked the air, then beckoned Chip to him all without so much as a glance in Chip's direction. As Chip hiked back, the subject came into view.

Barely visible in the rock, an Alpine ibex kid stared out at them with giant brown eyes, his horns mere stubs. Chip scanned the surrounding area for the rest of the herd as Pax inched closer. A wall of snow slanted upward above the rock to the right. To the left, a steep slope disappeared into the tree line and beyond. Not seeing them didn't mean they weren't there.

Chip grabbed Pax's shoulder. "Don't get too close. This isn't a petting zoo."

Pax shrugged him off and went anyway. "The light isn't quite right back there. And I think the kid is hurt. Look at the way his legs are folded under him at an unnatural angle."

The kid bleated and attempted to dislodge his hoof from between the rocks.

"Move on, Pax. No good comes of this."

"And leave him here to die? Are you completely void of all feeling? You're worse off than I thought."

Ouch. Chip retreated a few steps, nibbling on his emergency whistle. Pax was off his trolley to be interacting with wildlife, much less baby wildlife. With a steady hand outstretched, Pax moved toward the offending hoof. The kid blinked seemingly unconcerned. Chip held his breath, willing Pax to free the kid and book it out of there. Two tugs and the kid sprang into action as did Pax's trigger finger. The clack of the shutter blasted like a machine gun in the stillness. The kid danced to the side, bleating.

Cor!

A full-sized ibex charged onto the scene with horns lowered and slammed into Pax's crouched body, tossing him effortlessly. With a sickening thud, Pax hit the ground and rolled, curling into a ball as the ibex continued the assault. Too close to the ledge for Chip's liking. The shrill of Chip's whistle turned the ibex's attention on him. An invisible hand squeezed his throat.

"Help." Pax moaned.

Chip blew the whistle, doing jumping jacks and staying light on his toes. The air was too thin for this. The ibex lowered his horns and charged.

That's right come to me!

A blur out of the corner of Chip's eye snapped him to attention. Opa sprinted at the animal and blasted an air horn. The ibex peeled off in a flash.

Opa squatted over Pax. "Can you hear me?"

Pax muttered something.

Chip ran to them. "Y'alright?"

"Grab my pack. We have to hurry and get out of here." Opa probed Pax's torso. "What hurts, Pax?"

"Leg, arms, back, head, everything."

Opa unfolded Pax limb by limb. Blood stained the leg of his trousers. He was lucky he wasn't dead. Chip extracted the medical kit and Opa bandaged Pax's leg then lifted him to his feet.

"We have to get off this ledge. Your ribs may be fractured. Open." Opa placed pain pills on Pax's tongue, then pressed a water bottle to his lips. "Can you walk?"

Pax nodded. Opa grabbed Pax's fallen camera. "Let's go."

What just happened? Had he really just taunted an angry ibex? A shiver raced along Chip's spine and he tucked his scarf tighter around his nose and mouth. As he knelt to tie his laces tighter, the shock settled into rage. Chip stood, ready to blast Pax with an "I told you so" but a dull rumble under his feet stopped him. The trees quivered in response.

Panic zinged through him. Had the herd returned to finish them the job?

Opa shouted and waved his arms from a distance, his eyes wide. "Chip, run. Chip! Run!"

"Run?" From what? Chip broke into a sprint.

Fear radiated from Pax's face in waves as he glanced above Chip's head. Something was very wrong.

A wall of snow bowled Chip over the ledge.

No.

He fought to keep his face unburied as snow tumbled in a cloud around him. The avalanche picked up speed, rolling and flipping him out of control.

Pax.

Chip bulleted down the mountainside, his speed frantic. With each bounce, the ground punched the air from his lungs, spinning and tossing him further. Ahead, the white expanse disappearing into blue sky. His arms flailed as he grabbed for something, anything to stop him from going over the ledge.

Angels. God. Whoever is up there. Help!

The avalanche's power swept him over. His body sailed through the air then pounded into the ground and kept sliding. The terrain turned into dirt and rocks underneath him. His boot knocked against brush. Chip's hand closed around a bush limb. His arm absorbed the force of the stop, a small price to pay to halt the high-speed tumble. Rocks and residual snow skittered around him, pelting his clothes in protest of his defiance.

Someone heard his prayer. It was no small miracle that the sprout of greenery held his weight.

"Help!"

The wilderness swallowed his scream. The wind howled in response. With slow movements, he patted his pocket for his emergency whistle. Nothing. A string of foul words escaped his lips.

"You're not going to die. They're going to find you. Just don't look down. Look at the sky. That beautiful blue."

More debris scattered down the incline as Chip searched for a toe hold. His battered arm wouldn't hold him much longer. The toe of his boot found a crevice. He tilted his head to look over his left shoulder.

Snap.

The limb ripped loose. Chip's fingers scraped at the rock in vain. Gravity toyed with his frame, bouncing and rolling him off every surface possible. With each new hit his body submitted to, black spots dimmed his vision.

His limbs no longer responded to his brain's demands. The mountain wanted him as a victim. Blackness edged out the light until slivers remained. Then complete darkness.

Voices. Unrecognizable sounds prodded Chip into a thread of consciousness. Something warm rested on his head and touched his eyelid. Light seared his eye in a blinding blur. Everything hurt. Where was he?

"Paaah" escaped his lips.

A glimpse of brown skin registered before the darkness welcomed him once again.

Cold pressed into his cheek.

"Stay with me. We're getting you help." The voice of an angel.

She spoke nice words, but the agony shoved him toward the nothingness that beckoned him. Fighting meant more pain.

His time had come.

Chapter 3

Mali, Africa
August 2008

To the hospital staff's great relief, Madison discharged Amadou and his donor from the hospital a week after his surgery. Amadou had taken full advantage of his father's intimidation by telling the nurses stories about how General killed others for disagreeing with him about the flavor of foods. Their horror fueled his royalty complex and in turn they ran themselves ragged trying to keep his highness happy. A week was all the staff could handle and she had meetings in Bamako to attend.

Kidney transplant patients usually stayed in the hospital for at least two weeks hooked to monitors of every kind, but General didn't know that nor did he realize that his son wasn't taking anything more than pain killer and vitamins. Whatever unqualified doctor told him it was a kidney problem probably wouldn't know if she'd performed a transplant or not. The less General knew, the better off she was.

Early the next morning, she packed a bag of clothes and snacks in her white Ford pickup truck. Twisting the key, she begged the vehicle to start. Like any old man he had to clear his throat before speaking. Then she twisted again. He didn't cooperate. She stormed to the front of the vehicle, bashed two fists on the hood, and kicked the front fender to show him she meant business. This time when she turned the key, he sputtered to life. His rumbling hum was strangely comforting.

Her ever-present shoulder tension dissolved as the hospital disappeared in her rear view. She loved her job, but breaks were too few and far between. River plains gave way to sharp-edged rocks bordering basins of brown and green—landscape ripe for discovery and exposure. The grassy fields and open spaces called her name in a wild way. The concrete of Quebec City couldn't give her the same thrill.

The pock-marked dirt smoothed into mellow blacktop as soon as Bamako's buildings appeared. Her jolted insides settled into their normal places once more. The orange tower was in plain sight today. At twenty stories, the bank was the tallest building in Mali's capital and plopped right on the bank of the Niger. What use was a huge bank where a majority of the population couldn't afford to spend a day's wage on a meal out much less put it in a financial institution for safe keeping? Nevertheless, Mali was making progress. And she loved that she was a part of it.

Anticipation roiled in her chest. Ahead, a long line of vehicles waited to exit the highway, moving inches at a time.

"Traffic in the middle of the week? What is going on?"

She glanced at her fuel gauge. One-fourth of a tank left. One of these days the truck would have enough and give up the ghost. Not today. Not here. Thirty minutes passed as they crept forward. Small clouds of smoke rose over the buildings. Fifteen parked vehicles blocked her from the city streets.

Bam. Bam.

Her truck rocked to the side. Madison gasped and lurched to the middle of the bench. A shirtless man pounded her window, his face striped with bright paint. Saliva dripped from his dangling tongue.

He shrieked and thumped her window with the base of a flaming torch. She shrunk back and gripped the pepper spray on her keys a little tighter. What she wouldn't do to have a gun stashed under her seat.

Malians believed that everyone had a little devil inside them. This man clearly had more than his share. He yanked at her door handle. Her foot tapped the gas pedal, rocking the truck forward. The handle slapped into place. She leaned across the seat and slammed the lock on the passenger door down.

He disappeared. Where was he? Left. Then right. From the driver's seat she checked her side mirror. He threw his body against the hood of the car behind her. She sank against the wheel.

A parade of similarly clad men trailed him, dancing and humping the air. They waved bats, torches, and garden shears in their hands. Mental images of the damaged flesh made her cringe. When she returned to Canada, martial arts and self-defense were going to be the first classes she took.

She released the brake to close the gap in front of her. Police directed vehicles to the left. At this rate it would take hours to reach her hotel a few blocks away. To the right, crowds of people swarmed the streets waving colorful signs with a mixture of French and Arabic writing on them. Posters of men in *keffiyehs* hung on walls and covered street signs.

A flash of movement drew her attention. Columns of police ten men wide marched around the corner, their helmets barely poking over the full-body shields. Their path led them right where she waited, giving her a front-row view of the automatic weapons strapped to their sides. Garden shears didn't stand a chance.

The car in front of her turned leaving her truck vulnerable. The policeman directing traffic motioned for her to stop. Screams and the sound of breaking glass pierced the air as she cranked down her window.

He jogged over to her and leaned in. "Reverse. More police are coming."

The blast of a horn captured his focus.

"What's going on?" Her shouts didn't get his attention. She tapped his arm. "What's wrong?"

"They're protesting the presence of the French military. The Muslims are making it a religious battle. Stay out of the way. You don't want to get in the middle of this."

Waves of police lines pushed through the streets. A loud boom thundered over the high-pitched shrieks. Smoke lifted from the protesters' ranks. The traffic director's eyes widened as the crowd's volume rose to a fevered pitch. Her grip tightened on the steering wheel. Why couldn't people protest peacefully? Finally, he waved her forward. Cars from behind her whizzed past her in their effort to leave the disorder behind.

One last turn brought her hotel into view. A giggle escaped her lips as giddiness replaced her fear. Safe. She swung her truck into a parking lot and shut it off. With her bag in hand, she strolled into the lobby of the hotel.

Tile-covered floors accented the textured brick walls. People of all races and ages wandered around the lobby. Some huddled in groups while others power-walked to their destinations. No one paid any attention to the protest coverage on the television inside the bar.

This five-star hotel with air-conditioned rooms, a pool, and tennis courts had a room reservation with her name on it. The visa-renewal meetings and updating her medical certifications would sap her energy, so a little bit of luxury was her reward to herself for the hard work and long hours. This was her week to refresh herself.

She checked in and dropped her bag in her room. Clean, tidy, and quiet. It didn't take many trips or a medical degree to know a room wasn't cared for. Outside the window, paths of large stones led to netted sitting areas and a large pool. That blue water would have to wait. Her stomach's protests propelled her out the door as she weaved her way through side streets of dirt. Ina sent her with a shopping list of medicinal herbs to get from the medicine man in the market.

In the city center, the market curved around the bend between two long stretches of buildings. Sounds bounced off hard surfaces as if competing to be heard, bringing life and energy to the city. Clothes, fruits, vegetables, and hand-carved statues lured her through each display. Brightly clad women with babies strapped on their backs and baskets on their heads glided through the busy thoroughfare, dodging carts and bicycles with ease.

The plant man's booth was easy to find. Floral aromas wafted through the space ripe with sweaty bodies. Dried plants swayed in the breeze hung in rows overhead a gray-bearded man. Ina's shopping list was a bag filled with ten cloth swatches containing samples of each item she needed. Ina promised she didn't need to know the herbs' names, because the medicine man would know.

Medicine man nodded his hello and motioned at her options. One by one she brought out nine of the swatches and set them on his table. A smile lit his face. He sniffed each sample and bowed to her. He turned his back and pounded plants into nothing on a stone surface. His movements were fluid and hypnotic. She could watch him all day. He broke the spell by handing her a brown bag stuffed with more twine-bound cloth swatches.

She retrieved the final sample, an herb Ina fixed for her when she couldn't sleep. Ina said it soothed "mind and soul pains." Whatever it did, it was one-hundred-percent effective and she couldn't argue with that.

Madison dropped the swatch in his hand and held up three fingers. He bowed again and scooped a handful of fresh pink-yellow flowers from a box. He didn't pound and grind the petals. He sprinkled water on them and crushed them together with a rolling stone. He dipped his finger in the runoff and rubbed it on Madison's wrist and neck. Then he scooped the remains into a swatch and tied it. She paid and returned his bow. She didn't remember the last time she felt this relaxed walking through a market full of people.

Animal skulls, pots, papers, and jewelry of brilliant colors filled every available space. The peddlers guarding them enticed her to look at their merchandise, complimenting her beauty. Maybe it was time for a new boubou.

A series of shouts interrupted her perusing.

She whirled around.

Her eyes scanned the crowds for angry men with torches but found none.

There. Three stalls down, a man knelt over a pregnant woman lying in the street. The woman's face twisted with pain. Madison's brain argued that she was off-duty, but her feet didn't listen. Helping was engrained in her DNA.

She crouched beside the woman. The man gripping the woman's shoulders glanced at Madison and let loose a string of words in Bambara, but Madison only recognized the word "help."

"Sir, do you speak French?"

"*Oui.*"

Madison blew out a breath of air. "How far along is she?"

The man shook his head and shrugged. Either he didn't understand the question or he didn't understand French. Or both.

"What's your name?"

His wide eyes shifted and he shrugged with a smile. He definitely didn't understand French.

She placed her hand on her chest. "I'm Doctor Madison." The words came out slow and loud.

He straightened his back and raised his eyebrows. "Doctor?"

Madison nodded. The man spoke gently to the woman. She nodded and clutched Madison's arm with the steel of desperation.

The man put his hand on his chest. "Sam." He pointed to the woman. "Fanta."

Madison patted Fanta's arm. "Fanta, let's get you out of the street."

She slid her arms around Fanta's shoulders and glanced at Sam. He nodded and mirrored her movements. They lifted her to her feet. Madison plucked at her lip with her teeth. Where could this woman have a baby? They wouldn't make it to the hospital from here, but the road was no place for a baby either.

Fanta gasped, bent over, and her face pinched with strain. A harsh exhale came from her mouth. The baby wouldn't wait much longer.

Jogging to a vendor's booth, she waved to him. "Excuse me. Is there a house or business nearby that this lady could have her baby in?"

The man shrugged and smiled. He didn't speak French either. Fanta's muffled hisses ramped her pulse a few notches. Madison ran down the street, glancing into doorways. The back door to a quiet warehouse stood open. She returned to Sam and Fanta and pointed to the warehouse door. Sam nodded as he wiped sweat from Fanta's brow. Together, they carried Fanta off the street.

Inside the warehouse, Sam propped Fanta against the wall as Madison grabbed a discarded piece of plastic. They needed supplies.

"Sam."

Sam's worried expression shifted to Madison.

"Clean water." She mimicked washing her hands and drinking. He nodded. "Towels." She lifted her shirt to scrub her face. He nodded again. "Scissors." She imitated scissors with her fingers. "And clamp." Pinching her fingers together, she stared at him willing him to understand her. He nodded one short nod but didn't move. "Go."

She shooed him with her hands, repeating her request with hand motions.

Sam disappeared into the marketplace.

Madison returned to Fanta's side and checked her dilation with her bare hand. That broke so many levels of sanitation and protocol that she didn't want to think about it. Although Fanta couldn't understand her, she explained the process anyway.

"Fanta, you are doing great. We're going to start pushing, but we'll try to time this so your husband returns with our supplies before that sweet baby comes." He had better be quick about it or the baby would pop out onto the dirty warehouse floor.

Time slipped by between coaching Fanta through breathing and helping her push. The possibilities of complications made her cringe. She wasn't superstitious, but a warehouse seemed more appropriate for death. Not today. What mattered was that this mom and baby made it alive to the hospital post-delivery. The head crowned just as Sam reappeared at her elbow. He set the supplies on the plastic and smothered his wife's face in kisses.

Her heart twinged. Someday.

Sam shook her shoulder. "Doctor? Doctor?"

Smiling at him, she blinked and moved the supplies at her side into position. Everything she'd requested he'd found. Fanta continued her timed breathing as Sam grasped her hand and spoke to her. With three more pushes, a beautiful baby boy made his entrance into the world.

A half-hour later she had both mom and baby cleaned and resting in post-delivery bliss with Sam hovering over them. What did it feel like to be in that moment of love and pure adoration—to know what family truly meant? Fanta caught her staring and raised her hand to her heart with a smile. Madison covered her heart too, but to soothe the ache resonating there.

Therapists had told her that family meant something different to everyone, but she didn't believe that when she saw the look on the women's faces when they held their newborns against their chests. At ten years old, she'd asked her counselor, "Did my mom ever feel that way about me?" The bumbling response gave her no confidence. That was the last time she went. They couldn't heal her or fix her, so why waste time letting them try?

That despair lodged deep in her soul. Married friends said she had plenty of time, but they forgot in their found happiness that the desire didn't ease at their reassurances of "someday." If she didn't find someone that treated her like Dr. Cavine had treated his wife Amber, then she might be forced to do something crazy like speed dating or a singles' cruise. After surviving two years in the Mali bush, surely she could manage the courage to get a date.

Chapter 4

In and out, Chip faded. A few seconds here and there, convinced that each time he closed his eyes again it would be his last. A constant whir brought him toward wakefulness. Memories of the avalanche invaded his peaceful moment. Panicked, he sat upright.

Pax? Opa?

No one. They'd probably taken a break for coffee.

He flexed his right foot, then left. Fingers on his right hand and left moved on command. His head tilted to the side. Wires from circles stuck to his chest snaked behind the headboard.

The room was unremarkable. A small window let in a thread of light, illuminating a fan humming in the corner. White-painted, cinder-block walls met a concrete floor. A wooden door gapped in its frame. It was like no hospital room he ever remembered seeing. The lack of hanging art or signs tripped his silent alarm. Europe had better health centers than this in the mountain villages, didn't they?

He folded back the sheet that covered him.

Naked. Not even courtesy socks. He would have preferred the chance to begrudge a scratchy hospital gown.

And he had a catheter. This was a new low.

The door squeaked open. Chip yanked the sheet over him, rocking the bed. Two thin women—one short, one tall—strolled in wearing colorful flowy trousers, fitted t-shirts, and achingly bright smiles. Both were pretty in their own right, but they dressed more like spa employees than nurses.

"Hello, Monsieur Chapman." The short woman produced a blood pressure cuff and stethoscope from the bag she carried. "Good to see you are awake this afternoon."

French accent. Chip flinched. "Cold stethoscope." The woman gave him a half-laugh as she stared at the wall, listening. "Where am I?"

"A medical center." Conspicuously vague. The tall woman, her skin more brown than black, spoke with a thick French accent as well. Her voice sounded familiar. "You are lucky to have survived your injuries."

"I feel lucky. Has my family arrived yet?"

The short one clicked a few buttons behind him and peeled at the sticky circles on his chest. "No, love. You had no information on you and there's a world of Chip Chapman's out there." She giggled to herself.

Chip cleared his throat. "I seem to be at a distinct disadvantage here, as you know my name somehow, and I know neither of yours."

The short woman stopped and looked him in the eye. "I'm Janice, and this is Adrienna. We've been caring for you since you arrived. We wouldn't have known your name except you were so kind to wear your dog tags under your clothes." Janice motioned and Adrienna stepped beside her. They grabbed the pad underneath him and heaved up, rolling Chip to his left side. "Let me extract your catheter and we'll test out your legs, eh?"

Janice moved the sheet and extracted the tube before Chip processed her words. At least it was over.

She jiggled a bedpan and set it on a chair beside his bed. "Use this when you need to."

He flinched.

Adrienna set a stack of clothing next to him. "Do you want help putting these on?"

"I'll be fine," Chip said.

They busied themselves in his room with their backs turned. They weren't going to leave?

Easily done. Chip pushed his arms into the t-shirt, biting his lip to suppress the roar of pain in his temples. Cursed arrogance. The simplest task of sliding on loose trousers evaporated what little energy he'd mustered. He couldn't stand to get them on, so he laid on his back to pull them up. Sweat trickled from the nape of his neck along his spine as he worked to get a good breath. Fresh on and already the clothes stuck to skin.

They finished their tasks, their smiles still in place. So many questions he wanted to ask, yet he panted like a dog on a hot day. They didn't seem to notice his discomfort.

"We'll inform the doctor that you are awake." Adrienna made a note on a clipboard. "He'll stop by shortly. Do you think you can stand if we support you?"

No, he'd tried, but he nodded anyway. They each grabbed an arm and Janice counted to three. He pushed. They pulled. He growled. They released his arms.

"Very good." Adrienna's sultry voice soothed his agony a fraction. "For as long as you've been in that bed, that was remarkable progress."

Remarkable, his—. "Exactly how long have I been in this bed?"

Adrienna's lips parted as her glance shifted to Janice. "Three weeks."

Was that a look of guilt? "And the day I was found was…"

"August 3," Adrienna said.

"And today is?"

"August 26."

"Who found me?"

"A hiker."

"How did I get here?"

"You were flown here."

"To this..."

"Medical center," a male voice said, followed by a long productive cough. "I'm Dr. Thomas, Mr. Chapman. Should I call you Baxter or Chip? Both were on your tags."

Adrienna slipped out of the door as Dr. Thomas limped in. There went his answers.

"Chip is fine—"

"Excellent. Lay back for me, Chip. The ladies told me you were awake, and I was beside myself. Thought you might be in a coma for longer. Found, rescued, and still alive. I'd say you owe that man your life." Dr. Thomas chuckled as he pressed his stethoscope to Chip's chest. "Or at least a thank you dinner."

"Did the man leave his details?"

Dr. Thomas lifted Chip's shirt on one side, then the other. "Even better. He's been here almost every day to check on you. When a seasoned hiker comes across a young man's body on the side of a mountain, he's likely to feel invested in the story.

Certainly doesn't happen often. I imagine you have hiked quite a bit. Ever happen to you? No, I suppose it hasn't." Dr. Thomas finished his exam. "You've made significant progress, Chip. The ladies will be getting you on your feet a little more each day. Hope you won't give them too much trouble." Dr. Thomas winked.

Chip grunted. Trouble, no. Questions, yes.

"It takes a strong person to pull through what you did, Chip. If you use that strength for good, you'll have great things in store for your future." Dr. Thomas paused, as if to let the thought soak in. Then he tapped his forehead. "I'll make sure the kitchen sends you nutrient-rich meals so we can expedite the healing process. See you tomorrow."

A clang yanked Chip from his post-Dr. Thomas slumber. A teen winced and reversed a metal cart into the hall for a second attempt at clearing the door frame. Her trembling hands unwrapped the dishes, mumbling possibly in French while she did so. The food didn't need an explanation. His stomach was eating itself, so it could be a beloved pet toad and he'd still eat it.

"*Excusez moi.*" One of the only phrases he remembered from French class. "Where am I?"

She shrugged with a smile. The international gesture for "I don't have a clue what you said."

He snagged a notepad and pencil from her cart and wrote, "*Je suis in ____ in le monde.*" His French teacher should be proud he remembered that much.

She tilted her head to read. "*Monde?*"

"Yes, world. France, Switzerland, Russia, China, America, Africa? Where?"

The girl's eyes lit up as she pointed at the floor. "*Oui, Afrique.*"

Chip's heart pounded in his chest. She was playing with him, right? "Here? *Afrique?*"

"*Oui, Mali, Afrique.*"

The black spots hovered on the edge of his vision as his breath came in short bursts. "*Merci.*"

She bounced out of the room, motioning to the cart chattering a mile a minute. Nothing else she said mattered. His knowledge of avalanches was limited, but someone couldn't fall off the side of a mountain in France and slide all the way to Africa. Even if it felt like it. He had to call his family.

Grabbing the bread roll from the tray, Chip shoved it into his pocket for later.

One, two, three. Stand.

Too much, too fast.

He steadied himself with a hand on the wall. His feet shuffled despite his mental commands to walk normally. He kept his eye on the door. Finally there, he leaned against the wall and rewarded himself with a bite of bread.

Predictably dry.

Two more bites, then he stuffed it back into his pocket. He cracked the door open a hair and peeked into the hall without budging from his spot against the wall, more from exhaustion than any thought of stealth. No one wandered in either direction. No backlit signs guided him to the exit. And most curiously, the halls didn't have a ceiling—only a metal roof perched on posts spanning the rooms and walkway. Like stables, except not as nice.

Neither direction seemed promising, so he started left. What kind of person finds a body in the Alps and ships them to Mali for medical treatment? It was too extreme to be true. At the end of the hall he warded off the dizziness swarming in his head with another bite of bread and turned right, swallowing against the pain. A computer, a phone, a letter mailing station—he just wanted to contact Pax and Opa. The hallway led to a solid door that wasn't latched. He shoved it open and stumbled outside.

Dirt roads lined with tall brown grass snaked in every direction. The sun blazed against his face, proving that—against the odds—the ridiculous happened on occasion. Around the corner, an SUV sat in front of a set of stairs leading into another building. Someone to give him answers. The dirt burned his bare feet and the humidity made him itchy. Gritting his teeth, he swung his legs faster. His back gave out a body length from the rear fender. He dragged himself on his elbows into the SUV's shadow. This was a terrible mistake.

Between panting and groaning, he glanced at the license plate. The plain white with black letters and numbers meant nothing to him. In the back window was a square sticker of green, yellow, and red. Looked like a flag, but from where? He blinked. The fuzz wouldn't clear. He shoved his elbows into the dirt as he hauled himself beside the SUV. Just before he let his eyes fall shut, dusty boots stopped next to his face.

Chip awoke in his bed again as Adrienna tightened the blood pressure cuff around his arm.

"I'd like to contact my family and ask them to come get me."

"Good morning to you too, Chip." Adrienna hummed to herself. Morning? He must've passed out and slept all night. "I read your mind. I brought a pad of paper for you this morning so you can write down all their contact information for me."

That was easy. A little too easy. Chip wrote out Opa's address and contact details.

He tapped the pen on the pad as he scrutinized Adrienna's features. "Think they'll be able to find me here in Mali?"

Adrienna blinked but not a muscle more moved. "Mali? I think you mean France."

"I don't think I do. I've spent lots of time in France. This place is like no hospital I have ever seen there."

"It's a medical center."

"And if this was France, why did someone on your staff tell me it was Mali?"

"Who said that? Never mind. It doesn't matter." Adrienna's lip twitched. "Breakfast will be brought in soon. Then Janice wants to get you on your feet. Maybe today we can get you to the door and back."

Chip snorted. "I made it outside onto Malian soil yesterday by myself. I think I can make it to the door today."

Adrienna's lowered her chin. If she weren't lying to him, she'd be one of the prettiest girls he'd ever seen. "I don't want to discourage you, Chip, but I think that was probably a dream. Your body is still recovering." She shrugged. "Wild dreams and delusions are very common after traumatic injuries. Not to mention, pain medication is also well-known to create lucid dreams. Don't be too hard on yourself. You'll recover in no time."

She breezed out of the room. Dreams and delusions? No way that had been a figment of his imagination. Had his fear placed him subconsciously in Mali? The food cart girl would prove him right. But when the breakfast arrived, a middle-aged man was pushing it.

"Breakfast is here," the man rasped as he barged into Chip's room without a knock. "Good morning, Chip. Glad you are feeling better. I'm Loris, the center's administrator."

Chip faked his polite smile. He was not in the mood for a friendly chat. If Loris had a social clue, he'd excuse himself and leave.

"I brought a few items of paperwork with me that I need you to sign." Loris placed a packet of papers in Chip's hand which was reaching for the food. "I've highlighted the places to sign and initial."

The packet was at least ten pages thick and—
"It's in French." Chip handed the packet back to Loris. "I don't read French."

Loris swatted at an invisible fly. "I'll walk you through it. First is a treatment consent form. It's standard. We normally would have had you fill this in before you were admitted, but your circumstance was abnormal." Loris held his finger on the signature line until Chip signed. Loris flipped through the pages before Chip could study the words he didn't understand. "The next section is our privacy policy and after that is our financial commitment page. You promise to pay us in a timely manner and all that."

Chip wanted to smack Loris's pudgy finger from the signature line. He never signed documents before reading them.

"I'd like a copy in English before I finish signing please."

Loris frowned. "We don't have any copies in English. You need to sign this one."

The hair on Chip's neck bristled. Another push and he'd rip the pages up in his face. "I need time. I don't think that's an unreasonable request."

Loris huffed and plopped onto a chair. "Fine, I'll sit right here until you are ready. Unfortunately, our policy is that we can't leave you alone with the papers lest you alter them."

Chip doubted that very highly but said nothing. Between English and German and his tiny bit of French, Chip picked out a few words in the document that he understood. He dragged his finger across every line as Loris squirmed. Served him right for trying to rush Chip into something.

At last, he signed on the line knowing as much about the document as he did when Loris handed it to him.

Loris grinned and offered him a mock salute. "Now that you've signed, we have the little matter of the bill to take care of. We ask that this be paid before you are discharged."

Another packet landed in Chip's hand. This one had numbers. He scanned the pages. The nausea grew in proportion to the numbers.

"Have you gone absolutely mad? One hundred and twenty-four thousand Euros? For what? All I've seen the staff do is take my blood pressure and force me to stand."

A dark shadow twisted Loris's features, then changed to indifference. "I'm not privy to that information, Mr. Chapman. However, I do know our medical team is very thorough in their work."

"I don't have that kind of money to give you. I might have a fiver in my billfold. Wherever that is." Chip sat straighter. "As administrator, you should know I haven't seen a thread of anything that belongs to me since I woke up. This place is outrageous."

"Don't get upset. It's not good for you. I'll see about having your things brought to you." Loris collected the paperwork and patted Chip's arm. Now he was being patronized. "Don't worry about the bill right now. We'll contact your family and revisit the topic then."

"They don't have that kind of money either."

"Well, we have a few options for the interim. Our financial department is quite creative in ways that you can get started paying the debt. Focus on healing today and leave money for tomorrow." Loris sauntered to the door, a smug smile on his face. "Eating will help you get your strength back. You'll need it."

Chapter 5

Bamako, Mali

Madison stared at the lady across the desk. This could not be happening.

"I'm sorry, Doctor. We can't renew your visa for another year without proof of reasonable income."

She'd had a fantastic week. And now this. She had passed the Mali medical boards with flying colors, one of the many perks of graduating from Canada's top medical school. The Mali Medical Review Board renewed her certificates with no problems once they saw her test scores.

Clearly, the lady misunderstood. "Madam, I listed my proof of income on my renewal documentation."

"We saw that. However, in order to approve this application, we need you to earn an income within the country. We granted you a one-month extension until you provide proof that you are earning a reasonable income."

"What about the income I make from the hospital? That has to count toward something." Madison shuffled through the papers to find the one with the figures on it.

The lady tapped her stack of the copies. "According to this paperwork, the money that the hospital brings in goes straight to the nurses and assistants."

Penalized because she used the hospital's income to pay to the local staff? A dull throb that started at the base of her neck spread across her whole head. This had never been a problem before. The hospital hadn't made much since the government over-promised and under-delivered, leaving locals to foot the bill.

Stay calm. Be civil. You are a doctor. "How do I prove income to you?"

"We need three reputable witnesses to vouch for your business efforts, an itemized ledger for proof of how much money you are making, and an additional one hundred Canadian dollars for the administrative processing fee."

Always more money.

The lady stood and extended her hand. "Thank you for coming in today, Doctor Cote. We will see you in one month."

One month to make poor people pay what they didn't have. Madison gritted her teeth. She straightened her sagging posture as she marched out the office door. Her nationality made her a puppet, allowing officials to tug on the string of her visa status to get whatever they wanted.

The cloud of frustration followed her to the resort. If anyone ever cared about her opinion, she'd tell them how to fix their government and its greed. In her room she dropped face first onto the bed and yelled into the pillow. That made her feel a tiny bit better. The hospital didn't have her on the schedule until the next evening, and she couldn't deal with much more.

The luxury of the pool called her name. Donning her swimsuit, she wrapped herself in a swim cover. Time to even out the pronounced farmers' tan. Heat soaked into her bones, wicking away the stress of the day. She swam for an hour with the pool to herself, then went inside to the bar for freshly squeezed orange and mango juice.

Above the bar the television played news clips dated from last week about the French military's arrival. The obvious display of their weapons struck fear into the hearts of the regular citizens. Plenty of people made their displeasure clear at the protest earlier in the week. What was happening to this country?

"Recycled news doesn't make for good television, does it?" The comment came from a woman of medium build with dark curly hair and tan skin a few feet down the bar. She twirled a straw around her glass and smirked.

Madison laughed. "Western television producers would be appalled."

The bartender handed her a tall glass of juice. The sweet aroma made her mouth water. She paused before starting to her room. After today's excitement, she didn't want to be alone yet.

She motioned to the seat next to the woman. "Mind if I join you?"

"Please." The woman's dark curls bounced as she nodded. "I work with all men, so amiable female company is always welcome. I'm Sabine." Her face had a permanent, perfectly white smile.

"Madison."

"What brings you here besides this happening bar?"

Madison relaxed against the chair back. She liked Sabine already. "Renewing my medical certifications. What about you?"

Sabine wrinkled her nose. "Waiting for orders."

Sketchy. "Exciting."

"As exciting as government business can be."

"The French government?"

Sabine's eyebrows lifted. "What gave it away?"

"Your accent sounds regional to northern France."

"A little outside Paris. That's quite a party trick." Sabine laughed.

She bowed. "I specialize in people."

"Where do you practice?"

"At a small hospital on the Niger closer to Amdalay."

"It's dangerous down there."

General's words scrolled through her mind. She pushed the thoughts aside. His threats deserved not a minute more of her concern.

"Is the French government concerned about something in that area?"

Sabine tilted her head. "Keep your eyes open for suspicious activity. Drug trafficking is Mali's number one problem."

Of that, Madison was sure. "Those poor locals who live around the routes must receive the brunt of the violence."

"Like you wouldn't believe." Sabine's phone buzzed. She read the screen and sighed. "Looks like I'm dining alone. Again. Would you like to join me for dinner on France's dime? There's a place nearby that gets rave reviews that I've been wanting to try, but my male coworkers call it 'chick food.' They won't go near it."

Madison grinned. "I'd love that."

An hour later, they met in the lobby. Sabine led the way to a sushi joint four blocks from the hotel.

Sushi in Africa. This experience would get a mention in her journal, for sure.

Madison lifted a piece of *maki* to her lips. "You are right. This chick food is incredible." She washed down her bite with a sip of wine. "Now that I can trust your tastes—tell me—is there a man in your life?"

With a grunt, Sabine poked the air with her chopsticks. "Co-workers. They're all teddy bears in grizzly bear bodies."

"That doesn't sound like a bad thing." Would asking for an introduction sound desperate? "Lots of women in Quebec would kill for a man with a grizzly bear body."

"So the crime rate is pretty high then, eh?"

This girl had a sense of humor like no other government worker she'd ever met. "Must be. I should've gone into government work if that's where the attractive men are. What does Mr. Perfect look like?"

"Tall, bearded, a beautiful smile, and muscles like The Hulk."

"Sounds too good to be true."

"Which is why I'm still single." Sabine pointed her chopsticks at Madison. "Yours?"

"Adventurous, but dependable. Selfless, but driven. Just different enough to catch my eye—and my heart."

Sabine raised her glass. "To Mr. Elusive."

Madison grinned. "To catching the one who doesn't want to be caught."

On the walk to the hotel, they exchanged email addresses. It was nice to have company. Sabine promised to introduce her to one of her co-workers when Madison returned to Bamako in a month. And she was already nervous.

The next morning, Madison tossed her bags into her truck. After a three-minute drive, she parked and walked toward the market place where she'd delivered Sam and Fanta's baby. Sam was in his stall. His whole body reacted when he saw her.

"Doctor friend. Doctor, thank you," Sam said then shouted to a man in the next stall. The man walked over and stood with them.

Sam spoke using large hand gestures.

The man nodded and turned to Madison. "I'm Salif, and Sam would like me to translate for him since his French is not good." Salif listened to Sam. "He says, 'Thank you for delivering my baby. Fanta and the baby are very healthy, thanks to you.'"

Sam disappeared into his stall and returned with a crate in each hand. He extended the crates to Madison. She turned to Salif who shrugged but interpreted. "Doctor, I have saved for you my prize hen and rooster in my gratitude. Together these two have the most magnificent offspring, plump and good to eat."

Her jaw dropped and a little laugh escaped. A small gift she could understand, but this? "Sam, I can't take your prize hen and rooster. How will you survive?"

He grasped her hand as Salif spoke. "I have other hens and roosters to sell. But I would give you all of them for helping my wife deliver the baby. I could have lost them if you hadn't been there."

Sam shoved the crates toward her. Delivering a baby didn't deserve this man's most valuable possession. It barely merited a "thanks" in Canada. She held in the rejection sitting on the tip of her tongue. The song and dance of insistence and refusal was Western thinking. She grabbed the crates. "I am honored."

"Come back any time, Doctor. What I have is yours."

"I will care for the hen and rooster as you would." She had no idea how to care for chickens. "What do I feed them?"

"Anything. Chickens eat anything. But if you want them extra fat, my secret is hen pellets." Sam pointed further into the market. "The man at the end of this row will sell you some for a good price. Tell him I sent you." Madison's gaze tracked Sam's finger pointing. "Be sure to haggle hard with him. If he doesn't treat you fairly, I will come take care of him." If the pellet man sounded trustworthy, he might be the only man in Mali who didn't take advantage of a foreign woman's money.

Madison nodded and thanked him one more time. Her cheeks hurt from smiling. She muscled the awkward-sized crates through the crowded market path. Inside one crate, the rooster fluttered and squawked as if he had lost his mind, while the hen peered out the slats, moving her head to watch the happenings. They might make for fine dining if she ever had the heart to kill them.

She stopped in front of the stall filled with burlap sacks. A man called to her, but she didn't understand.

Madison shrugged. "French?"

The man's arms opened wide. "What can I get for you today? Anything you see here is for you. Would you like some fine grain for making bread?" He bent over a bag and started to scoop grain.

"No, no grain. I am a friend of Sam's. He said I need pellets for my chickens."

The man paused. "Sam? I don't know a Sam."

She pointed back to his stall. "His wife Fanta just had a baby."

"Oh, you mean Cheick Oumar." The man slapped his thigh. "He is a brother. He says you need hen pellets." With a wide arm swing, he motioned to his bags. "Then hen pellets you get."

They sparred with the price and she left with almost eight pounds of hen pellets for less than her drinks cost at dinner last night. The walk back to her vehicle took a lifetime at her snail's pace. Ladies with bulky bundles perched on their heads sailed past her.

Their way made so much sense when her hands were full, but she didn't have the head balancing mastered. When she was little, she'd thought only people with flat heads could do it. She'd been disappointed when she found out everyone's head was as round as hers.

At last she made it to her vehicle. She dropped the chicken crates in the truck bed and slapped the bags of pellets next to them. Their beady eyes peered out at her as if daring her to eat them. Raising chickens and selling eggs could make her an income. Her breath hitched. This would work. In one month, she'd show the government that she could do the impossible if that's what they wanted.

Outside the market she drove the winding roads headed for the highway. Once on RN5, she headed south. In too short a time the smooth pavement dumped her on to potholed dirt that jarred her to the bone. Frankly, she could walk faster than she could drive these roads as she weaved to avoid the dips and pits. A bewildered squawk accompanied every bump. The chickens might take a few days to recover from the journey.

Up ahead, a figure moved into the road. She slowed. Pedestrians often waved at drivers to stop and pick them up, but if you stopped for one, you stopped for them all. As she neared, the man stood in the middle of her path, waving a big gun in the air. She sucked in a breath at the sight of the camouflage uniform. What was wrong? She stopped close enough to see his finger hovering near the trigger.

Military or police—they meant business.

Her heart raced as the man marched to her window. If she pulled away, he would get her plate number and find her. Or worse, he would shoot at her. Dying wasn't on her agenda, but African prisons were only one tier away from hell. Her fist tightened around the window crank as she rolled the window down. Heat blasted in.

"Can I help you, Officer?"

The man's eyes narrowed to slits. "I noticed you were exceeding the speed limit."

Not on these roads she wasn't. "No, sir. I was actually going under the limit."

"You were speeding. I saw you. I'm going to need you to come with me to the station."

Madison glanced around. This stretch was strangely void of the normal pedestrians. It was him and her. "How would I go with you to the station? I don't see a vehicle."

"You will drive me." The officer's chin lifted. He glared down his nose at her, daring her to defy him.

"I absolutely will not drive you."

The man blinked and stared. Rage seized his face when her words registered. "Your fine is going up with every minute I stand here at your window."

"A fine? How much money for you to drop the charges?"

"Five hundred thousand francs."

"That's extortion. I will give you ten thousand francs."

The man's eyes shot daggers at her as he fingered his gun. "Four hundred thousand francs."

"Twenty thousand francs in cash to you."

"You insult the government of Mali with such an offer. Pay your fine. Do not make me use force."

"I don't have that kind of money on me. If I did, I still think the fine is exceptionally high considering I was so far under the speed limit that you could have caught me on foot. Be reasonable."

He pointed at her. "You are under arrest for refusing to pay a fine, speeding, and refusing an officer's demand."

What? She'd never been under arrest in her life for an actual crime much less a fabricated one. The officer left her window and stalked to her passenger side, his gun pointed at her the entire time. She banged her forehead against the steering wheel. For the first time in her life, she was headed to jail. Not any random jail—an African jail. She'd be lucky to make it out of this alive.

Chapter 6

Sabine Roux adjusted her headset as the sweat dripped from her neck to her spine where it joined the other droplets in a waterfall down her back. The oppressive gear would save her life if a stray bullet found the armored surveillance truck, but couldn't it come with a built-in cooling system? She'd do anything to be in that pool she'd spent so much time in the last few days.

"Move in." The whisper came in her ear.

Nine of the beefiest men she'd ever met exploded from the van parked behind her truck. They moved in groups of three toward the door. Headquarters handpicked these guys. They were grim reapers with the stealth of ghosts.

And every single one was like family.

In front of her, one monitor displayed a grid of their helmet cameras so she could keep an eye on the operation. The other gave her a three-sixty of the perimeter.

A laser cut through the lock like it was melted butter. In seconds, they crept inside. The front group peeked around a corner and jerked back. Hand signals said four terrorists stood between them and an almost-successful mission. Silencers on the guns smothered the sound of the shots. The front group signaled, and they moved forward as one around the corner.

A large room opened in front of them. Few windows surrounded the top of the wall near the ceiling. Nothing large enough to fit bodies through in case of an attack. The helmet cams gave her a view down the hallway. There were more doors than their intelligence had accounted for. Her team crouched on alert, pointing their guns at various entry points.

Another lock busted.

The first group dashed up the tiny staircase, not knowing what was waiting for them above.

She held her breath. The success of this mission determined her promotion, an elevated clearance status, national recognition for her team, an office with a door instead of a desk in a bullpen, and another foiled drug smuggling route.

Basically everything.

True, the smugglers would find another way to get what they wanted like dogs determined to get under a fence. Once they patched a hole, the criminals dug another. Al Qaeda of Islamic Maghreb, or AQIM for short, was at the top of the most creative traffickers she'd ever worked against. Their commander Amion Dirra dictated through terror, so no method was off limits.

Currently, three French citizens sat as hostages on the second floor of the building they'd breached. Ransoms for Western hostages funded AQIM's creation of Islamist cells around northern Mali. It was a war that France hadn't taken on lightly. Their intelligence from anonymous locals said they'd seen three blindfolded white men being led into the house days earlier.

The sound of silenced gunshots clicked through her headset. Then the camera bounced as the extraction team climbed the stairs. All the hostages were still alive and the guards were eliminated. She exhaled with force and lowered the mic to her mouth.

"Good work, guys. Let's get out of here before backups arrive. Dirra will be none too happy to find his hostages gone." AQIM suffered another blow. She didn't hate that feeling, but it almost felt too easy.

"Get them loaded and move out. Now." The team leader barked over the headsets.

The team retraced their steps, as the hostages limped with them. They were halfway out when her monitor sounded an alarm.

Already? "Guys, Dirra's backup was faster than we expected. They are approaching the north gate. Move."

The extraction team sprinted out the back door with the hostages while the others covered for them. The smugglers' goons headed inside the front while her team slid out the back gate. The truck bounced across rooted trails and mud paths with no tail before Sabine dared to look away from her monitors. The relief shot adrenaline straight into her bloodstream.

Ping. Ping. Ping. Ping.

What was that? She cocked her head.

"Get down." Ralph only yelled when he panicked.

"Ralph, this is no time to pa—"

Boom.

The truck rocked. Gunshots drowned out her shouts. She smashed her face against the floor and covered her head. The desk and bolted-down computers above her shuddered with the force. Ralph was right. This was definitely time to panic.

"Truck one?" She could barely hear her own voice over the noise.

"It's an ambush. We're still going. No one's been hit."

"Get us out of here fast, Ralph."

Dirra played hardball, attempting to explode the trucks with civilians inside. Losing the hostages would be a guaranteed demotion. What was lower than a paper pusher? Coffee lackey?

The exchange of gunshots seemed to go on and on, but the truck never stopped moving. Bile rose in her throat. Her motion sickness kicked in. Four swallows and the acid still burned her throat.

The jerking stopped around the same time the quiet registered. No gunfire.

"Truck one is all clear."

"Truck two, clear."

At the command base, the truck hadn't parked before she ditched her gear and jumped out into the sunlight. Fresh air. The ridged impression of the floor left a small indent on her cheek. She smoothed her hands over her helmet hair. The celebration from the guys exiting the other truck shot sunshine straight into her heart. She joined in on the hugs and congratulations. Her team deserved every win they could secure.

"Sabine?"

She froze. The gravelly voice of the extraction team commander was unmistakable.

"Yes, Colonel Catre." She turned to face him, bracing for his ever-present scowl.

He smiled at her. She stepped back. Meteor showers appeared more often than Colonel Catre's smile.

His hairy hand patted her on the shoulder. "You did well. Slipping out that south gate was a good call. A lesser agent would have lost time getting their team out." He held out an envelope. "From a grateful country. You deserve this."

The envelope felt like silk in her hand. This moment could change everything. Her insides danced at the potential. She slid a shaky finger under the seal. *Hold it together. You will be so disappointed if this isn't what you think it is.* The heavy foot of that thought tamped down hard.

How many times had she gotten her hopes up?

Too many.

She yanked the paper out of its envelope.

Dear Mademoiselle Roux,

Upon the completion and great success of today's extraction, we'd like to offer you a place on the Trafficking of Illegal Substances Investigation Team headquartered in Bamako, Mali. The move has been approved by your commanding officer and only awaits your acceptance.

Sincerely,

The Executive Team of the French Embassy

A squeal escaped her lips. She ducked behind the command station and punched the air. Oh, that felt good. This was what she had worked for every day of the last three years.

Success!

Time to go formally accept. She collected herself, turned around, and ran straight into the well-muscled chest of Burke Sandou, the man handcrafted to perfection by God.

"Why wasn't I invited to this little party?" His deep voice sent a rush of heat to her cheeks.

Some men lost their attractiveness when they opened their mouths. Not Burke. Women of all ages begged him to talk about whatever he wanted for hours. No matter how much she wanted his attention, she didn't beg.

She snagged her lower lip between her teeth and waved the paper in front of him. "A promotion."

Standing on her tiptoes, she pecked his cheek and then danced past him with another squeal. He smelled like fresh air and peppermint. Coming out from behind a building with Burke wouldn't look good. Then again, she shouldn't care. She was headed to the big leagues—an office in the French Embassy and a title that smacked of superiority.

She almost felt guilty for leaving him behind, but heavy footsteps sent a thrill through her chest.

He was coming after her. A warm hand wrapped around her bicep.

"How about a celebration before you leave us out here in Timbuktu?" He grunted. "Literally."

"Hm." As if she had to think about it. His face was so earnest. She shrugged. "Okay."

He relaxed. "Good job on the extraction today."

"A compliment? That means a lot coming from you."

Burke laughed out loud. Music to her ears. This was why she would never be able to work on his team. She'd be distracted.

"Before a celebration dinner, I challenge the newest promotee to a boxing match."

Hard to say no to that.

She tilted her head. "Accepted." She punched his arm lightly. "See you in the ring, thirty minutes."

He gave her a look of approval.

After donning her sleeveless top and shorts, she crossed the common area to the gym. The usual gym rats paid no attention to her. Other females garnered enough attention in their skimpy clothes. That wasn't her style. No need for hungry males to get any ideas about her other than that she had earned every letter in the title behind her name.

Fifteen minutes of stretching had her limber and ready to take on The Hulk. She jumped rope for a couple of minutes to burn the extra energy. Burke was late. According to Colonel Catre, if you weren't early you were late. One minute after their meeting time, Albert walked in. Sabine ducked her head to hide the disappointment that was, no doubt, broadcasted across her face. Albert was Burke's best friend and—apparently—his backup plan.

"Hey, Sabine."

She stopped jumping rope. "Hi, Albert. Here for the spar?"

His face scrunched up. "Burke sent me to apologize. Colonel Catre called him to review the bust tomorrow."

That sucked the wind right out of her celebration sails. Silence settled between them. A man who didn't keep his word wasn't worth her time. Albert shifted his feet. He always seemed so awkward, so opposite of Burke.

"Well." She forced a pleasant expression on her face. No use in verbally battering poor Albert. "You look ready for a fight. Do you want to spar since I have all this energy and nowhere to put it?"

Albert wet his lips and looked at the ground. "Sure, but I wouldn't want to hurt you."

Sabine laughed. "So thoughtful. Don't worry about me."

To Albert's credit, he handled her pounding with good humor. She couldn't tell if he was being nice or if he really couldn't keep up. He tapped out after an hour and a half of sparring. What was left of her energy she burned lifting weights. She took her dinner to go from the mess hall and ate it while she packed. It was a disappointing end to the day, but better to leave with no desire to stay than wish she could stay longer.

The next day, she packed her car and headed to Bamako. She dressed conservatively for her first day in the office. Her new boss, George Armand, met her at security and introduced her to everyone they met on the way to her desk. There were so many, she didn't have a chance at remembering them. At last, he stopped in a doorway and motioned her in.

"It's not a lot, but I think you will find it comfortable and easy to personalize." George winked.

The heavy wooden desk and ornate draperies of red and gold screamed of decadence. A filing cabinet and a bookshelf filled one wall. Two chairs for guests sat opposite her luxury roller chair. Her computer monitor and phone already hummed in anticipation of her use. Her first case came in a thick folder lying on her desk. Her new project—the drug smuggling line from the border of Guinea to the northern Islamic-dominated regions of Mali. This wasn't a quick bust-and-file type of job.

"That file is your welcome present."

Her fingers flipped through the papers in front of her. "I would've liked it better had it been tied with a giant red bow."

George laughed as he plopped into one of her guest chairs. "You can read through the file yourself, but the main problem is General Abdou Karim. His grasp in the area is very tight and has been for over a decade. Before that, his father controlled the area with a more tolerant take. Karim has been on our radar for a while, but according to sources his business is growing rapidly. We need more proof of his drug smuggling."

"Who's inside?"

"He keeps his inner circle tight. At the moment, our contacts are outsiders. They're not included in any of the runs nor are they knowledgeable as to who he buys from at the border. His business has grown exponentially in the last few months, based on what we can gather from our informants. Our military is putting heavy pressure on routes south of the city, so he's bound to get sloppy."

"I'll find my way in," she said.

George left her to it.

Not three minutes later, a slap against the wall made her jump. "Got any leads for the Karim case?"

David, George's boss, stood in the doorway. She'd met him less than an hour ago. His welcome seemed fake then, but now she knew he was possibly the most impatient man to ever live.

"I have a few ideas." Burke's team was the best in the business for this level of investigation.

"What's the best one?"

David wouldn't approve of using the extraction squads for research. "There's a doctor from Canada doing charity work near Amdalay—"

"No. Won't work. We don't involve other countries unless absolutely necessary. Keep on it. Your predecessor caused a lot of damage with his laziness. I hope we don't have a repeat on our hands. Our mail room doesn't need any more sorters." He slapped her wall again before he walked away. That would get annoying. If he stopped by too often, she'd need an extra hour in the gym to recover.

What a miserable man.

She cradled the phone against her ear and dialed a number her fingers knew well. Two rings, then nothing. She grinned.

"Gordo, I need a sturdy steed for a big-stakes race."

"Nothin' new there. Why can't ya find another provider?" His stilted words meant someone was in the room with him.

"Because you like the lifestyle our appreciation affords you. As does your wife." They danced this tango every time. His ears heard everything but only cash loosened his tongue. "Who do you know in Karim's camp?"

A huff. "I'm not associated with anyone in the network anymore. I earn an honest living." Being a rat was as honest as they came.

Sabine scribbled AQIM onto her notepad. Her file mentioned Karim sold to Al Qaeda but missed mentioning he wore their patch. "How long are his arms?"

"His fingertips rest in Western Europe."

With that kind of reach, why hadn't he been higher on the priority list before now? "Give me something, Gordo."

"My cousin's wife's nephew used to be a cook for him. Might still be. Don't know how reliable he is. Bossman keeps communication from his camp really limited so there aren't any leaks. Call me in a couple days. I'll have more."

Sabine dropped the phone into its cradle with a grunt. He'd deliver. He always did. Another flip through the file sounded a quiet warning bell in her head. Something wasn't right with this case. The list of contacts was empty. Karim couldn't be that good. There was always a way in. Everyone talked and would tell you what you wanted to know for the right price.

A thrill sent a tingle down her spine. The hunt was the best part. One thing was sure—her desk wasn't moving to the mail room in this lifetime.

Chapter 7

"Any word from my family?" Chip lowered himself into the wheelchair next to his bed.

Three days of consciousness was far too long to be stuck inside. And way too long to be alone with his thoughts.

"Nothing yet. Loris will let us know." Adrienna set what was left of his things in the corner of the room, their condition tattered. "We couldn't find any identifying items on you except the dog tags around your neck. It was smart of you to wear them. Hope you didn't lose anything important."

Only his passport, pilot's license, driver's license, money, and a credit card. It was probably buried under at least a meter of snow somewhere. "I'll survive."

"Good, because in the meantime, Dr. Thomas said a trip around the grounds would put some fight in your lungs." Adrienna held the handles steady. "You're an outdoorsman obviously, so that is where we will go for you to find complete healing."

She knew nothing of where Chip found healing, what eased the festering wounds deep inside. And there were many. More than healing, he wanted answers. When Adrienna wheeled Chip into the hallway, he sucked in a quick breath. The ceiling was exactly the same as he'd remembered.

Ha—he wasn't loony. Adrienna turned right and wheeled him to a door not far from his room. As she backed the chair outside, the anticipatory triumph welled in his chest.

Then vanished.

In front of him was trimmed green grass, symmetrical flower beds, and gravel walkways. A concrete lion spewing water from its mouth stood in the center of the space, watching over the grounds.

"We're a medical center that uses alternative procedures to heal the brain. Once the brain is healed we step in when absolutely necessary since the body knows how to repair itself." Adrienna stopped the wheelchair next to a golf cart that had handles and extra padding on the passenger's side. "The cart will be easier on you than trying to push a wheelchair through gravel."

As Chip positioned his hands on the armrests, Adrienna shoved her forearms under his armpits and heaved. A laugh escaped Chip's throat and a tennis-grunt from Adrienna's. His body rose an inch off the seat until he had mercy on her and pushed himself up with his legs. Whatever scent she used in her hair made him inhale deeper.

Adrienna stilled. "Are you okay, Chip?"

Faking a groan, he settled into the seat. "I think so. I'm looking forward to being pain-free again." That was the truth.

Ducking into the cart, she sent him a sympathetic smile. An awkward tension hung in the air until the golf cart jerked forward.

"We call this place *La Retraite* which in English is The Retreat. Two brothers built it to what it is today. You met Loris. He is one of the administrators. In addition to our medical center, we also have a trade education center for adults and a school for boys, but we'll drive past those places in our tour. The first place I want to take you is the garden."

The cart crunched between the buildings into the open.

"It's more like a farm than a garden," Chip said. The expanse was a field by any measurement in the UK.

"To your right is the fruits and vegetable section. The fruit trees border the garden. Everything you see is used in our kitchen." Adrienna veered left. "Here is my favorite part. We have wildflowers, rare flowers, and some that were imported from France."

"From France?"

Adrienna clapped her hand on Chip's arm. "Ah, to France. My French is better than my English as you can tell." From where he sat, her English sounded fluent. "Everyone has a responsibility in the garden. Mine is the wildflowers, because they are hard to mess up." She tossed her hair and sent him a sheepish grin. "I don't have the best reputation with keeping plants alive."

Her shrill giggle set him on edge. He didn't join in on the humor. "Bonny good you're better at keeping humans alive then, eh?"

They powered on as Adrienna continued her monologue on the Retreat's history. The dining area, the housing complexes, more fields with people scattered around, a library, and deserted trade classrooms—what was going on? Of all the places to be brought for medical help, why was he here? They left the classrooms headed back the way they came.

Pop.

The cart jolted to the driver's side. Adrienna groaned and let out a string of French words. She got out and tossed her hands in the air.

"Translation?" Chip asked.

"Flat tire." Adrienna propped her hands on her hips. No one was around this area that they'd seen.

With a huff, she retrieved his wheelchair from the back. "Hop in. We're going to find help."

A spare tire was ratcheted to the side of the cart, but not a cell in Chip's body desired to walk Adrienna through the tire-changing process. He swayed in place as Adrienna wrestled the wheelchair over the gravel to the trade classrooms. Once inside, she maneuvered him around crudely built wooden desks and tables covered in layers of dust. Behind the classroom was a workshop. Welding equipment and various metals covered the room. Adrienna grumbled as she stopped to make a path for the chair. On a table next to him sat brushes, shiny black metal parts, and tubes of oil. The set-up looked so familiar.

Almost as if it were the parts to a—

Adrienna stepped between him and the table, pushing his chair from an angle. "I'm going to have to talk to the administrators about the poor shape of this room. It's embarrassing. The coolest thing to see is that ancient samurai sword on the wall over there. Inspiration comes in all forms, I guess."

She shoved his chair out the door, dissolving his chances of getting another look at the table.

Out back, the trimmed grass wasn't as green and the path was free of gravel. Adrienna knocked at the next door and then tried the handle. She pushed him into a mechanic's shop which was in considerably better condition than the welding shop.

"Silly to think a mechanic might be available to help us fix our cart, hm?"

They passed through two more sets of doors and heard shouting. Adrienna stopped inside the doorway of a massive aircraft hangar that had no hangar door. Toolboxes lined the walls as well as boxes of parts. Chip's mouth hung open. A Cessna Turbo Skylane's wing extended within his arm's reach. Behind that, a Pilatus PC-12 filled most of the space. To own and maintain the two required hundreds of thousands of Euros.

"I'll be right back." Adrienna disappeared around the Cessna's tail.

The Skylane was in pristine condition. Chip wheeled himself closer. The tail number began with an F, France's airplane registration code. A hint of relief swept through him.

Had he been dreaming? Mali was a random place for his subconscious to choose. Maybe it was a vision that had meaning?

Around the other side, the stairs to the Pilatus hung to the floor, tempting him to touch her. Beautiful planes and so well-made by the Swiss, but he needed faster and louder. If he could hear himself think, it wasn't good enough.

A door slammed. Harsh voices echoed in the hangar. Adrienna and Loris strode under the nose of the Pilatus. Adrienna waved her hands as she spoke and Loris responded with a firm tone, his face pinched. When they spotted Chip, they went silent. Loris's face immediately donned a forced smile.

"Hello, Chip. Adrienna was telling me about the mishap with the golf cart. I get upset when something puts my staff and guests in danger. Typically, our carts are reliable so I hope you don't think negatively of our safety standards."

Chip shrugged. "Not at all."

Loris patted the Pilatus's stair handrail. "Do you like planes?"

That was an odd question. As if Loris knew the answer already.

"As much as the next guy does, I suppose. I think I saw something like the smaller one in a museum once," Chip said.

Loris's eyes narrowed into slits, giving his face a snake-like appearance. The whites were yellow as if stained by age and sunlight. "Adrienna thinks that all planes are alike, but to me they each have their own personality. Don't you think, Chip?"

Much like women, they could be fickle and charming in the same instant. "If by that you mean they look like other creatures in the world, I agree.

This big one looks like a shark and the little one like a dog wearing a hat."

Adrienna laughed and Loris gave a disapproving hum—the one that all pilots give when someone makes an ignorant comment.

"What gives them personality to you, Loris?" Chip said.

"Their color and shape add to the appeal, but I think the personality comes from how well they handle the sky." Loris laid his hand over his heart. "The dearest ones have quirks and endearing flaws."

"And he could go on about them for days." Adrienna's tone was humored yet familiar as if she were well-acquainted with Loris's airplane speeches. Much like a daughter would to a father. Their skin color was a near match. She grabbed the handles of the wheelchair and pushed Chip towards the door.

"We're taking a different cart so the mechanics can fix the one we had."

Adrienna settled Chip in the new cart. "Now we can finish the tour. Lots left to see."

The tour didn't interest him much, but he wouldn't tell her. Chip studied her face. "Loris is your father?"

It really wasn't a question and she knew it.

Her expression faltered a bit. "He is."

"You two have similar traits." Mainly that neither seemed trustworthy and both could talk for a long time. "In a way, you're heiress to this place."

"My cousins will take over the family business. I'm going to continue to be a nurse." Adrienna lifted her chin. "It's my gift."

He wouldn't argue that she could lift a surprising amount of weight in proportion to her size and take a blood pressure. As for her actual nursing skills, that remained to be seen.

"Good for you. Carve your own path, I say." Although Loris seemed more the arranged-marriage type than the girl-power type.

Her shoulders sank as they rounded a curve. "It's harder than it sounds." She cleared her throat. "Ahead is our school for boys. My father and uncle noticed a lack of men stepping in to raise boys, especially orphans, in this country. Their response was founding a school that would teach boys to be men. After the boys pass our curriculum, we send them on to impact the world in different capacities. While they are here, they help keep the property nice as well as helping in the kitchen, shops, and other areas of learning we have available."

"What ages?"

"Studies have shown that boys between the age of nine and fifteen are the most impressionable, but we won't accept any under the age of eight or over sixteen."

"No doubt that makes for a lively campus." He had yet to see a boy running around the place as he had when he was that age.

"Their part of campus is. They aren't given free rein since we have so many other places where we'd prefer the guests not be disturbed." Adrienna parked and helped him to his wheelchair. "Loris thinks that you might be a great fit for our language department while you are here. Aside from studying French, we teach the boys English."

Dread buried his curiosity. Pax and Opa would come for him before then. They'd figure out how to pay the big medical bill. Somehow.

The rising panic fractured his focus on the school tour. The boys' classrooms were very basic. Cement floors saved on ruined carpet. Benches beat broken chairs. The boys did intensive studies since they didn't stay long after they finished the curriculum. Attached to the classroom building the dormitories featured long rooms of bunk beds and foot lockers. Nothing about the school facility welcomed a student to make it their home away from home.

A bell rang and then a second one.

"We're just in time to attend chapel." Adrienna wheeled him outside and into a chapel.

The whole room smelled like unwashed bodies. No one spoke as they waited for someone to lead them. Very well trained. Most boys he knew would have cut up any chance they could. Chip glanced around at the thirty or so boys. In the corner sat a group of women and girls.

No one in the room was white. In fact, he hadn't interacted with any white people since arriving. France boasted about their diversity, but there wasn't any diversity here to speak of. The realization did nothing to suppress the tightness in his chest. What if this was Mali? The service started and Adrienna murmured along with the voices.

He leaned over to her ear. "Why are there girls in here?"

"Those are my cousins."

All of them?

The person leading the service spoke a few words and motioned to the sides. Everyone dropped to his knees while eight boys grabbed containers, lit something inside them, and wafted smoke over the group as they walked by. The boys placed the containers on pedestals and returned to their seats as the smoke began in earnest.

He took a whiff and coughed.

Adrienna smiled. "The smell of the incense takes some getting used to, but once you release your spirit to rise with the incense, you will feel relaxed and happy." She inhaled deeply.

The smoke stung his nose. That wasn't incense they were burning and inhaling. It was marijuana.

Chip coughed and gagged. Adrienna spread her arms wide and raised her face to the ceiling.

His head ached. He grabbed the wheels to his chair and spun himself around. At the doors, he attempted to push one open. It didn't budge. He tried another.

Trapped.

The marijuana was starting to alter his perception. Tucking his nose into his sleeve, he breathed deeply but still could smell the drug. He pushed at the door again. This time it opened.

Thank God.

He wheeled himself through and turned to acknowledge the door holder.

It was the girl that had brought him breakfast. She was real. He hadn't imagined her. Her wide eyes stared at him, exposing the awful truth. His encounter with her couldn't have been a dream. He was in Mali, Africa.

Everyone spoke French. Orphan boys. Planes. French paperwork. No paved walkways. Blisteringly hot days. Gun pieces on tables. Weed passed off as incense in religious services. If that was what he was allowed to see, what was actually going on behind the scenes?

He had to get out of here, but he was stuck in a wheelchair his body unable to run.

Chapter 8

Mali, Africa

Why?

Why had this happened to her? Wasn't she a good person? She'd paid her dues to life with the junk she had gone through in her childhood.

Madison's handcuffs scraped against the leg of the table. The holding pen, they'd called it. A dark room with one light and no windows, the third-world version of an interrogation room reserved for the worst criminals. If dodging potholes at a glacial pace landed her in the dangerous category, she needed to remind them they had bigger fish to fry. The terrorist organizations ruining the country, for example. She was no national threat.

But police corruption ran rampant throughout Mali—heck, most of the continent.

Footsteps passed outside the doorway. While she suffocated in the stuffy room, they were out there watching TV. Her fingers tingled. She tugged at the cuffs. The table didn't budge, but the metal bit into her skin. The officer had taken no thought of her wrists when he squeezed them as tight as they'd go. She couldn't have been the first woman to tell him no.

Her head thumped on the table. She groaned. No man, especially no self-respecting officer, handled being told no by a woman. She'd kicked him right in his sensitive ego. Rookie mistake.

Worst of all, he held her passport. Her prize chickens, they could have, but her passport and visa were her lifeline.

The door banged open as the injured-ego officer marched in. His eyes weren't crazed anymore.

"Stand up."

She stood as far as the cuffs would allow. He bent to unlock them. Now would be the perfect time to channel her inner James Bond and knee him in the face. Only she wouldn't make it out alive if her escape depended on her martial arts skills.

He shoved her forward through the door. "Walk."

His fingers pinched her upper arm as he hauled her to a small lobby with an empty desk. He backed her against the wall and pulled a Polaroid from the drawer. Did he have to push her so much?

The camera pointed in her general direction, but the guy didn't bother to see if she was in the frame. "Name your crime."

"Speeding."

"Louder," he said.

"Speeding."

The flash blinded her eyes when he pushed the button. He set the camera on the table with care, more care than he was taking with her. She almost asked him if he was done throwing a fit, but he yanked her chains first. She stumbled and caught herself. His laugh about sent her over the edge of her control. Inside the cell, he unlocked her handcuffs and pushed her one last time for good measure.

"Get comfortable."

She muttered a few choice English words at his back. Where was common decency? The cell door slammed in her face. She rattled the door in disgust. A man occupied the cell already but didn't open his eyes as she plopped onto the floor.

Thick, corded cables stretched across the small opening in a crisscross pattern, clearly a low-budget cell. The short ceilings, lack of windows, and tight space resembled more of an animal cage than a holding cell. Three bodies packed the opposite cell to capacity. The stench of human waste and unwashed bodies overwhelmed her. The other cell's occupants regarded her with silent interest. She was their entertainment.

Sweat beaded on her forehead. The heat had her sweeping her hair into a bun. Already she considered shedding layers. Except that the longer she sat on the dirt floor the more thankful she was she had worn trousers. Since med school, not much had fazed her, much less caused the physical reaction that presently boiled in her gut. Proving an income to the government had been a nuisance, but being in jail gnawed ulcers into her intestines. She switched from hyperventilating to holding her breath to avoid puking.

Her gaze shifted to her male cellmate, propped against the cell's back wall. Asleep, his chest rose and fell in an easy rhythm. Relaxed almost. His face was somewhat handsome. He didn't seem like the criminal type, but then everyone looked peaceful and kind when they slept.

Deep creases pulled across his forehead, stressing his pale face. A strange comfort eased her mind. Another foreigner was in this predicament with her. If someone was coming for him, they might get her out, too.

She squeezed her eyes shut. Her mind ran through every option it could conjure up in an effort to avoid this cell. Useless. Hope was all she had. No one knew where she was. No one at the hospital would notice her absence until tomorrow. The offer of money didn't interest the officer after he'd declared her under arrest.

Cursing her foolishness, she vowed that if— no—when she got out, she would buy a satellite phone immediately. The Canadian Embassy would be on speed dial for such emergencies.

Was she allowed a phone call? It didn't matter. Everyone she wanted to call didn't have a phone— the hospital, Ina. Roger was probably smart enough to have one, but she didn't know his number. What a wretched mess she was in.

It was too much. A huff escaped her lips. She, Madison Cote, was two breaths away from crying for the first time in over thirteen years.

"Don't cry."

Madison twitched. She eyed her cellmate. Had he said that? He hadn't moved, so maybe she'd imagined it. Her head drooped against the wall. The caustic anxiety wore her energy thin.

English.

She gasped. The voice telling her not to cry had spoken in English, not French. She bit her lip. The people in the other cell appeared to be locals. Highly unlikely they spoke English.

Her gaze shifted once more to the man. This time he met her confusion with intensity in his jade-colored eyes, his expression flat. Neither of them looked away. That would make her a coward and she wasn't about to let him intimidate her.

"I'm glad you didn't cry." His voice was deep and melodic. And German. "I could hear it in your breathing."

There was no use in trying to deny it. Her eyes widened. "I didn't know my breathing was that loud. I'm sorry to disturb you."

He tilted his head but didn't answer. The tension knotted in her shoulders again. Exactly how much of a criminal was he?

"So why are you in?" she asked.

The silence stretched deep and wide, as if he misunderstood her or found her question too intrusive. She didn't pursue it.

He shifted his weight. "I ran a roadblock and they shot out my tires."

This guy didn't mess around. His story could easily have been hers. "Sounds extreme."

His head moved with slow nods.

The awkwardness grated her nerves. "I'm in on false speeding charges."

"I heard."

She raised her eyebrows.

The corners of his lips tilted upward. "The low ceilings make everything echo, Madison Cote of Quebec City, Quebec, Canada."

Well, that was embarrassing. "And your name is?"

"Duke."

"So, Duke. Is there a way to get out of here?"

"An elaborate prison break scheme might work."

This wasn't going as she'd expected. "You watch too many movies."

Duke motioned to the room around him. "Clearly."

"This is going to sound ridiculous." She leaned toward him. "But do I get to make a phone call for someone to come get me?"

A dimple appeared in his left cheek, but he didn't smile. What a shame. "You have someone to come get you?"

They probably wouldn't supply the Canadian embassy's number, but she could ask. She nibbled the inside of her lip. Her situation amused him. If she said she did, he wouldn't help her. If she said she didn't, he might help her or take advantage of her. Her ability to lie ranked low in her skill set.

"I do have someone." Lots of someones under the age of twelve. She pressed her fingers into her shoulder. "To come get me, I mean. But that someone doesn't have a phone for me to call."

His bare feet had red spots that looked like burns. She leaned closer, but he tucked his bare feet under his tattered jeans and raised his eyebrows. "There isn't a phone here anyway. You'd be better off sending a message via carrier pigeon."

No phone. His words sucked the remaining oxygen from her dying ember of hope. "Is that what you did?"

Duke snorted, the creases in his forehead disappeared for an instant. He opened his mouth but snapped it shut again. The sparkle in his eyes faded.

"No, I did not send a carrier pigeon with a message."

"So who is coming for you then?"

His head fell against the wall. "God, I hope."

He stretched out on the floor with his forearm over his face. His frame filled three-quarters of the length of the cell. He couldn't go to sleep on her.

"You think you'll recognize him when he walks in?"

Duke didn't move. "Who?"

"God. You said you hope he comes to get you. Do you think you'll recognize him?"

Duke's beautiful eyes searched hers, staring straight at her vulnerability. "I wouldn't know him by looking, but I think I'd know who he was when he said my name."

She pulled her knees to her chest. He must know him well then. "When he comes for you, put in a good word for me, if you would."

"Okay."

His words balmed her anxiety-riddled soul. Things might work out after all.

"Duke?"

"Hm."

She shouldn't ask if she didn't want to know the answer, but she'd find out sooner or later. "Do they feed you here?"

"Once a day."

"Water?"

"Twice a day."

"Let us out of the cell?"

He paused. "Never."

Chapter 9

From the spotted shade of a small tree, Chip watched Adrienna stagger out of the chapel with a boy holding each arm. They laughed loudly at something she said. The burn in his chest radiated to his stomach. He and Pax knew too well what came after the high. Rage. Hate-filled stares. Shouting. Fists hitting flesh. The taste of blood. Pleading. Tears.

Did the boys know the poison they inhaled? Did they care?

"Chip, these are my *copains*, Tag and Jab. *Je* love them. I also love *chapelle*. I feel calm and happy. If you don't have religion, you should get some." Adrienna swayed as she grabbed for the wheelchair handles and giggled when she missed. "Or you can borrow some of mine, Chip. You should always be confident about the destiny of your soul. You can think about it over lunch." Chip's chair jerked forward. "I feel like I haven't eaten in days."

Adrienna's companions grew quiet while they walked. Probably focusing on staying upright. At the front of the line to enter the eating area, the religious leader handed each boy a pill.

"What is it?" Chip asked.

"*Prêtre* gives each boy a tablet so the health of their bodies is aligned with the health of their souls." Adrienna feigned a whisper. "Personally, I think it's just a vitamin."

The leader bowed his head when Adrienna and Chip reached him. He extended a pill to Chip. Adrienna waved her hand, letting loose a long string of nasally vowels as she wheeled him by.

"*Prêtre* doesn't ever give me one. Dad says it's because I'm a girl and the tablets are meant for boys. Although you're a boy, I told him you were a guest of our medical center, so you didn't need one." Adrienna dipped next to his ear. "Besides, we are already working on the health of your body with our own medicine."

Her breath against his ear sent a tingle along his spine, making his shoulders twitch. "What medicine do you give me?"

She shrugged. "Dr. Thomas oversees that. He's a great doctor. He studied in North America somewhere." She pushed him until his feet bumped against a flimsy wooden table. "Sit with the boys while I get us lunch."

As soon as Adrienna stepped out of earshot, Chip nodded at Tag and Jab who'd already grabbed their plates. "Do you speak English?"

They grinned at him.

"A little," Jab said.

"Do you like being here?"

They nodded.

"We are lucky," Tag said. "Some boys in our village were not chosen because they were too weak. With this learning, we are given the chance to become something more than our fathers and grandfathers."

Jab nodded. "They give food and bed and clothes. We had no school in villages, because we work. Here we learn new things and become men. We return home a better person."

Jab shoveled food into his mouth and swallowed without chewing. Chip's chair jammed into the table. A hand swept over his head toward Jab's plate. Jab and Tag leapt to their feet as the offender snagged a handful of Jab's food and tossed it on the ground. Jab tackled the boy to the ground, rolling him over.

After five half-hearted kicks to the chest and face, Jab and Tag left the boy on the floor surrounded by food particles. They laughed as they returned to their seats nonchalantly. The caveman display went uncorrected. No one stopped to help the offender whose nose bled all over the floor. In a way, he'd brought it on himself. Adrienna stepped over his body with a loud giggle and placed both plates on the table.

"I hate when I miss the exciting stuff," she said.

The plate of rice had small bits of what appeared to be a vegetable. Next to that was a green glob. Chip much preferred the presentation of the meals delivered to his room. There he was given silverware at least. The thought of giving eating utensils to thirty boys who were high as Mont Blanc made him cringe.

"We do physical training after lunch," Tag said.

Adrienna clapped, but her eyes were bleary. "You should go with them, unless you're tired. I always take a nap after chapel and lunch."

His adrenaline levels flowed at an all-time high. Sleep was the last thing he wanted. He had to get more information on how to get home.

He motioned to Tag. "I'll go with you."

A gong sent vibrations through the table. Like a football team after half time, the boys surged out of the door beating their chests. Adrienna sighed and giggled after every other bite. Chip swallowed what he could stomach and spread the rest around the plate, biting his tongue to keep from snapping at her to hurry up. When she finally finished, she wheeled him to the training building and left him inside.

No girls allowed inside.

No exceptions.

The main room was chaos. Pairs of boys beat on each other in a dirty free-for-all. Neither structure nor sportsmanship showed their gentlemanly heads. From the corner two men surveyed the brawls.

After a few nods, one man weaved through the crowd and raised his hand beside a pair of fighters. A hush fell over the rest of the boys as they formed a half circle to watch, leaving Chip's view unobstructed. The height difference between the fighters was laughable. The little one was quick and scrappy whereas the big one covered more distance in his powerful swing.

If the lesson was how to choose a fair fight, then the teachers picked the perfect example of making the wrong choice. The surge in his chest screamed that nothing at The Retreat was as it seemed. The moment the man handed the little one a knife, Chip's breathing stopped.

What was the idiot thinking?

It was sick. Perverted. Unethical. Neither side would win.

But he couldn't stop watching.

The little boy sliced at the bigger boy. The knife empowered him, made him brash. In a heartbeat, he went from his heels to his toes—defeated to invincible. Onlookers whooped with each charge and hissed with each retreat. The bigger boy dodged and watched. He had more body surface to keep track of but his hands never left his face unguarded. The blade bit into the bigger boy's forearms leaving a trail of blood. The little one roared and beat his chest, working the crowd.

The bigger boy launched at the boy's torso. Surprise flashed across the little boy's face as they crashed to the ground. When the bigger boy staggered to his feet, the little one stayed on the ground, the knife protruding from his side.

Everyone went silent. The man barked out instructions and four boys carried the little one out of the room. Still but alive.

And the nightmare continued.

Chip exhaled.

"Pride is a deceptive drug, isn't it? Makes us feel out of reach."

Chip clamped his hands around the armrests and glanced left. The second of the two men stood next to him, his gaze on the boys.

And stupidity in giving a boy a knife ranked up there with the wickedness of pride. Chip clenched his jaw.

"I hear the rage in your silence." The man clucked. "You are a man of action like me. We demand justice by the rules of warfare. These boys, what do they know of either?"

Apparently, the whole campus knew he came in with dog tags. They were imitations that Opa made them wear when hiking, but he didn't bother correcting him.

Instead, he flexed his fingers around the armrest. "Life doesn't offer kindness equally, so some boys learn the ways of men much sooner than they should."

The man tilted his head and studied Chip. Then he broke out into a big smile. "We have much in common, *oui*. You must come to my home for dinner tonight, okay? When Adrienna comes to care for you this afternoon, tell her that Abe asked you to dinner."

He clapped Chip on the shoulder and disappeared out the door. Chip rubbed his face. The boys filed out of the room except a lone boy mopping the blood spot.

The bigger of the boys, the winner of the fight.

His reward was a mop and a bucket.

Chip had been that boy—beaten down, cheered against, hoped to fail. Mum always said, "Negativity attracts negativity." Time after time, he'd chosen positive actions, holding his heart in hands begging for someone to notice him, appreciate him, and approve of him.

That changed as a pre-teen when he decided to go into the Air Force. Chip approved of himself and that was enough.

It'd have to be.

Adrienna gaped at Chip when he relayed Abe's message. Her explanation of "because Abe doesn't usually like strangers" brought him no comfort. Nevertheless, she appeared on schedule and handed him an over-sized collared shirt to pair with his medical center sweat pants. His unease had grown as he contemplated his escape options and found he had none without a strong body. Creating a plan to execute was what he did best, but without all the facts he was left empty-handed.

They loaded into the golf cart. Adrienna tapped the steering wheel and didn't say a word. Why was she so jittery about eating at Abe's house?

Abe's house was a sprawling estate—not a mansion by U.K. standards, but a single-story building that was as long as it was wide. A gate let them into an open grass courtyard where dozens of other golf carts sat. A place this big had to have staff.

Cement walkways surrounded the courtyard. Three bright parrots perched on a carved statue. They eyed him and squawked as he rolled by.

Once they entered the house, they weaved through a network of well-lit hallways. Children skipped by calling out to Adrienna with enthusiasm. She didn't offer a word about the house's school-like aura with countless doors and off-shooting corridors. Instead she chattered about the kids she saw.

Loud voices carried down the hall. Laughter erupted as they approached the open door. The aroma of meat greeted them.

Inside, pots and pans clattered, keeping time for a woman with a bowl on her head, dancing in the middle of the kitchen. She dipped in a low bow, but the bowl didn't budge. Chip clapped. The dancer sent him a wink.

"You should take your act on the road," Adrienna said.

The ladies laughed. They waved goodbye as Adrienna wheeled him further in the maze. When the twelfth kid stopped to give her a hug and a kiss, he couldn't contain his curiosity.

"They're my cousins." Her mumble was hushed as if the walls were listening.

"Which makes Abe your..."

"Uncle."

"And he has twelve kids." Abe obviously loved children if he had that many kids of his own in addition to the orphan boys.

Adrienna snorted. "He has more than that. You'll see them all at dinner."

She cut her explanation short by knocking at a door. The door opened revealing lush tan carpet and a group of men sitting in front of a television. A man thanked Adrienna and wheeled Chip further into the room. Chip could have walked, but he was enjoying playing the invalid for the time being. A variety of preserved animals and mounts decorated the green walls. Abe had kept the taxidermist busy with his kills. Overstuffed armchairs sat in front of a huge flat screen TV showing the Olympics.

"Ah, Chip, our honored guest." Abe strode into the room, drawing everyone's attention in his direction. "Glad you made it this evening." Abe held out his hand and a glass was put into it. "I checked with Dr. Thomas. He said you can have scotch neat."

The room went cold then hot as Chip grasped the glass with a murmured "thank you." How strangely coincidental. A scotch neat was Father's addiction of choice. Something about the burn gave dear ole Dad a thrill. Chip wouldn't drink it. Not out of fear of addiction, but because Abe could have handed him an unopened bar of Toblerone and Chip still would be searching for a place to dump it.

Chip's wheelchair stopped in front of the TV. Three men greeted him with nods and returned their attention to the screen. Brazil's men's football team ran circles around some team with rubbish defense.

"Great Britain is doing well in swimming," Abe said, settling himself in a chair next to Chip. Imagine islanders winning at water sports. "We need to succeed at something. Not qualifying in football this year was a national embarrassment."

Abe chuckled and the other men laughed with him. A little too loudly. Chip lifted the glass, inhaled, and swirled the brown liquid around. Right before he got sloshed, Father always said savoring a drink showed respect to the drink and the buyer, especially if it was expensive. Abe's scotch emitted an aroma like no scotch Father had ever kept stocked. Whether it was better or worse or not scotch at all, the devil he didn't know set him on edge.

A man whispered in Abe's ear then held open a side door.

Abe clapped. "Dinner is ready, my friends. Please come find your seat."

Chip's wheelchair magically moved into the huge dining room. Three long tables formed an open square with chairs and benches on both sides of each table. Women and children filled two tables on both sides. Adrienna sat closest to the men's table. He caught her eye and motioned at the kids with raised eyebrows. She nodded.

All his kids. There were only four adult women besides Adrienna. Wives? Nannies? Concubines? He leaned back to look at Adrienna, but her gaze stayed on the table. Next to her, Loris bared his teeth at Chip in a mock smile. Daddy wasn't ever far away. Didn't he have nineteen other kids to worry about, too?

Chip sat directly across and one down from Abe. Neither of his neighbors engaged him in conversation, so Chip kept to himself. Bowls and platters of food waited on the tables. The priest stood with lifted hands, silencing the room. Chip checked the air for smoke. Nothing.

"*Notre Dieu.*" The rest of the words blended into an unintelligible string of monologue.

The *Amen* was barely finished before the talking began again. As everyone served themselves from the communal platters, a beautiful woman glided into the room and set Abe's plate full of food in front of him. He caught her hand and kissed it. Her face beamed the "I love you" that she didn't say.

Abe motioned her closer and kissed her with unbridled passion. Twenty kids from one woman made sense if there was that much steam in the relationship. Chip glanced behind him to see if the other women noticed. The women had.

Trying to make sense of Abe's relationships made Chip's brain hurt. He busied himself with filling his plate and taking table cues from his neighbors who were deep in conversation.

Eating rice with your fingers? That was a giant waste of time. Hunger overruled his hesitation. Chip dug in. No mysterious glob of vegetables were served at this meal.

"Chip, tell me. Are you an experienced hiker?" Abe bent over his plate stuffing in the food, his expression friendly.

Chip shrugged. "I've hiked since I was a wee boy. Some would call that experienced, but others would only count the times I hiked a certain difficulty level."

"I cannot figure out how it was you fell down a mountain."

The scene replayed in his mind for the millionth time. Pax's ridiculous need to save the animal. Opa's blaring horn. His need to cool off before lashing into Pax for being such an idiot.

"We were coming down from the summit, and an avalanche hit out of nowhere. And unfortunately, I'm not that fast of a runner."

Abe paused and then laughed. The rest of the men laughed with him. Black fuzz on the top of a little head appeared next to Abe's elbow. Abe scowled when a hand patted his arm. Chip sucked in a breath. If Abe had wanted to be disturbed by

children, he'd have sat at the table with the kids.
Poor kid.

Abe glanced at the child and then at the woman
behind him. Her face scrunched in embarrassment.
Or was that a hint of fear? Abe swung the child onto
his lap. She couldn't have been older than three and
already had piercings in her ears. Abe handed her a
piece of meat from his plate and spoke in her ear.
Her eyes lit up as she nodded, munching happily.

Perhaps a man with that much love and
tenderness for his family wasn't a cold-hearted
monster who delighted in letting boys stab each
other to teach them a life lesson.

When the evening was over, a guy helped him
into a golf cart to take him to his room. The warning
flags waved a little less vigorously now. He'd be
leaving soon anyway. As soon as Loris heard from
Opa, they'd come get him.

Chip's chauffeur drove without a word until the
radio on his belt squawked. He answered, listened,
and answered again. The chauffeur stopped the cart.

"I'm sorry, *monsieur*. I am needed immediately.
The medical center is ahead." The chauffeur pointed
to the well-lit entry across the way. "I must leave
you here."

Chip exited as the cart peeled away taking his
wheelchair with it. The man must have forgotten

that Chip was still recovering. They weren't far from the classrooms which led to the mechanic shop and aircraft hangar. Without a hangar door, Chip could sneak in and find the answers he was looking for. No one was out here to see him.

Turning on his heel, Chip retraced the path to the classrooms. He stayed next to the building, away from the lights at the front. His stomach churned with each step closer. Past the mechanic shop, he stopped.

Light poured onto the grass from windows adjacent to the hangar. Chip peered in. No one was inside. He slid in and crawled under the Skylane to get to the entrance.

The door hung open.

With a glance over each shoulder, Chip hauled himself inside the plane. In the pocket next to the captain's seat was a handful of papers. Chip yanked out the airport directory. Europe 1995. No key in the ignition so he couldn't check the fancy GPS.

A muffled shout sent his heart racing. A voice responded. Chip ducked. His pulse thumped in his ears. Could he for once sneak around without getting caught?

The hangar lights flickered on. Chip crawled behind the second row of seats. Beside him two stacked duffel bags blocked his view of the luggage compartment door. He hugged his knees to his chest.

A loose wrench lay in front of him. He snagged it for protection. Who was he kidding? He grabbed it to make himself feel better.

The voices grew closer and stopped outside the plane. A loud thud made him flinch. Hands pushed a bag to the opposite wall of the compartment. Three more bags came in after it. The hatch snapped shut. Chip relaxed. These guys couldn't leave soon enough.

As Chip leaned in to peer between the seats, the plane sagged and a dark head appeared in the doorway. Loris. The two men exchanged quick words. Then the aircraft moved and the lights disappeared. Chip's grip tightened on the wrench. The slam and lock of the cabin door took the air from his lungs.

A flight was happening tonight. As in now.

The weight and balance consequences of the plane could be dire, but he was willing to risk it. He was ready to go home. And this was his chance to do it.

Chapter 10

Mali, Africa

Night had never been so black. Madison paced the width of the cell.

Two strides, turn, two strides, turn.

No one had come to discuss her release. The sole visitor to the cell had been a small boy who left two bowls of porridge made from cardboard particles. It settled into her stomach like cement. She took her time eating since she wouldn't have the privilege of ingesting any more for another twenty-four hours.

Human rights activists would have had a field day with this place.

She saved her small cup of water, drinking sips at a time. The last thing she wanted to do was use the human waste pail in the corner with Duke only a few feet away. During the day, she would sweat off most of the liquids she took in, but she'd have to use the pail soon enough. Thinking about it made her palms clammy.

Little had been said between them all day. Duke had kept his eyes closed most of the time, so she used the opportunity to study him. His physique, hidden under his t-shirt and jeans, seemed toned from work instead of the gym. His tan skin and calloused hands suggested he'd seen years of hard work, but she didn't dare touch him to find out. Unless there was a medical emergency.

A medical emergency.

Maybe they would free her if she told them she was a doctor. Or like everyone else, they'd ask her to diagnose their ailments without letting her go. They might keep her longer if they could get free medical advice out of it.

"Are you trying to wear a hole in the ground with that pacing?" Duke's low voice made her jump.

"Not a bad idea. Do you think I could escape under the cables if I wore a hole deep enough?" She cringed. Her voice was abrasive.

"You could, but how would you get past the guard?" He sounded somewhat amused.

"Well, I'd need a distraction, I think."

Duke tsked. "You won't find one of those around here."

"Are you saying you wouldn't want to escape if I could get us out of here?"

"We'd get no further than the door before they caught us."

"But if we did, I have a vehicle outside. We could try to outrun them and hope they weren't armed."

"Doesn't work. You have a vehicle here? How did that happen?"

"It's a pathetic story actually." She closed her eyes. *Please don't ask what happened.*

"I'm all ears. I love a good story."

"I said it was pathetic."

"I have time and lots of sympathy."

He wasn't letting this go. She exhaled and told him what happened. The whole incident sounded ridiculous when she retold it.

"And you didn't think to get out of there when he told you he was taking you to jail?" His pitch raised in disbelief. She felt five years old again.

"He had a huge gun and his trigger finger was twitchy. Those roads have so many potholes that he'd have caught me on foot after an axle snapped." An edge crept into her voice. "Some of us prefer not to be shot at by the police. Anyway, I figured he would bring me to the station, make me pay a fine, and let me go. I didn't think they'd actually put me in jail and hold me for ransom. It wasn't exactly in the 'Mali for Dummies' guide I read, you know."

Duke kept silent, so she continued. "Why? How did you get here?"

"They hauled my wife and me here in their police cars after they shot the tires of my car."

Married? Not surprised. "Your wife? What's her name? Is she in the cell across from us?"

"No, Anna Grace is not."

That didn't make sense. "She got out, but didn't take you?"

"She's dead."

She covered her mouth with her hand. "Duke, I'm so sorry." The silence magnified the pain. "What happened?"

"Same as anyone else. She was alive and then her body stopped working. Now she is dead." The sharpness in his tone slid into her heart like a knife. Death—the ultimate failure.

"How long ago?"

"Too long, yet not long enough to forget her beautiful smile or the sound of her laugh." His voice broke, but he cleared his throat to cover it.

She sank to the ground close to him. The heat radiating from him added to the stifling heat seeping in from outside. She ignored the urge to move. He didn't seem to be the type that wanted a shoulder to cry on. What he needed was an amiable companion to keep him from his misery. And her own.

"Tell me about yourself, Duke."

He said nothing.

"Please?" She slid over so her shoulder touched his.

A sigh escaped his lips. "What do you want to know?" His voice was soft.

"Where are you from?"

"Austria."

Ha. She knew his accent sounded German. "What brought you to Mali?"

"We came to teach agriculture near Bankoumana."

"You're upriver from the hospital I work in."

"Are you a nurse?"

Madison coughed. "Doctor."

"I offended you by asking if you were a nurse?" She could hear the humor in his voice.

"Would you be offended if I called you a gardener?"

"Point taken."

She giggled. "I didn't go through a million years of med school for nothing."

"Then I suppose I should give you the honor due your position and start calling you Doctor."

"Call me whatever you like, Doc, Doctor...Your Highness."

"Madi?"

Her heart pumped double-time. Her voice squeaked out at a whisper. "No one's called me that since…"

"Since?"

"Close to eight years."

"That's a while."

Madison shifted. "Are you planning on starting your own coffee shops in Europe with your crops?"

"A great idea, but we're not growing coffee beans."

"That's too bad. Westerners are suckers for a good cause."

Duke's deep chuckle made her heart swell. She had to hear that sound again.

"To renew my visa, the embassy said I need to prove a substantial income from within the country. The hen and rooster dying in the back of my truck are my best plan."

"Sounds like they're fleecing you. There isn't much by way of health care outside the city unless witch doctors are your style. Don't you have plenty to do with working at a hospital?"

"The hospital income doesn't count since it goes to pay the staff, not me."

"What about your chickens? You could sell eggs or the whole chickens once they are old enough."

"Don't people already have their fill of chickens with the ones running around like they own the world?" She shrugged. "I know nothing about raising chickens, nor do I have time to take them to a market to sell them."

"Know anyone who could take them for you?"

His questions jabbed her pride. Why did everything return to her being alone? "No one that I trust."

"If we ever get out of here, I'll raise your chickens and take them to the market for you. I take produce to markets several times a week. You can keep the profit."

He'd said we. Maybe he hadn't given up yet. "How is that fair to you? You raise my chickens and take them to the market yet you make nothing for it? That isn't right."

"It's plenty fair, because I get all the eggs I want." He paused. "And you'll let me use your vehicle since mine was taken by the police and I have no money at the moment."

Hysteria bubbled inside her. Then she burst out laughing. It felt good to laugh.

"All right, Duke. You have yourself a deal. But there are conditions. I must see you several times a week so I can use my truck. It's my lifeline. Driving is the only way I get away from the hospital. I'd go insane without it."

"Except when you go home every night."

Home—what did that mean anymore? She stared at him.

The lightness in his tone dropped as his brow furrowed. "You said driving is the only time you leave the hospital, but that's not true. You have to go home every night."

Madison paused as the reality of how pathetic she was dawned on her. Should she really admit she lived in the hospital? She'd already promised to share her vehicle with him. It couldn't be worse than General knowing where she slept.

"I sleep at the hospital, Duke. I don't go to a separate house each night."

"You work and live there." His tone was one of genuine curiosity, but still felt belittling. "Why?"

"It's free and fairly safe. There are always people around. And if one of my patients needs medical care overnight, I am present to guide the nursing staff. It's easier that way."

"And how often does the overnight staff need your assistance with a patient?"

His nosiness tested her patience. "Every so often."

"How often?"

She glared at him ready to take his criticism. "Rarely."

"Then why don't you come live with me?" He relaxed against the wall as if he'd volunteered to watch her pet goldfish, not share a living space. "It'd be free of charge."

His proposition stole the wind from her sails of justification. He was dead wrong if he thought by lending out her wheels she would be willing to sleep with him. It was just like a guy to think that's what a trade involved.

Her disappointment morphed into panic. "I'm sorry if I gave you the wrong impression, but that is not the arrangement I was looking for."

His hand closed around her arm. "Not like that. You're here in Mali. You don't have any connections. You have no one to call when you need something."

Madison jumped to her feet and paced. He'd overstepped his bounds. "You know nothing about me. You don't know who I know here or how I protect myself."

He grunted. "A few minutes ago, you said you didn't have anyone you trusted to take your chickens to the market. And if you can't trust someone with your chickens, then I know you don't have anyone to bail you out of here."

Oh, she hated his smug words. "Yes, I do."

"Who? Who do you know and trust that can pay your fee?"

She could say anyone's name and he'd have no idea. With her chin tilted upward, she let triumph seep into her tone. "Monsieur Karim."

Duke sputtered. "Please tell me, not General Abdou Karim."

She gasped. Of all the people she could have named, he knew the General.

"It is, isn't it?"

There wasn't a chance she was admitting that.

"You are close enough to General Karim for him to rescue you? I didn't take you as the kind of woman who would willingly be in a warlord's harem."

Caught in her own lie. "I'm not. And no, I don't know him well enough. I lied." She rubbed her neck. She was digging her own grave with Duke. "I didn't really expect you to recognize his name."

Duke let out a laugh. "Madi, everyone south of Bamako knows who he is. He runs everything from Bankoumana to the Mali-Guinea border—"

"I know. I know."

"I was trying to be nice by giving you a place to stay that got you away from the hospital." His voice sunk lower. "And I would feel guilty leaving you stranded without your vehicle."

"That's a kind offer. I'll think about it."

"I promise nothing morally reprehensible will happen. It's one Westerner helping another survive the Mali wilderness."

"And Anna Grace? What would she say about it?"

He looked at the ceiling. "She would have had you living with us in a heartbeat. She wouldn't have taken no for an answer."

"But living alone in the same house as you…"

"Well, she'll have to trust my judgment in helping a stranger. Let's be honest. We both know that it won't be long before something else happens that could be prevented by the presence of a male you trust."

"You think highly of yourself."

"Not highly of myself, but very poorly of the male species in the area who would willingly take advantage of a single, unprotected woman and not think twice about the damage done."

Everything in her longed to deny his words, but she couldn't. Morals for survival in Mali sure didn't look the same as they did in Canada. Her mentor would have a fit. Or would have had a fit had he stayed alive long enough to see her move to Mali to use her skills.

"If we make it out of here, I will board at your house for the sheer purpose of having someone watching my back. As a doctor, I will return the favor if you need medical attention."

"And don't forget that you have to prove that you are making an income." He sounded satisfied.

"Yes, that too." Fatigue washed over her, but it'd be a miracle if she could fall asleep.

"Since we have that settled, let's talk about your friendship with General Karim."

A crack of thunder interrupted her protest. The first drops of rain tapped on the roof. She loved the clean air the rain brought with the breeze. A light patter turned to pounding downpour in seconds. The roar was deafening.

"Here we go." She barely made out Duke's words over the noise.

"What?"

He grabbed her hand and pointed to a corner. "Sit there until the rain stops."

Why? Lightening lit the cell through the cracks in the walls. Rivulets of water trickled in from outside, turning their dirt floor to slop. Duke dug at the mud and stuffed it where the floor and wall met.

The water found a path around his blockades. The crevices he made drew the water away from the rest of the floor, leaving a few dry patches. Rinsing the grim from her skin sounded heavenly. Madison cupped her hands and leaned toward the water.

Duke grabbed her hands. "No, don't touch it."

"I want to wash my face."

"It's not safe." Thunder shook the walls as the lightening illuminated Duke's scowl. "The water is overflow from a pond behind the jail."

"It's not fresh water?"

"You saw the sores on my feet. It's filled with parasitic Guinea worms."

Chapter 11

We are going to die.

Chip was more positive now than the last twenty-six times he'd told himself that during the ten-minute flight. Loris piloted the plane as if he were taking his jalopy out for a Sunday cruise. He did none of the usual pre-flight checks of the engine or the propeller. Just opened the throttle and away they went.

No concern whatsoever that they could fall out of the sky in a fiery ball of burning metal. Besides that, he didn't make any calls on his radio. If he wasn't checking with an air traffic control tower, he should have at least radioed local traffic. The odds were slim, but air collisions did happen.

The baggage compartment was stale and hot. If Loris had cool air going, none of it reached Chip's hiding spot. The bags next to him omitted a nostril-singeing odor. To make matters worse, Chip couldn't see the horizon or a flicker of a light signifying civilization. To fly over France for three minutes without tiny dots glowing below seemed unlikely.

In through the nose. Out through the mouth.

Don't. Puke.

His dinner waited at the base of his throat, taunting him. His hand gripped the wrench tighter. A vision of whacking Loris on the head and taking the controls floated through his mind. It'd be safer than enduring this nightmare. He peeked between the seats, angling himself to get a better view of the GPS yet again. With the updated avionics getting a visual on the screen wasn't the issue. Figuring out where they were without zooming out was.

The map listed no nearby airport names and the route line ended in the middle of a green patch. Landing in a forest would explain why he hadn't seen lights. If Loris was trying to stay incognito, it'd make sense to not radio out.

Chip's stomach floated into his chest as Loris dropped them out of the sky without a hint of finesse. Had the man bought his pilot's license from eBay?

The engine's hum grew louder. They'd be landing in the next few—

BAM.

Chip launched toward the ceiling with a surprised squawk. He righted himself in time to be tossed again. His teeth pierced his tongue. Blood oozed down his throat. The plane went airborne again.

We are going to die.

His nails bit into the seat back.

With a grunt, Loris managed to stick the landing. Third time lucky.

The plane bumped along, jarring Chip's internal organs out of place. To be fair, Loris was carrying an extra one hundred and eighty pounds that he didn't know about. Not that Loris did any of the normal calculations before taking off. That would have required him to not have a death wish, to own an actual pilot's license, and to care if his plane was intact at the end of the flight.

When they came to a blessed halt, Loris cut the engine and hopped out. Distant shouts greeted him. Fresh air permeated the cabin. Chip scrambled into the seat in front of him as the luggage compartment latch clicked. His heartbeat throbbed in his temples. The duffel bags disappeared one by one including the two that had hidden him from view.

Loris's rasp faded, so Chip peered out the window. Spotlights flooded the side of a metal warehouse. Men swarmed like ants, carrying bags and pushing crates. He reached into the front and twisted the key, turning on the GPS. The screen loaded and beamed in his face. He checked over his shoulder. Loris still had his back to the plane.

Three taps.

That couldn't be right. He zoomed out and reloaded the connection to the satellite. The results said the same thing.

The dot placed him in the middle of nowhere in Mali, Africa.

With a twist of the key the cabin resumed its darkness.

How? Why?

What made him a prime candidate for international kidnapping?

Chip glanced over his shoulder. He froze as his insides seized.

The window framed Loris's demonic grin and crazed eyes staring in at him. Rage tore through Chip's body as he jumped from the plane.

"What have you done?" Chip swung the wrench at Loris and connected with his shoulder. "What. Have. You. Done?"

Loris laughed. "Baxter Charles Chapman, beloved brother and grandson. Days away from joining the Royal Air Force. Tragically missing after an avalanche in the Alps. What a treat for Adrienna and I to have found and helped a promising young man in such desperate need of medical care."

"Do you troll the Alps looking for victims to take hostage?" Chip clenched his jaw to keep from spitting. "Why lie to me? What do you want?"

Loris grinned. "The lists are too long and detrimental to your fragile psyche. Quite the past you had." He pulled a joint from his pocket and lit it. "The best part about this situation is that you are in the bush of Mali. If you try to escape, you'll be destroyed by nature, or we'll find you in a heartbeat. We have eyes everywhere. White skin is visible any time of day." He took a long drag, held it in, then blew it toward Chip's face. Weed. "Don't worry. We'll take excellent care of you. Our honored guest."

"Like you do for those boys you drug and then pit against each other?"

"We're teaching them to become men. Something your father obviously didn't succeed in teaching you." Loris's lip curled. "Tell me. Did you cry when he hit you? Or did you hide whenever you heard his footsteps?"

An explosion of fury blinded Chip as he smashed Loris into the ground. His fists connected with bone and flesh again and again. Loris laughed underneath him. Chip threw his weight into his punches, splitting skin and drawing blood.

An arm wrapped around Chip's neck and dragged him backward. Loris stumbled to his feet as he swiped at the blood dripping from his eye and lip.

"That was the manliest thing I've seen from you yet." Loris retrieved his fallen joint and pressed the embers into Chip's forearm, burning his flesh. "Come at me like that again and I will feed your immobile body to the army ants. Alive."

The arm tightened around his neck. Blackness took over.

Chip jolted awake as the plane pounded the earth. His wrists were hogtied to his ankles behind him. As the plane came to a stop, he closed his eyes feigning sleep. Loris rustled around and popped the latch to the main cabin door. A few seconds later the baggage compartment latch sprang open.

Hands gripped his ankles and yanked. The coarse carpet gave his face a rug burn. His feet went out the door and dragged the rest of his body with them.

Thud.

Gasping and coughing, Chip rolled over.

Can't breathe.

His limbs sprung free of the ropes. On his hands and knees, he sputtered until his lungs worked again. Loris was nowhere to be seen. Chip's golf cart driver from earlier in the evening waited for him with an angry stare.

Annoyed that he had to babysit again? Angry because he got in trouble for not putting Chip in his room? Wishing he could be home with his family or asleep in bed? Probably all of the above.

If only he'd been willing to risk hijacking that plane, then maybe he'd be free of this mess.

Or dead.

The next morning greeted him with sore limbs, but for the first time in ages he felt rested. Stronger. No lingering grogginess clouded his brain as the events of the previous night replayed. And—instead of anxiety—a measure of peace settled in his core. The unknowns outweighed the awful truths. Now was the time to formulate a plan.

Seventeen minutes past her usual time, Adrienna slipped into his room—head down, shoulders slumped, shirt untucked. Her monotone questions about his pain levels shut down any doubt that she'd heard of last night's happenings. Her fingers fumbled with the blood pressure cuff. When Chip touched her arm, she recoiled. Her gaze met his. Her dilated pupils gave her a glazed look.

She was high.

Again.

"Don't touch me." Adrienna's hiss was loud and slurred. Chapel didn't start for a few more hours.

He lifted his hands in surrender. "What happened?"

"As if you can't tell." Her lips lifted in a sneer. "Like you can't see the mark of 'whore' all over me."

Chip scanned her clothing for clues he'd missed. Nothing stuck out to him. "I don't understand."

"Dangled like bait by my own father in a room full of disgusting boys. Boys that Tag said bragged about threatening to rape the girls in their village if the girls had something the boys wanted. It's evil. And Dad said, 'She's the prize. Succeed in your mission and you will be—'" Adrienna choked back a sob. "I'm a reward." She sank onto the end of the bed. "This is your fault." Her voice lowered to a whisper.

"I—"

Adrienna waved a finger at him. "I was leaving the day Loris found you on the side of the mountain. His daily hike usually lasted an hour and a half. All I had to do was finish packing and make it to town in the truck. But he found you. At first, we were going to take you to a local hospital, but then he heard who you were on the radio." She sniffed. "If you hadn't dropped off the side of that mountain, I would be in Gibraltar with Daniel living the life I want."

Chip sighed. "Instead you're in Mali, playing nurse to the guy who destroyed your dreams while

Daddy drugs you and parades you in front of sex-starved boys who want to be men."

"He doesn't drug me." Adrienna jumped off the bed, pacing and swaying. "He lights incense at our morning prayer time and tells me it's Allah's will for my life that I do as he says. This is how it's been." She lifted her hands. "What else can I do but help him load you into the plane, nurse you back to health, and wait for my chance to live my life?"

What if he could fix this—for her, for himself? "I'm sure there's a way you can get out for good."

His excitement sank with her as she crouched against the wall. "Not this time." She swiped at her cheeks. "Maybe not ever."

Chip wholeheartedly believed she couldn't see a way out in her drugged despair. As much as he needed answers, Adrienna wasn't his source. She was a puppet in The Loris Show, bound by his manipulation.

The door banged against the wall as Lucifer himself strolled in, wearing another in his collection of button-down shirts paired with creased khaki trousers. Adrienna leapt to her feet.

He clapped his hands together, quite pleased with himself. "Ah, *ma belle fille* and today's lucky co-pilot."

The level of disdain that Loris inspired far surpassed Chip's contempt for his own father.

Perhaps it was because the man wouldn't be held accountable that Chip hated him more, as if that was a small slice of justice that Chip could dole out. Without a word, Adrienna pecked Loris on the cheek and left the room. Chip propped himself against the headboard of his bed. Loris's wide-eyed pleasure morphed into a squinty assessment. The urge to squirm slithered along Chip's spine. He tensed, forcing his limbs to remain still.

With a manufactured yawn, Chip stretched. "Going flying, mate? Have a smooth ride."

"Were those tear stains on my daughter's cheeks?" Loris took a step toward the bed, his posture coiled. "Was it you that made her cry?"

Chip curled his lip. "She takes my blood pressure and checks my vitals every day which lasts three minutes, tops. I'd guess her father would know more about what would make his daughter cry than I would." When Loris's lips pursed, Chip threw in, "She really seems to love you with the way she talks about you. It's like you can do no wrong."

The lie hung so heavily in the air that Chip could see it perched above Loris like a cartoon piano hanging by a thread.

Loris broke into a grin. "As far as daughters go, she is a gift."

Chip nodded, his chest releasing the pressure.

Loris continued, "Since my plea for a son went unheard, I had to make the best of what I got. I raised her well." Bitter words had to accompany the sweet. "Now, get out of bed. You're co-captain today. We leave the room in one-and-a-half minutes. Wheels up in ten. Cooperate or both you and your family suffer."

Chip contemplated a childish stare-down but opted for staying appropriately demur. If submission was what Loris wanted, then that's what he'd get. For now.

At the plane, Chip started his pre-flight checks, audibly muttering about flight safety and the reason the checks are mandatory in the aviation world. Flaps, lights, fuel, landing gear, propeller. Surprisingly, the plane was decently well kept.

"What do the fuel gauges read?" Chip glanced at Loris who glowered from his place against the plane. The baggage compartment popped open easily and the door lowered without protest.

Loris slammed the door shut almost smashing Chip's fingers and locked it. "They don't." His rank breath gagged Chip. "Get in the cockpit."

"Do you want to crash and burn to death when the cargo weight prevents us from taking off?"

"In the cockpit—now."

Chip growled as he complied. "You're going to get us killed."

"Then your sad little family won't have to mourn your miserable life twice." Loris jerked the cabin door closed behind him and had the plane airborne before Chip had his headset in place.

Loris's words sank into Chip's soul, dampening the small flame of hope left burning. His family mourned him and he hated that he was causing them so much pain. But he'd survived an avalanche. Each day he woke up he was grateful for that. He missed the mountains, the crisp air, the comforting jingle of the cowbells on the hillsides, morning chats with Oma and Opa, and especially his knuckle-headed, frustratingly messy twin. By now, he'd have been at boot camp wishing for home in a different way.

"Get comfortable with this route. You'll be flying it frequently."

So long as he was useful, he wasn't dead. Chip's fingers twitched as a variety of colorful versions of "no" popped into his mind. The end point on the navigation system inched closer and still they cruised along at altitude. A dull throb pulsed in Chip's forehead. He massaged it with pressure. Loris was too careless to be a licensed pilot. A couple more seconds went by. He cleared his throat.

"Mind if I practice my field landings today? It's been a while." It was the fakest kindness that had ever spewed from Chip's mouth, but at least his words were honest and dead sincere.

Precious seconds ticked by until Loris grunted. "Fine. Don't wreck my plane."

Loris would accomplish that on his own. Chip lowered altitude as they neared the landing site so they wouldn't have to drop out of the sky. Turning in line with the dirt strip, he floated above the trees and kissed the ground with a smooth landing. Loris stomped the brakes on his side, skidding the tires and throwing them against their seat belts.

"Don't get out." Loris leapt from the plane door, taking the key with him. He disappeared into the trees with the bags of cargo and returned carrying a solitary bag. As he neared the plane, he broke into a run. He tossed the keys to Chip.

"Firewall it."

Chip shoved the power lever to the maximum as dirt sprayed around the plane. A rock hit the window but was deflected.

Loris watched over his shoulder and banged his fist against the dash. "Go. Go. Go!" Fear edged into Loris's voice.

With zero finesse, Chip yanked the plane into the sky. Blue blanketed his front window. For once, he ignored the instruments and protocols.

A loud pop behind them made Chip flinch.

Loris cursed. "A bullet pierced the cabin." He seized the controls and spun the plane into a nosedive.

In a matter of seconds, they'd hit the trees and be dead.

Chapter 12

Mali, Africa

Voices. Raised voices pulled Madison from her sleep. She squinted her eyes. Her world was sideways, but her pillow was so comfortable and warm…and moving. Up and down. Sitting up, she cringed at the sight of Duke sleeping under her head. Thank God he wasn't awake yet to see she had fallen asleep on his shoulder. After the rain stopped, they crowded onto the driest part of the floor they could find and let the exhaustion take over. She couldn't remember if Duke allowed her to use his shoulder or if it happened naturally.

"Madi, put your head on my shoulder and close your eyes." Duke's whisper was barely audible.

She pursed her lips. His habit of talking with his eyes closed made her want to smack him. "Why?"

"Trust me on this."

Was he mocking her? After their amiable talk last night, he didn't seem like the kind of guy to make fun of her. She did as he said and dropped her head onto his shoulder and closed her eyes.

"Now what?" she said in a whisper.

"Don't move."

More parasitic worms? A gut-wrenching scream halted her internal rebellion. Her eyes popped open in reflex.

"Keep your eyes closed, Madi. Some things you can never un-see."

She clamped her eyes shut, her pulse racing. The screams and the dull thud of objects hitting flesh turned her stomach. They'd come for her next. Duke placed his head against the top of hers. He started murmuring. She angled her head to focus on his words.

"Sunshine, puppies, chipmunks, Tim Horton's coffee, snow, Christmas…"

This game she could play. "The Rockettes, Andrea Bocelli, pepperoni pizza, pina colada, hockey, soccer…"

"Football, not soccer," Duke said.

"Whatever. Olympics, swimming pools, ripped muscled men…"

Duke cleared his throat. "…beautiful, flexible, athletic women…"

"Flexible is overrated."

He snorted.

The screaming stopped. A cell door slammed. If she kept her eyes clenched shut, she could ignore the damage done. She exhaled. Everything was going to be okay.

A rush of air tickled her ear. Then, white hot knives pierced her skull as she was lifted by her hair. She roared through the blinding pain. Twisting her head to see her captor added to the intensity of the fire.

"Duke?" Her shrill voice sounded foreign to her own ears.

Someone hissed in her ear. Duke. Where was he? A thud of flesh hitting flesh. A moan and a cough quickened her breathing almost to hyperventilation.

No!

Duke's limp arm flopped on the ground in her peripheral vision. Her head jerked left. Her body followed. They had come for her and taken Duke out to do it. She backed into her captor and threw her elbow into his stomach. He grunted and loosened his grip on her hair. Whirling around, she slammed her foot into the first shin that came into view. A howl deafened her. She backed right into another man's grasp.

Rage burst in her chest. She would not be their next victim. "Lay another hand on me and General Abdou Karim will add your heads to his collection."

The grip lightened and she tossed the hands off her arms with ease. The two guards consulted with each other in Bambara. They stared at her.

She was ready to take them on with her bare hands. "What?"

"You are a friend of General Karim?" The question gave her no hint of fear or mockery.

Threatening them hadn't been the smartest idea, but it was the first name with Mali clout that had popped into her mind. As the reality of what she'd done sank in, regret arrived on its heels. Was General Karim on their most wanted list? Or were they on his payroll?

The guards left the cell and disappeared out of sight. Madison dropped to her knees beside Duke's sprawled form. She pressed her fingers into his neck. His heartbeat pulsed in steady response. She rolled him on his side and opened his eyelid. Good dilation.

He groaned, rolling away from her.

"They're gone."

His eyes scanned the length of her in concern. "Did they hurt you? Are you okay?"

"My head will be a little sore, but otherwise they didn't hurt me."

He cradled his head in his hands.

She sat on her heels. "Anything broken?"

"I don't think so. How did you get them to leave without hurting you?"

Why did she spout Karim's name? "Well, I may have told them that if they touched me General Karim would slit their throats."

Duke's jaw dropped. "You didn't. You namedropped Karim again."

Madison pressed her lips together. "I did."

Pushing to his feet, Duke stalked to the front of the cell. With his face pressed between the cables, he peered to the left. She held her breath to listen for any word that might tell her fate.

"This could go so badly. We talked about this." He sunk to the ground. "This could mean big trouble for you."

The words had been a reflex. Like wrestling with kids during her elementary school years, the fear had overtaken her and she called uncle before she had a chance to process the consequences.

"Next time, think it all the way through before you say something. Your spur-of-the-moment words could get you killed."

"They'll kill me for saying General's name?" She swallowed, but her mouth was dry.

Duke shrugged. "We'll find out."

It had been almost one full day in the jail and yet it felt as if weeks had passed. Daily abuse and fear of harm wasn't a life she wanted to get used to.

If she dug a hole and buried herself, she wouldn't have to deal with General. Her body flashed hot and cold. Waiting would kill her if they didn't.

Time dragged on, but the guards didn't return to her cell. Her daily ration of cement appeared and still she waited. Darkness crept into the corridor between the cells. The occasional chatter from the guards' room ceased. They headed home for the night while she stayed locked up like a caged tiger.

Madison rubbed her eyes. Her clothes reeked of body odor. She plopped onto the ground perilously close to whining about wanting a bed and a pillow. Fatigue pounced on her like a chubby dog jumping for a treat. Duke did one-handed push-ups, alternating hands. She should join him to stay fit, but instead she closed her eyes and succumbed to her lethargy.

"Doctor." Warm breath fanned across her face. "Doctor, wake up."

The soft French words woke her in an instant, and she stared into the eyes of General Karim. Deja vu. General smiled and brushed the hair from her face, his touch gentle like a lover's.

What had she done?

Three men filled the cell holding lanterns while Duke stood against the wall, his arms folded watching the scene. His face had suspicion written all over it.

"General, what are you doing here?" She was afraid of the answer.

"The better question would be what are you doing here, Doctor? But I already know how that came about." He chuckled. "Speeding, were we?" She had not been speeding. She'd been trapped. She grunted.

"Your price is very high, beautiful Doctor. Lucky for me, I have connections that will lessen that price for me."

"You'll get me out?" Dare she hope she could see the outside of these walls instead of carried out in a body bag?

"I can, but I have a proposition for you." General turned and motioned the other men out. Then he squinted at Duke.

"General, he doesn't speak French. He is no threat." She didn't know if Duke spoke French or not. They'd only spoken English together and she hadn't bothered to ask him.

General shifted his attention back to her. "Here is my proposition. You leave this place on my conditions. You can agree to both conditions, but you must accept one. Understand?"

She nodded. This would not be good.

"The first condition, which is my favorite, is that you agree to that relationship I suggested before."

Madison bit her lip. There was no hiding that from Duke if he did speak French.

"But because I'd rather not force affections, I have a second option for you. If I pay for your release, you help me with a small project which I will tell you about tomorrow."

Duke coughed, thumping his chest as he moved into the corner line of her sight. He definitely spoke French. She didn't want to see the judgment on his face.

Madison stalled. "Keeping secrets, General?"

"You could say that."

Duke shook his head.

If it wasn't something terrible, he'd tell her here. "What kind of project?"

"You'll find out tomorrow."

Leave her fate with a warlord who wanted her for his own? Or stay under the thumb of police who hated her?

"All right, General. I accept the second option."

A hum of disapproval came from Duke.

"Very good." General nodded at his men. "Let's get going then."

She laid her hand on his arm. "I have a favor to ask though."

His hand covered hers. "I love it when a woman barters with her freedom on the line. Let's hear it."

"I would like Duke to come, too." She could already see the rejection forming on General's lips. "Duke is a man of agriculture. He could advise you as to your crops."

His rejection morphed into a thoughtful assessment of Duke. She'd tossed her hand onto the table, not knowing if General had crops like most of the others in this region.

Please take the bait.

General looked back and forth between them. He stalked out of the cell and spoke in clipped words to his men. In the light of the lantern, he leveled a stare at Madison.

"Fine. He comes."

She exhaled in relief and sneaked a glance at Duke's expression. He scowled, his fists clenched.

"I'll drive you home, Duke," Madison said.

"I'm not going." He sat in the dirt. "I won't be any part of what you've agreed to. I'd rather die in here than agree to a blank check from a terrorist."

Stubborn man. She stepped inches from him and whispered, "In exchange for daily abuse from the police who care nothing for your life?"

He didn't move. "Karim wants to add you to his harem, Madison. Are you really willing to risk cooperating with a project he has for you? That's foolishness."

"It's a chance at survival—a much better one than being stuck in a jail cell with little food or water until we die from starvation or some horrible disease."

A shadow crossed Duke's face.

Madison stopped. "Is that what you want? To die in this hellhole?"

"I'm not sure being a slave to a criminal is a much better choice. Who knows what kind of unsavory things he has planned."

"Would Anna Grace want you stuck, Duke? Don't you want to live in her honor?"

Madison hated her words instantly. What was wrong with her? She was desperate to save a man who didn't want saving.

As Duke's jaw pulsed, she bit her lip. "Sor—"

"If I don't like it, I walk away."

"You can't. I live in your house and you promised to raise my chickens."

Duke shook his head. "That was before this."

His words stung, but she deserved them. After one day, her future included Duke and she wasn't ready to surrender that yet. But if he stayed in jail, she really had no chance.

General returned to the cell with his lantern held high. "Is everything all right?"

Her gaze didn't move from Duke's. "Yes, General. I was explaining your kindness in getting us both out of here."

"Let's go then," he said.

General left. Madison grabbed Duke by the hand and followed.

Outside the jail, General handed Madison her truck keys. "Did they touch you, Doctor?"

Madison nodded.

"I will see that they pay for that." General held her truck door open. "One of my men will see that you get home safely."

Deep breaths of fresh air cleansed her lungs. "No need, General. I will see you tomorrow at the hospital."

"I insist that my men see you home."

"Thank you, General, but no. I saved your son's life, remember? It's what I do. You can trust me to be at the hospital. Come see me tomorrow afternoon and you can tell me about your project."

Duke closed the passenger door. General scowled as Madison slid into the driver's seat.

"I will see you in the morning. If I don't, there will be consequences," General said.

Madison started her truck and drove to RN5. "Thank God we're out. I never want to see that place again."

"I want no part in criminal activity, Madi." Duke's voice was firm. "None."

"Stop with the disappointment, Duke. My mentor always taught me that if I was asked to do something unethical, go as far as my ethics allowed and then improvise, because my life depends on it."

"So how far do your ethics allow you to go on this one?"

"I'll find out tomorrow. Until then, I want a good night's sleep and a place for my chickens to get fat so I can sell them."

"Madi, you aren't in the least bit worried?" Duke's tone pitched higher with each word.

Her grip tightened on the steering wheel. "Terrified out of my mind. But do you have a better idea?"

Duke stared out the window. "Fine, we'll do this. I hope you know what we're getting in to. We have to be smart so we don't get our heads handed to us on a platter."

Chapter 13

"Answer my question." Chip dogged Loris around the tail and under the wing. "Why is there a bullet hole in the plane?"

No answer.

Chip opened his mouth to ask again.

"Because a bullet pierced the metal." Loris mourned the jagged metal edges with whispering and petting. "The why is not your issue."

Not his issue? One bullet to a fuel tank and they'd have been fireworks. One bullet to the engine and they'd have been tree ornaments. One bullet to the floor board and the shorted control wires would have made them a propelled missile. The carelessness gave Chip an eye twitch.

Lifting his face to the sun, Loris inhaled from his joint, held it far too long, then made his face disappear in a cloud of nose smoke. "Get in the Pilatus."

The tension of Chip's jaw blitzed his temples with a sharp stab. No doubt by now Adrienna's drug-induced confessions would be shuttered behind a corset of duty to her father and the veil of her customary elegance. However, her vulnerability tugged at his core. She didn't see it yet, but he could help her. And when she truly embraced him, he'd get them out of there.

Inside the Pilatus cabin, eight boys filled the cargo area. Dark tees and green trousers replaced their student uniforms. Sturdy boots and a small pack at their feet outfitted them for whatever came next. Their blank expressions and quiet whispers gave nothing away.

Chip slid into the left seat and studied the dashboard as Loris prepared for takeoff. His European pilot's license permitted him to fly aircraft this size, but Father spent more hours in a chartered Pilatus than Chip had in total flight time. To learn the plane from Loris would likely be a study of how not to fly, but it beat out counting the cinder blocks on his room walls.

Mentally rehearsing football stars' statistics barely kept his tongue from spewing the sarcastic comments that formed as he watched Loris meticulously follow pre-flight takeoff lists. Did the smaller mistress not deserve the same amount of affection? Step by step, Loris acquainted Chip with the cockpit. Chip asked questions and received short answers.

By the time the necessary checks were finished, Loris growled into the microphone of his headset. "Dear Allah! Do you hear yourself? The sound of your voice is a shard of glass in my ear. I would rather eat nails than listen to you talk. No more."

Foreigners usually fawned over British accents. Maybe that only applied to female listeners. Four minutes into the flight Loris flicked off the intercom switch between them.

Oh no, this was far from over. Chip turned it back on.

"You have bulletproof windows and the world's shortest time between startup and takeoff in your Skylane. How often do you get shot at on these runs?"

"How often did you expect to get shot at in the Air Force?"

"Completely irrelevant."

Loris snorted. "Duty is the same regardless of who employs you."

"Business is different than serving king and country."

"False. Your flying is for your sanity as much as this is for mine. I sell and buy to provide for my family, but I don't have to fly to make those drops. I fly for me." An alarm interrupted his speech. He pushed the button and lowered a lever.

"We're the same, you and me. You can serve your country in a thousand ways—eight hundred and fifty of them from behind a desk in relative safety. Yet you chose to fly for the Air Force. You're a risk-taker. You live for the adrenaline high. Don't pretend you have a more noble cause than everyone else."

Loris yanked his headset from his ears. Conversation over.

"You're so wrong." The drone of the engines swallowed his whispered words—words he didn't believe as they left his tongue.

Thirty-eight minutes later, Loris read the landing checklists. A strip of lush green grass awaited them in the distance. As they drew closer, dark specks grew legs and ran around the field after a white ball.

Chip grinned. The boys had a welcome party. Young boys ran alongside the taxiing plane waving frantically.

Loris opened the latch, letting the stairs fall into place. Chip crouched in the cockpit door as the boys filed out. Then he followed them down and waited at the bottom. Two men greeted Loris. One watched the approaching line of boys, holding a duffel. The other corralled the younger boys. After wide gestures and some laughter, Loris took the bag and pointed the young boys to the plane.

They gathered around Loris, giving him high fives. He emptied candy from his pockets, a huge smile on his face. Loris had more personalities than late-night TV. Skipping and hopping, the nine boys ran circles around Loris all the way to the plane. Faded shirts boasting American universities or sports teams either exposed rounded bellies or bared thin shoulders. Two boys wore shoes—one in over-sized sandals and another in glittery flats that looked like girls' shoes. Chip suppressed his smile and swallowed his comment about the glitter.

The boys smoothed their hands over the railings as they danced up the stairs into the plane. One by one they disappeared inside. A knot hardened in Chip's throat as he took his seat. They were still kids and they had no idea what was coming. They didn't deserve to be drugged into submission.

Loris waved at the cargo area. "These boys are yours. Stay with them today until dinner. You'll teach them English until they graduate. Get them to trust you. If they don't, do whatever it takes to make them. Their future survival depends on your teaching skills."

Survival depended on English? The world was changing and English speakers grew with the bleeding heart of western charity, but when did survival in Africa count on it? His mind's referee tossed yet another flag into the air. Another question with no immediate answer.

When they landed at The Retreat, the assigned guide didn't talk to the boys except when necessary so Chip filled in the gaps. They giggled at his attempts to communicate. Sekou, Paul, Alou, Bodox, Razak, John, Fode, Malick, and Nafy the glitter-shoed boy. The boys' energy matched a football locker room on game day.

The first stop was the uniform shop—a glorified storage room with a bulky desk. Whatever the uniform man said made the boys strip down and stand in line. When they handed over their old clothes, the man measured each boy for shirts, trousers, and boots. Their size was awarded accordingly.

Despite the similarities to prison processes, the boys received the better end of the trade. No jumpsuits for these kids. Fode, first in line, slid the socks on his hands like gloves. With a grunt Chip grabbed a sock and pulled it onto Fode's foot. The boots slipped on without ties—a well-thought-out shoe for boys who never had worn shoes before.

Nafy left the line before he reached the front, a frown furrowing his brow. He grabbed Chip's hand and led him to a corner with a bench. They sat with their backs facing the uniform desk. Nafy held Chip's gaze for a moment before placing his glitter shoes in Chip's lap. Nafy whispered pointing to Chip's pocket.

Money? Chip pushed them back. Nafy shook his head and set them firmly in Chip's lap. This time, Nafy held one hand on Chip's and the other over his heart.

"*Hakɛto.*"

The plea hit its mark. Chip left the shoes on his lap as Nafy rejoined the line and collected his uniform. Once dressed, Nafy stroked his clothes. The other boys laughed as they did the same. Nafy leaned in and rubbed his sleeve across Chip's cheek.

Chip smirked. "Nice."

Nafy nodded. "Nigh-suh."

Close enough. Chip clapped his hands. Pinching his shirt, he said, "Shirt." The boys stared, so Chip grabbed Nafy's sleeve, too. "Shirt."

They giggled and said what they heard.

"Shh. Irt." He pointed at them. They mimicked him. "Shirt."

As Chip continued sounding out English words for clothing, Nafy tucked the glittery shoes into the back waistband of his new uniform trousers. The looseness of the shirt barely hid the bulk. Nafy skipped to Chip's side, jumping to give him a high five.

"Nigh-suh," Nafy said, his grin capturing his whole face.

The orientation guide directed the group to the sleeping quarters. Each boy chose a bunk bed and learned to put a sheet on his mattress. Chip grabbed Nafy's arm as the other boys left the room. He pointed to the lump on Nafy's waistband and raised the mattress.

Nafy's eyes widened. "Ah."

He yanked the shoes from his waistband and set them under the mattress, his care painstaking. When he was satisfied no one would touch them, Chip already had his hand waiting for a high five.

Outside they joined the group in line for lunch. The chapel doors burst open, reverberating across the yard. The boys from chapel raced to the cafeteria in the briskest non-running speed walk he'd ever seen. According to Adrienna, men didn't run unless absolutely necessary. Adrienna apparently knew little about men, especially about men topping out the ozone, they're so high. In both cases, food was a running matter.

Nafy sidled up to Chip at a table. The new boys huddled together, the table dwarfing their small frames. As the room filled, the energy simmered, ready to boil over. The boys chattered to each other sending the stray word his way. Chip scanned the room. Adrienna's friend, Jab, caught his eye with a wave.

"You are stuck with the new group, eh?" Jab said, pulling a chair over to Chip's table. Jab said something that made the boys laugh. They chatted to him and repeated the words they'd learned.

Jab shook his head. "They're learning your accent."

"It could be worse. They could have French accents," Chip said.

Jab threw his head back and laughed. "Good joke. They don't see many white people. They're orphans from a displacement camp in Safo, except that one." Jab pointed at Nafy. "He still has a mother and is someday going to kill the man who murdered his father."

Little Nafy with the glittery shoes and infectious smile wanted to kill someone?

"What displaced them?" Chip said.

Jab spoke to the boys, clicking his tongue in response to each story. "I think you mean who, my friend."

Nafy's small hand crept towards Chip, so he pushed his half-eaten plate to the middle. The boys jumped on the food like wolves.

"Who then?"

Scrubbing his head, Jab glanced around them for eavesdroppers. No one paid attention to their small table in the corner, but Jab's somber expression screamed that they would if they knew his next words. Chip leaned closer.

"Karim." Jab's whisper tiptoed across the space between them.

The name meant nothing to Chip. He raised his eyebrows and shrugged.

Jab glanced around again. "General Abdou Karim—the famous warlord, the richest man in the country."

Chip shook his head still not seeing Jab's fear.

Jab growled. "Abe, the man who is responsible for these boy's families dying, owns and runs this school."

Chapter 14

Mali, Africa

An alarm buzzed near Madison's ear. The sound rang in the space around her more than usual. She surged upward on a shot of panic, then relaxed. She was in her new room in Duke's home. The pale daylight gave the room a homey feel that a flashlight in the dark couldn't.

According to Duke, the brick house had been built by western missionaries a few decades earlier. They'd vacated when war came. Bricks were a rich man's building material. The rest of the buildings in the area were hardened clay. The chief had been so delighted to give Duke the house that Duke wondered if the words "teaching agriculture" must have translated into "no more famines—ever."

The night's sleep had been refreshing. The real bed was heaven on earth compared to the jail cell's floor and her little hospital cot. Across the small room, a bowl of water sat awaiting her morning cleaning. A small cloth waited beside the bowl. She scrubbed herself raw and threw on some clothes from her overnight bag. Her scrubs would be waiting for her at the hospital.

Madison emerged from her room and walked toward the open front den. Duke stood over an open fire. His face was shaved and his hair trimmed.

"Good morning."

Duke didn't take his eyes off the fire. "Good morning."

This was awkward.

He stirred the pot that dangled over the fire. "I fed your chickens this morning. Put them in the same space so they can get started with producing little chicks and eggs to sell."

"Do you need the truck today?"

"If you don't mind. My help was supposed to take the produce to market in my absence but hasn't done a great job from what I can see. They ran unsupervised for too long." Duke extended a bowl toward her. "Here, I made you breakfast. A small-scale sandstorm would blow you over with no problem."

She dished some of the warm oatmeal substance into her mouth. So much better than cardboard particles. "Thank you. Not just for breakfast, but for the water and a nice place to stay."

Duke glanced at her. The warmth in his smile sent heat through her. A shared space with him might not be as easy as she thought. She finished her breakfast, grabbed her bag, and walked outside.

He followed, snagging the keys from her hand. "I'll drive you."

She paused outside the truck, unable to keep the frown from her face as he jumped into the driver's seat. Was he taking possession of her truck or trying to be nice? She hadn't had to share a vehicle before. One of the few perks of being alone.

The drive to the hospital was slow going, filled with potholes. It took twice as long as expected. When Duke pulled up to the hospital at last, vehicles armed to the teeth were parked around the building.

"What is going on here? Armed Forces Day?" Duke smirked at his own joke.

The day had barely started and she wanted it to be over. "Looks like General Karim is making good on his promise to tell me his plan."

Duke tapped the steering wheel. "What are the chances that I can drive us away so he never finds us?"

"Probably slim. He has connections."

"Then let's get this over with."

They shared a look before exiting the truck. She didn't know him well, but her senses told her she could trust Duke to go with her to the very end. She had to hope it didn't come to that. Duke pushed his lock into place and then closed his door with a grunt.

"Who am I kidding? They could shoot me and take the keys if they really wanted the truck," Duke said as he joined Madison on their walk inside.

The men manning the armed trucks didn't spare them a glance as they went past. Madison couldn't help but stare at the giant weapons slung across their backs. They caused so much death and destruction. The sight of them near her hospital made her insides coil. She led them to a side entrance instead of in the front.

Hawa stopped her in the hallway. "Doctor, you're back. Where have you been? We've been so worried." She glanced behind her. "General Karim is waiting for you in your office."

"Please have someone remove him from my office and have him wait for me in the common area."

"Doctor, no one wants to talk to him. They're afraid."

Madison sighed. "I will handle it. Thank you, Hawa. Please let Ina know I have returned and am in a meeting with General Karim."

"Yes, Doctor." Hawa scurried away.

"Hard to find good help, isn't it?" Duke whispered near her ear. "Won't find many people willing to take on Goliath." He chuckled.

Madison faced Duke and looked him straight in the eyes. "You'll be in there with me the whole time, right?"

Duke's smile disappeared. The laugh lines around the corners of his eyes faded. "I'll be there. But won't he get suspicious of my presence? He thinks I don't understand French."

"He may. He may also try to kick you out, but I'm not going to let him if I can help it." She squeezed his hand.

When had she started holding it? Didn't matter. It felt right and he didn't pull away. Holding tighter, she led him to her office.

An armed guard stood against the hallway wall. The sight of him slowed her march. He nodded his approval, as if she needed his permission to enter her own office.

How had her life come to this—fearing for her life every day? She wanted to run, but Karim wouldn't wait forever. She dropped Duke's hand and opened the door. In an instant, she missed the assurance his touch gave her. She glanced around her office. The familiarity eased her mind a fraction. A day ago, she'd been so sure she would never see this place again.

What was that smell?

There in her chair behind the desk sat General Karim with his feet propped up, smoking. The smoke choked her until she coughed.

"You don't like the smell of marijuana, Doctor." General Karim laughed.

"General, it's the hospital's policy that there is no smoking allowed in hallways or in the rooms."

General stood as she shuffled around the chair and faced him. "My apologies, Doctor. I am almost finished. Would you care for a little breath of heaven?"

She coughed again. "I would not. I have inhaled enough of it." There was no oxygen left for her lungs to intake.

General dropped the stub to the floor and pressed his boot over it.

"I'm disappointed you give me no kiss of thankfulness. After all, I saved you from much violence and humiliation in that jail cell. The men who touched you received correction for their deeds. The least you can do is reward me with a touch of your lips."

He stepped toward her, his arms extended. She cleared her throat. Move or tolerate the embrace? His hands settled on her upper arms and his eyes bored into hers. His crooked grin never left his face, but he made no move to kiss her.

"When I did not find you here this morning, I was afraid I would have to come track you down. As fate would have it, I did not have the good fortune of the exciting hunt. And it would have been most thrilling to hunt for such a prize. Look at me, beautiful Doctor."

Madison swallowed hard and shifted her eyes upward to his face, a breath away from hers. His dark eyes gleamed with pride. One of these times he'd close the short distance between them.

"I'm delighted you called on me to help you. You think me capable then."

"Please, General." She stepped out of his grasp. "No better time than the present to talk about your project. I have quite a bit to catch up on after my unexpected extended absence."

She retrieved a pad of paper from the desk drawer. General stayed across the desk. Behind General, Duke silently watched from where he stood against the wall. No doubt, her interactions with General had thinking negative things about her, yet he said nothing.

Madison picked up her pen to study it. "What do you propose, General?"

"Such a direct manner. I like it. In return for rescuing you from jail, I want your help with my business. I think the international cooperation would sit very well with the others."

"To be clear, General, which business are we discussing?"

General raised his eyebrows. "I have more than one business? I suppose I do, but my fascination with you is more of a hobby than anything."

"I don't understand."

"Who could ignore the beautiful doctor who bathes herself at twilight in the Niger? And, for the moment she is exposed, leaves the world breathless with her beauty."

She cringed. Humiliation sucked the air from her lungs. The earth could swallow her now. For once she had no words to defend herself, no red herring to cover her vulnerability. He had watched her bathing, come to her rescue in the jail, and clearly wanted more than she was willing to give.

Next, he'd require what was left of her dignity. And Duke heard every word. She cared—far more than she should have—what he thought of her. There was no recovering her composure. Was it worse that a terrorist thought she was beautiful? Or that he had watched her bathing in the Niger?

"General, the business proposition."

"My need is two-fold. First, I need a place to store the goods I obtain for resale." General glanced around the room, his intention very clear. "Second, I need you to transport the goods down the line for me."

"And by goods, you are referring to..."

"Marijuana."

Drug trafficking. Her head spun. Of course. Mali's worst problem according to Sabine. She plopped into her desk chair.

"You understand, Doctor, the French decided to punish those of us who are actually making a reasonable living in this country. They prefer we stay a third-world country, that we starve or die from diseases easily cured in the world of modern medicine. They eliminate the highest paying livelihood to ruin the happiness of those selling and those buying. It is an inhumane cycle."

His reality orbited light years away from her own. Was he really delusional enough to think recreational drugs brought happiness to the world?

"The French troops who recently landed in northern Mali have been tasked with finding the trade routes we use. Traffic on the main roads will be stopped and suspicious people will be further examined. But since you are female and a Canadian doctor, the French won't think twice about your passing through or the contents in your vehicle. They are looking for locals or Muslims, not Westerners."

How convenient that her identity might get her a pass instead of getting her noticed for once. She bristled at that.

"How much will I earn?"

General yawned as if bartering with her future was a non-event. "Storage is worth five thousand francs a month to me. Successful runs are eight thousand."

"And my debt to you is how much?"

"Two hundred thousand francs."

Madison sputtered. "That's outrageous. That will take me over three years to pay that. I saved your son's life. Does that count for nothing?"

"Of course, it counts. That is why you are being charged for half instead of the whole amount."

A year and a half. Still too long. Madison closed her eyes. The government hadn't guaranteed her one more month in the country if she didn't show proof of a reasonable income. General ducked his head to light another joint. She raised an eyebrow at Duke. He shook his head.

Her heart dropped. He'd walk away from this—and her—in a flash. "I have a job to do here. My care makes a difference. I can't make drug runs for you every day."

"I don't expect you to, Doctor. Not at all. We don't make a run every day. Once or twice a week we move our merchandise along the route. Until then, it needs to stay in a secure location. Our business is expanding and this little hospital is the perfect place for storage. Are we agreed on this, Doctor?"

Common sense screamed no. "If I don't agree, then what?"

He shrugged. "Then you pay me back in full right now and I take your hospital by force for my own uses. Its unassuming nature suits me well. You still would work for me but you lose your hospital, your patients, and your visa. Eventually, you return to your home country knowing you signed the death warrant for the innocent locals whom your heart yearns for."

She shoved the vision of the children dying from curable diseases from her mind. Cavine had cared for them better when he was alive. And she was bringing this disaster to their doorstep. Her choice was clear. How much different would storing drugs be from allowing unnecessary prescription drug refills in Canada? Marijuana saved some people's lives, right?

For the good of everyone, she would do this. The check to Karim was signed when she agreed to his conditions in the jail. Acid burned an ulcer in her stomach. She could feel it. She wouldn't make it out of this in one piece.

"My patients come first." They wouldn't have to suffer any more than necessary because of her selfishness. "Any shipments that need to stay here must not arrive in a giant armored vehicle, okay? I don't want your men armed around my hospital. It scares people away from the help they need. People walk for hundreds of miles and I won't have you harming them because you want to make money. Are we agreed?"

General beamed. "As smart as you are beautiful. Your choice of men isn't complementary to the sharp mind you have in your head."

He walked around her desk and crouched in front of her chair.

"Your assistance is greatly appreciated, Doctor. I assure you that your cooperation will be nicely rewarded."

She pursed her lips into the best smile she could muster for him. "I will see you to the door, General. In the future, please remain unarmed when you step into my hospital. It draws unnecessary attention to you."

"My hospital, you mean."

"Your weapons take the lives of my patients. The only armed man who would be attractive to me is the man protecting me from an intruder in our home."

An earnest expression spread across General's face. "I can be that man for you, if you'd let me."

That was enough. Madison sprang to her feet. "Thank you, General. I will keep that in mind."

"Now let's talk about the man's repayment to me. What did you call him?"

"Duke."

"Ah, yes. The man of agriculture is greatly useful to me. I will require his assistance and knowledge in growing my goods. Several times a week he will assist my workers. They will pick him up from here and take him to my fields."

Duke stalked out of the room. Madison kicked herself for getting him into this.

"I will let him know." With forced kindness, she strode to the door. "Have a pleasant day, General. I'll see you in the near future. And, please, don't tell the staff about our new arrangement. I will be here to work with you myself."

General stood in the doorway, the picture of complete control. He blew a haze of smoke in her direction from a cigarette he'd lit seconds ago. "You'll do your first run tomorrow." Then he disappeared.

Her shoulders sagged as she sank into her chair and buried her face in her arms. The door clicked. She didn't look up.

"I'm glad that's over." Duke's voice soothed her frayed nerves.

She peeked at him. His arms crossed over his strong chest. What a mess she'd gotten him into.

"Go ahead. Yell at me."

"I don't know what morals your parents taught you growing up—"

"My parents never taught me morals because I never knew them. And my foster homes worried about keeping me fed and out of trouble, not about sound morals. But my mentor did teach me that you do what you must to survive and find the first exit."

"You told me this before." His sharp tone snapped her from her explanation.

Her ears burned. "Then don't act so disappointed that I'm not quite such as saint as you."

"I shouldn't have spoken like that. Please forgive me." He scrubbed his face and exhaled. "My wife hated when I interrupted her."

"I can see why, Mr. Goody-Two-Shoes."

A smile played on Duke's lips. "Why are you here, Madi?"

"What? What do you mean?"

"I mean what brought you to Mali? Why work in a hospital here?"

It was too close to home, too personal. The walls of her heart snapped into place. "I'm here to change the lives of these people who have nothing close to the medical care of the west."

Duke's eyebrows pulled together. He strolled over and sat on her desk facing her. Leaning forward, he scooted her chair closer to him. "That's the answer everyone else hears from heroic Dr. Madison. I want the real answer."

Her pulse quickened. She stared at her lap. The pain of loss had eased but sadness remained.

"Dr. Cavine started this hospital. Mali was his country of birth and he cared deeply for the underprivileged of this region. Eight years ago, he was involved in a fatal car accident. He left me the money to finish med school with the condition that I spend some time working here after I graduated. I came in memory of him. His memory makes the hard times bearable. And I feel nearer to him each day I work. He and Amber were the closest thing to family I had."

"Would Dr. Cavine want you trafficking drugs in his hospital?"

"He would want me to survive."

Duke studied her, weighing her words for their sincerity. "All right then, Madi. If surviving is what you want, then that is what we'll do."

An idea sprang into her mind. Why not go to the very people she was trying to sneak past in the first place? "Tomorrow after the first drop, you and I are taking a trip. It's a long shot, but it may be the only way we get out of this alive."

Chapter 15

The surprise of Karim's identity swirled and twisted in Chip's mind. The boys attempted to engage with him, but the pieces falling into place occupied his attention. Everything he'd seen and experienced played a part in the whole picture.

Chills then heat scaled Chip's body. This was no retreat or healing center.

Not until the orientation guide led them outside the walls of the compound did Chip surface from his daze. The worn path wove through the high grass. Out of the grass rose dirt towers engulfing trees. One of the boys kicked the top of a smaller mound on the side of the path. As the ants poured from the dirt, the boys scattered laughing.

The laughing stopped as the sound of gunfire grew louder. They stopped on the edge of a circular field surrounded by trees. Man-shaped targets laid against trees opposite them. In a straight line eight-, nine-, and ten-year-old boys stood firing automatic and semi-automatic guns. The sight made his blood run cold.

This wasn't a school for boys to become men.

Karim harvested these boys to become child soldiers.

Pick the orphans no one would miss. Train them, indoctrinate them, and use them in war campaigns.

His chest tightened and he braced himself against a tree. The acrid smell of guns left a grit in his mouth. This was what Loris had wanted him to see, to know who he dealt with, and what they'd left the graduated boys to do. Chip flinched at the gunfire. Those muzzles could be pointed at him one day—a military man, a witness, someone who knew too much.

The group guide led them back to the compound. Little brown heads bobbed along the path in front of him. Innocent lives training to become killers or used as shields in Karim's war. A warm hand slipped into his.

Nafy grinned up at him, choosing to walk beside him instead of skipping to the front with the others. Maybe Nafy sensed his mood or wanted reassurance after the gun display. It didn't matter. He'd been that boy, trying to find reassurance and acceptance every chance he had. Chip held Nafy's hand a little tighter as the ache in his heart grew.

Chip dropped them off at dinner with a promise to see them in the morning. They didn't understand, but they repeated his words like they did. Dinner held no appeal tonight. He needed pen, paper, and a clear mind. Halfway to his room, the feeling of being watched made him glance behind him. A man with his hands in his pockets trailed him at a safe distance.

A babysitter.

Loris was no fool.

With quickened steps, Chip dodged into the hallway of his building in the opposite direction of his room and pressed his back to the wall. His stalker hurried in after him. Chip snorted. The man whirled around and faced him.

"Aren't you going to introduce yourself since we'll be spending so much time together?" Chip crossed his arms. He might be able to win a wrestling match against him if there weren't any surprises.

"I'm Sidi, your stay coordinator." Sidi was short but solid, his skin darker than most.

"And if I choose to terminate my stay, would you coordinate that as well?"

Sidi's smile exposed the gaps in his teeth. Mid-thirties, no more than forty.

"You and I will be taking many trips together, Mista Chip, but you will always return with me. Whether you are alive—" Sidi shrugged.

"Well, I'm staying in for the night so—"

"Me too."

So that's how it would be. "Then you can help me find paper. I have plans to make for teaching the boys English."

Sidi rifled through the deserted reception desk and emerged with a stack of paper and a pen.

"Don't forget to teach them words of love. It is important for all men to know this." He winked.

A hundred sarcastic responses bounced through his mind, but "okay" was all that exited his mouth before he shut himself into his room. On the first sheet, he sketched a map of the compound and surrounding area from what he'd seen on the approach to land. He labeled the buildings that he'd visited based on his room's proximity to the airstrip.

None—that's how many feasible ideas he had.

How would Opa get out of this ironclad fortress? Either something intelligent like hiding in a truck bed as it left the compound or simple like walking out the gate and surviving in the wild. He rubbed his bearded face.

Another tangible reminder of how life had flipped on its head. The whole situation was beyond absurd. He punched his bed. The plane was the only way that could get him out without testing the locals' loyalty to Karim. A test they'd pass with ease. White men couldn't hide in the middle of nowhere, Africa.

On the second sheet, he wrote a letter to his family. And on a third piece of paper, he scribbled categories of English words to teach the boys. How would they know what he was talking about if he didn't have pictures? He'd have to teach them whatever they encountered during the day. Flopping onto his bed, he closed his eyes to wait for the brilliant solution to drop into his mind.

The next morning, Adrienna let herself into his room carrying a covered tray.

Chip cracked open an eye. "You don't knock anymore?"

"This is my last morning visit to you. From now on you're medically cleared, so I thought we could have breakfast in your room to celebrate." Adrienna swept her hand over the spread on the corner table.

Maybe she did like him.

Chip pushed out of bed and slapped his hand over his heart. "Darling, that is so sweet."

Adrienna smiled but clucked her tongue. "No shirt, no breakfast."

Chip glanced at his pajama trousers and frowned. She'd seen him in less the first time she walked in his room.

She propped her hands on her hips. "It's good manners to be dressed at the table. And although I was your nurse that does not mean you're allowed to have bad manners."

Said the girl who just let herself into a man's room while he was sleeping. He finger-combed his hair.

"Well, it'd also be good manners to put a mirror in my room so I can make myself presentable before being in front of others." After sliding on yesterday's shirt, he sat down. "I'd like to shave, shower, brush my teeth, and put on deodorant. I stink almost as badly as those boys who smell like body odor all the time."

"When everyone smells the same, you only notice the person who smells differently."

"So that's a no on the deodorant. Can I at least shower, shave, and brush my teeth?"

Adrienna leaned forward, her lips parted. "I like your beard. It makes you look older and strong."

His jaw tingled as her fingers brushed his beard. "Strong is good, but how old is older?"

Her giggle broke the stillness. "My grandmother used to say that beauty is a garden full of scavengers, but wisdom is a garden with a fence. So I suppose you can be wise anytime you have a fence."

"That's quite the saying. She sounds wise." Chip stuffed his mouth with food before he continued with anything less complimentary.

"She also said that a man with a beard has something to hide and is not trustworthy."

He raised a finger. "Or he hasn't been given a razor since he woke up from being unconscious which means that maybe his health providers are untrustworthy." The joke rang truer than he'd intended, so he cleared his throat and raised his tea cup. "To your good health, since thanks to you I have mine."

Adrienna dipped her chin, her long lashes fluttered against her cheek. When she lifted her chin again, water pooled in her eyes. She tapped her cup against his. "To men who are kind, strong, wise—"

"—bearded—"

"And a welcomed reprieve from the wolves."

Her father, her main protector, made her afraid. The pain resonated in his core like a familiar song. He covered her hand with his. She sipped without raising her gaze, turning her hand to link their fingers. At last she managed a smile.

"Tell me how to fix this for you." He gave her fingers a light squeeze. "You deserve to live your life."

"How can you give me my freedom when you don't have it yourself?"

"I'd hoped you would help me with that. The best way out that I can see is—"

"—in the plane. I'd thought of that." Adrienna leaned back in her chair, but her voice remained a whisper. "I have to confess that the reason I did this was for a moment alone to ask you to help me. I don't know how we'd manage, but if we could make it to Bamako, we'd be free. I'll leave the country and you go to the embassy."

Him? He was her solution to the abuse, her avenue out of her torment. Hero Chip wasn't alive yet. He was supposed to be born in the Air Force. This version of himself still flinched at heavy footsteps and the smell of scotch.

She'd chosen the wrong guy. A wild animal mauled Pax because he couldn't step in. He needed rescuing as badly as she did.

"Sidi is my guardian. We'd have to disable him in order to get out alive."

Adrienna shrugged. "Dr. Thomas has lots of sedatives we could use. He doesn't keep the cabinet locked in his medical quarters."

"Loris doesn't give me any warning. How would I contact you about the flights?"

"I have a friend in the shop who knows I like to watch the planes. He thinks it's because of Dad. He usually lets me know when a plane is getting prepared." Adrienna tapped her head. "I've been planning this for a while now. Dad thinks I know nothing, that I see nothing. He will find out how wrong he is when I'm gone for good."

In his chest the fire sparked—a giddy hope. "I'll be your wings to freedom, Adrienna. I promise."

Her schooled features beamed with the first light of happiness he'd seen from her. Words of freedom gave power.

She threw her arms around him and kissed his cheek. "The time is coming. I can feel it. It's a new day, Chip. Maybe that avalanche wasn't the worst thing that happened to us after all."

Chip laughed. No—the worst thing that had happened to them was Loris. Once he was in their rearview, life could continue its happy path.

"Can you do something for me, Adrienna? Can you send this letter? Please?" Chip handed her a letter to his family that he'd written last night. "It just needs postage."

"I'll see what I can do. You could be home before this letter gets there." Adrienna filled her tray with dishes and gave him one last peck on the cheek. She winked as she sashayed out the door. "See you soon, captain."

Sidi poked his head in. "Mista Chip, we're needed at the airstrip."

This wasn't the flight. Adrienna wasn't ready, but she was right. He could feel it, too.

Soon.

Chip dressed for the day and walked with Sidi to the hangar. The Cessna was on the ramp waiting. Dr. Thomas joined them as they crossed to the plane.

"Glad to see you are fully healed, Chip. I'm in need of transportation to this airport." Dr. Thomas thrust a piece of paper with coordinates into Chip's hand. "Loris is occupied with the students today but said you'd be able to get me there." Dr. Thomas shifted on his feet nonstop. He apparently needed a large dose from his sedative cabinet. "I hope you'll forgive me, but I took the liberty of asking the team to fuel the plane. The task is time sensitive."

Chip plopped into the left seat and started the engines. The coordinates directed him to an airport right outside of Bamako. Why couldn't Adrienna have been ready? This could be his chance to get himself to an embassy or radio for help, but he'd promised her. He vacillated between justifying his leaving and deciding to keep his promise to Adrienna.

Someone would have changed the trajectory of his life if they'd taken him and Pax from Father at the height of the abuse. It was years before Oma and Opa finally barged into their lives and insisted on time with their grandsons. When they did, Father saw that he could be rid of his leeches for a while and was more than willing to grant the grandparents time.

Couldn't he save her by telling the embassy what was going on? But what would the British embassy do for a Malian girl? And he had no proof the students were actually child soldiers. He needed concrete evidence.

"Dr. Thomas, are you going into the city?" Chip said.

Dr. Thomas nodded. "Near enough."

"Can you get a couple things for me?" Dr. Thomas started to fidget so Chip continued. "I'm not used to going without deodorant or a shave."

A stuttered laugh came through the headset. "I think I can accommodate simple hygiene requests without concern."

One down. "And I would really like to get a thank you gift for Adrienna. She's been so kind to be my nurse. She loves to sing and dance so I thought it'd be nice to give her something to record herself and improve her skills."

"Does she? I didn't know that about her." Dr. Thomas fell into a coughing spell. He retrieved a flask of water from his bag. "I don't know if I can help you with that this time. I might have something at home that she could use."

"I don't think she'd mind something secondhand." Chip forced a laugh. "But—uh—I'd like to record a message for her and give it to her myself, if possible."

Dr. Thomas chuckled. With a pat to Chip's arm, he said, "I see, son. I will look through what I have. I'm sure there's something that would make a nice gift for her."

"Thank you, Doctor. It looks like we'll be landing in a couple of minutes."

Chip radioed into local traffic. If none of the pilots spoke English, he'd really be in trouble. Another example of how dangerous it was to fly in another country without the proper education. Being so close to the capital city meant a lot more air traffic of varying sizes. Chip scanned the skies but didn't see other aircraft so he landed and taxied.

Dr. Thomas had the cabin door open and a mobile phone in his hand before Chip exited the runway. Chip parked to the side and cut the engine.

"Just landed," Dr. Thomas said into his phone. "On schedule? Good—what was that? Hello? Are you there? Are you okay?"

A voice responded.

"What was that noise?"

An answer.

"A what?" Dr. Thomas shouted into the phone. Whatever the voice said made Dr. Thomas suck in air. "I'll be there in ten minutes."

Dr. Thomas grabbed the key from the ignition and jumped out with his bag in hand. "A bomb just exploded in downtown Bamako. Wait for me here."

Chapter 16

Bamako, Mali

"Someone will be with you in a moment."

The door clicked shut, leaving Duke and Madison enclosed in a French Embassy office. Her stomach groaned in protest of its emptiness. She didn't manage more than a couple of bites of the porridge Duke made for breakfast. Dread and anxiety had hounded her the previous night to the point she felt ill. If that wasn't enough, Karim, angry drug buyers, and the Mali jail fueled her nightmares.

Their first drug drop went without a hitch, but that didn't mean they always would.

The moment the guard waved them through the embassy's front entrance, her tension headache eased. Here she felt safe. If the French intended to solve Mali's drug problem, wouldn't they intervene in her situation? Or would they punish her?

Hope was the very reason they perched in straight-backed chairs waiting for someone to come to their rescue. The lush carpet and floor-to-ceiling windows seemed obscene compared to the stark homes of local Malians. Draperies with rich tones dimmed the daylight and suppressed the outside heat. Electronics hummed in the void of conversation.

Madison tapped her fingers against each other on her lap. What if they didn't take her seriously?

Duke arrested her hand in his. "Waiting isn't your strong suit, is it?"

Yet another of her shortcomings. Duke noticed everything.

She relaxed. "Not at all. Lucky for this embassy, you're the world's most laidback man."

Duke winked. Behind him, the door eased open. Sabine walked in. Madison almost laughed out loud. This was too good to be true. Sabine's tight bun and dark brown business suit stated that she was the person they needed on their case.

"Hello, I'm Sabine Roux." She extended her hand to Duke first. Recognition lit her eyes as she greeted her. "Madison."

An ally. She hugged Sabine a little too tightly. "What a welcome surprise."

"A recent promotion landed me in this office. I'm delighted to see you. You were supposed to email me next time you came to Bamako." Satisfaction stole across her features as she set a file on her desk and took her seat. Her bright smile faded a bit. "You aren't in any trouble, are you?"

"In a way. That's why we're here." Madison shifted. In her peripherals, Duke observed their exchange. It looked like this time he was happy enough to let her take the driver's seat. She cleared her throat. "I'm in over my head. Since I saw you last, General Abdou Karim approached me and wants me to run his drugs past the French checkpoints and store them in my hospital as payment for bailing me out of jail."

A grunt came from her petite form. Sabine squinted her eyes, biting at her lower lip. "Surreal. What are the odds?"

"I owed him."

"I meant what are the odds that he would approach you after we met and after I got my promotion to this job." Sabine pushed to her feet and stepped over to the window's edge, peering behind the curtain. "Who knows you are here?"

"No one as far as I know. I didn't tell Duke where we were going until this morning."

Her heart pumped faster. It did sound too coincidental. Why hadn't it occurred to her that General might have her followed since she was part of his team?

Madison gripped her chair. "Is someone out there? Did someone follow us?"

Duke shook his head. "I kept a close eye on the other cars around us."

"You need to be overly cautious." Sabine returned to her chair. "Tell me more about what happened."

"The short story is that on my way back to the hospital from Bamako a policeman pulled me over and threw me into jail where I met Duke. They demanded an extortionate price for my release. In the morning, they were about to—"

"—harm her," Duke said.

"In the spur of the moment, I told them if they touched me General Karim would kill them. I was desperate for someone with authority that they might fear."

Sabine's eyebrows shot up. "And General Abdou Karim was that to them."

Madison cringed, ready for her reprimand. "My contact with him until then had been brief. I performed a surgery on his son a month ago and he made it clear he wanted more of a relationship between us."

Sabine snorted. "Where was this story when we were at dinner?"

"Well, fending off the fathers of my patients isn't always dinner appropriate. At that point, I wasn't involved in anything but medical care." Madison gave her a half-smile. "When General

Karim rescued me from the jail cell, he required repayment. I was willing to comply to get out of there. It wasn't the smartest move, but I don't know what I would have done differently in hindsight."

Sabine nodded. "You made the best call at the time." Her eyes fell to their joined hands. "Duke, where do you fit into all this?"

"Madi promised General Karim that I would help him if he got both of us out of the jail cell. I'm to aid his gardeners with whatever they are growing," Duke said.

Sabine scribbled notes onto her pad of paper. "When did this happen?"

"Yesterday," Duke and Madison said in unison.

"You came straight here then. Have you made any drops for him?" Sabine asked.

"One this morning on our way here. Karim didn't want to waste any time in getting us to move his goods past the French checkpoints, and he was right. We didn't get any hassle going through."

Sabine hunched over her pad of paper scribbling notes. Her silence on the matter grew more intimidating by the second.

"Let me bring in a colleague of mine," she said.

The thump of the door shutting made Madison's heart sink. Sabine had been good company when she needed some in Bamako, but was she trustworthy? Would she punish Madison's involvement? Or did Sabine think she was bluffing?

Madison stood to pace. "French prison has to be better than Mali's jail, right?"

Duke huffed. "That's one way to get out of Karim's arrangement."

The large clock on the wall sounded off the seconds in a march toward her future confined in a prison cell. Madison massaged her neck. The door creaked open. Sabine entered first with a man behind her who looked every bit the part of a French diplomat from his styled dark hair to his expensive-looking suit and coordinating leather shoes.

"Madison, Duke." Sabine motioned behind her. "This is my colleague against crime, Monsieur Mane Komot."

Mane—the name suited him.

"A pleasure." Mane drew out his words.

He grasped Duke's hand. His manicured nails put hers to shame. He held hers for a long beat, bowing over it and kissing it.

Slimy. "You as well." Madison withdrew her hand, resisting the urge to wipe his kisses on her skirt.

"We'd like to take the opportunity to identify your vehicle and track its progress. You won't get any hassle going through our checkpoints. We are serious about stopping this problem." Mane peered down his large nose. "Do you have a satellite phone so we can contact you?"

Pay for a phone with no one to call her? Madison shook her head slowly.

"Nothing?" Sabine pursed her lips. She'd not needed one until recently. Madison shrugged.

Sabine pointed at Duke. "Anything?"

"No. Too big of an expense," Duke said.

"Except it could save your life." Sabine typed a note into her computer. "We will fix that for both of you."

They weren't going to jail, but they were still stuck running drugs. Not exactly what she wanted to hear. Mane leaned against the wall, looking well-fed and overpaid. His lips protruded as if he had an underbite. A French aristocrat if she'd ever seen one. He met her gaze with a bemused expression. Madison flushed. He'd caught her staring.

Duke squeezed her hand twice. She glanced at his widened eyes.

Oops. She smiled her apology to Sabine. "I missed what you said."

Sabine smirked. "I said, Mane suggested we check in regularly by phone when you know a delivery is going to happen. We may also send an undercover operative to your hospital to identify the goods and document what is taking place."

"The more you know, the sooner you can nab him and he will no longer be able to terrorize the people who need my help, right?" Madison said.

"We need more time to develop a fully executable plan." Mane brushed invisible lint from his sleeves as he spoke. "Feed us information as often as possible. If we have any plans, we will inform you. No need for you to be surprised and blow the operation."

"But you can get us out of this? I want to be clear that we want no part in his dealings," Madison said.

Sabine clicked her pen. "This is the break we've been needing on tracing the path of the drugs. I can't promise you it won't be stressful, but we'll do our best to keep you alive and out of jail."

Our best. Weren't those the exact words Madison used with her patients? They were far from the solid reassurances she longed to hear at this moment. The look on Sabine's face said she knew it wasn't enough. Was the French military's best going to keep her alive? She had her doubts, but for some reason she trusted that Sabine's best would come through for her.

"Our tech expert will get you the devices you need and you can be on your way." Sabine stood and straightened her suit.

Madison and Duke followed her lead. Mane's warm hands engulfed Madison's once more. With a slow bend at the waist, Mane brought her hand to his lips while keeping eye contact with her. There was something so unnerving about this man.

At last he released her hand and Duke grabbed her other.

Swallowing hard, Madison pasted a smile on her face. "Nice meeting you, Monsieur Komot."

"The pleasure is all mine." Mane purred.

As they trailed Sabine through the hallway and down a long set of stairs, Madison scrubbed her hand on her hip. Their footsteps clacked in the stairwell.

Sabine opened a door off the landing and led them into another beautifully decorated hallway. At the third door on the right, she stopped and knocked.

"Enter," a muffled voice called.

She slid the door open. "Robert, these are the recipients of the tech gadgets I requested."

"Good timing. I have them right here," Robert said.

Sabine took the satellite phones from Robert's outstretched hand. "These phones are close to top of the line and aren't cheap. Keep them on you at all times. Robert has installed trackers in the them so we can find you if ever need be. We won't always track you. However, if we have reason to believe you are in trouble, we can access your location regardless of whether the phone is off or on. The trackers work on their own energy."

The ten-ton brick sitting on her chest lifted a bit.

Sabine handed them each a phone. "My number is one on speed dial. Keep the phones charged with the solar panel chargers and don't lose them. Any questions?"

"Can we call each other?" Duke asked as his fingers tapped the screen.

Madison's phone dinged. A text popped onto her screen that said,

Not a bad perk for a terrible gig.

She grinned.

"For limited amounts of time. Don't incur too many charges or we'll send the bill your way." Sabine extended an open hairpin box to Madison. "These devices are needle trackers. There are one thousand in this box. Metal and waterproof with nanotechnology, these little pins send us location data. Slide one in each shipment you can. We'll track the locations with our technology."

Trackers. Phones. She could do this. The French would get the information they needed and shut

Karim's operation down. The plan seemed foolproof.

Sabine escorted them to the embassy entrance and embraced Madison. "We'll be in contact soon with further instructions. Stay tuned."

They said their goodbyes and found their way to the truck. Pedestrians passed the iron gate. Anyone of them could be waiting to report her to Karim. A shiver ripped down her back. The rest of the embassy sat surrounded by brick walls.

Inside was safer. Less dangerous—what she preferred her life be instead of the dangerous mess it had become. She patted her pocket. The bulk of the new phone pressing against her leg felt so foreign, but the security hugged her like a warm blanket.

"I hope we don't need to use it much, but I'm excited about the solar panel charger," Duke said. The Mali bush brought out the inner tree hugger in everyone.

Madison grinned at him. "Your nerd is showing a little bit."

Duke laughed, then slid into the truck. It chugged to a start without hesitation as if it knew Duke was driving, not her. The soldier on duty lifted a hand in acknowledgment as the gates opened. The street teemed with people and vehicles.

As they turned onto the main road, Madison scanned the area for loiterers staked out but no one gave them so much as a glance.

Boom.

A screech tore from her throat as she bent over into the footwell of the truck. Duke swore. General Karim had come for her. She squeezed her head in her hands, listening for the gunshots. Her heart pounded out of her chest when she dared lift her eyes above the dash.

Two hundred yards away, black smoke billowed into the sky. A hotel was in flames. People ran toward the building while others dragged bodies away. Most ran the opposite direction. Already, prostrate forms occupied streets and sidewalks.

Duke opened his door and sprinted across the street toward the flames. What if it was meant for her—a warning or just a mistimed detonation? If she was their target, they'd find her in the vehicle or out.

Quit hiding. Go help.

The chiding scraped her raw emotions. A groan escaped her lips as she got out and jogged after Duke. Sirens wailed in response to the pained cries from the victims. Hospitals and morgues would be full tonight.

Duke squatted over a limp, bleeding woman. His hands pressed into a wound in her chest. "I pulled a piece of metal from her. She's unconscious."

Madison pressed her fingers into the woman's neck. Her skin felt hot to the touch. Good sign. Blood streaked down her face from a gash in her forehead.

Layers of clothes hid her wound. Madison tugged to get a better visual. No success.

"I need the med kit. It's under the passenger's seat."

She took over keeping pressure on the wound as Duke dashed from her side. The chaos. The smell of burning flesh. The blood spilling onto the ground below. It felt so familiar. The med kit dropped near her hip, unzipped. Latex gloves dangled in her periphery. Shoving her hands into the gloves pulled her from her haze. Another wound oozed above the woman's right ear. Evidently, she hadn't been close enough to receive burns, but debris hit her hard enough to knock her out.

Duke cut her top open while Madison tended to her forehead.

"Looks like she'll need stitches," Duke said.

Madison dabbed an antiseptic wipe over the gouge and sealed the wound with steri-strips. "This should do her until the paramedics come." If they came.

A man approached from behind with a child in his arms. "Can you help my little girl?"

Madison nodded and ripped off the gloves. "Set her down."

A steady stream of people needing care found her on the side of the street. They brought news that the explosion was a suspected terrorist attack, compliments of AQIM. Somewhere along the way her supplies were restocked and a granola bar was stuffed in her hand, but she couldn't recall Duke leaving her side. With basic first aid knowledge, he'd assisted as many patients as she had and sent the more involved cases to her.

Around the time she saw her thirty-third patient, the fire yielded, leaving smoldering remains and black smoke billowing into the sky. In late afternoon she finished with the final person in her line. She stared out over the wreckage that the emergency responders struggled to control.

Exhausted chaos.

Police cars, fire trucks, and medical first responders lined the streets for as far as she could see. Some bystanders huddled on the sidewalks with blankets thrown over their shoulders. Others stared at the damage, disbelief warring with sadness. She felt it too, deep in her bones.

White sheets covering victims' lifeless bodies littered the streets. Worlds shredded to pieces in seconds. There was no logical reason or acceptable explanation as to why innocent people had to die.

Duke had left to help search through the rubble for survivors with seemingly boundless energy, but each of her patients sapped a little more strength from her. Her fatigued brained begged for a break, to be allowed to sink back into processing what had transpired in front of her. With a heave, she pushed herself onto her feet. Every muscle in her body ached from the aftereffects of shock.

Uninspired by a swallowed granola bar's energy, she lifted her med kit and trudged across the street toward her truck.

"Doctor. Doctor."

A child's voice stopped her trek. She placed her kit on the ground and waited as the boy ran to her. One more patient wouldn't kill her.

"Doctor, this is for you." He handed her a scrolled piece of paper and skipped away.

She unrolled the paper. A chill ran through her veins at the blood streaked across the bottom.

This was no thank you note.

Chapter 17

Bamako, Mali

Boom.

The building quaked and windows chattered in their frames. Her vase of flowers bounced from her desk and dropped onto the carpet.

What the heck was that?

Sabine jumped from her chair and threw open the curtains. Smoke billowed skyward from a building yards from the edge of embassy property. Pedestrians scattered, covering their heads. Madison and Duke had just left. What if they were involved? She punched out a quick text to Madison.

Shouting filled the embassy hall. Someone flung her door open as sirens ramped to a deafening howl, their message clear—get to the underground bomb shelter now. She joined the masses in the stairwell. As if in a trance, everyone moved together into a dimly lit hallway. Security guards waved groups of fifty into windowless rooms.

"I hate these dungeons," the man next to her said.

Sabine squinted. "Safer than out there."

He grunted and sidled toward a group of guys. She had no tolerance for simple-minded men. Lives had been lost and he was whining about the security measures. A guard motioned her into a room. She dropped into one of the chairs against the wall as the door closed behind them. Across the room, someone clicked on the television to watch the news for updates but recycled programs came on instead.

In less than a minute, a short man entered with a clipboard in hand. "Listen here. Looks like our lockdown might last a little longer than we hoped."

"What happened?" a woman toward the front of the room asked.

"We're trying to get accurate information. The embassy executives have activated the military to give a report," the short man said.

"Muslim extremists?"

The short man pursed his lips and studied his clipboard. "Could be. We'll keep you updated as we learn more. Until then, please stay in your designated area until released."

Concerned workers lobbed questions at the short man's back as he departed. If he knew something, he wasn't sticking around to tell them. She crossed her arms and watched the others. Fifteen minutes passed, and people grew restless. Someone called for the room to be quiet. Pictures and videos flashed across the TV screen of the French Embassy's front gate and then panned to the broken remnants of the building across the street. She moved closer to the screen.

"This morning, innocent bystanders witnessed the terrifying explosion of the Maisons de Jeunes that has left thirty dead and dozens more wounded. A stone's throw from the French Embassy, experts say the explosion is meant to send a message to the French government for trying to aid the Malian military in shutting down the massive amount of illegal drug trade crossing the borders. The drug traders may be telling France that further intrusion will result in more civilian deaths. Is the French government willing to have more civilian blood on their hands?"

Sabine turned and exhaled sharply. Who wanted to "send a message" to the French? Was it really the AQIM? She checked her mobile phone for a response from Madison but had no signal. How long would this take? Sitting wasn't comfortable and standing made her restless.

Center. Balance. Deep breaths. She slouched into a chair in the corner and closed her eyes.

Had Karim tracked Madison? There hadn't been any report in the news of a vehicle being the first to explode. If Karim had seen her entering the embassy with Duke, they'd be in serious danger. Was Madison trustworthy? Or was it a bait to taunt the French? When Madison had spoken of Karim, the fear in her eyes had seemed real.

It was the same fear that shone in her brother's eyes that night twenty years ago. If she had the chance now, she'd fill that intruder's body full of lead. What had Daddy said the robber was looking for? Gold? Years later, it still didn't make sense.

Sabine's parents had been so adamant about banning weapons from the house. Little good it did them. The man stole the most important thing from Sabine and her little brother—the ability to feel safe with the doors locked and family in the house. That feeling of defenselessness drove her to join the military as her repayment to that scumbag and a world of others who thought they could terrorize the innocent. Now, with her handgun under her pillow and terrorists in jail, she slept soundly every night.

But Madison didn't have the luxury of defending herself against Karim. Duke might be able to help, but Karim could crush them like bugs. Mane had insisted on Madison staying involved contrary to Sabine's objection. David the Insufferable changed his mind about other countries' involvement as soon as Mane said it was a good idea. And Mane's opinion carried more weight than hers as a newbie and also—she suspected—as a woman. Without Mane's knowledge, George quietly approved Sabine's request for the pin trackers outside their meeting.

After three hours of waiting and listening to the news blame the French for the attack, everyone returned to their offices. The short man didn't keep his promise to keep them updated, but they'd find out soon enough. She climbed the stairs, stepping aside for the claustrophobes who dodged and weaved up the stairs to get away from the crowd. One step into her office, she stopped.

Something felt off. Someone had been here.

Everything appeared to be in the general place she'd left it. Had her files always been stacked so haphazardly? She straightened them. Her filing cabinet housed everything confidential, locked away from prying eyes. She crouched in front of her cabinet drawers. The middle drawer contained a locked false bottom where she kept her notes on AQIM raids and the drug trade. But the drawer seemed untouched. Scratches marked the rim near the lock of her bottom drawer.

Had they been there before? Or was this new? She should have done a more thorough evaluation when she first arrived.

Her chair sat askew from her desk, how she'd left it as she ran from the room. In the chair she rolled forward. Too bad she couldn't fingerprint her things.

She located Madison's phone number on her mobile. As she grabbed her desk phone, the mouthpiece fell off.

Strange.

The bomb couldn't have loosened a phone mouthpiece. Retrieving the stray piece, she inspected her phone's interior before screwing it on. The threads on the mouthpiece were still in place. No reason for it to have dropped as it did. A metallic gray caught her eye. Was that a small recorder? Her phone had been bugged? Her heartbeat raced. Someone had taken the opportunity of the bomb to track her.

Who did she go to?

She grabbed her key and locked the door behind her. She marched straight to George's office.

He sat typing at his computer, his brow furrowed.

"George."

He glanced up and smiled. "Come on in."

She cleared her throat. "Actually, I was hoping you would accompany me." He squinted, puzzled. "For a smoke."

The sides of his mouth lifted. "No problem."

He locked his computer and joined her at the elevators. The doors closed them in.

"George, I don't actually smoke."

He grunted. "I know. You're too worried about self-control to do that."

She turned to face him. "I think my office is bugged."

His eyebrows lifted. "Are you sure? We have tight security and everyone that works here has been through a rigid background check."

"When we were released to go back to our offices, I knew something was wrong as soon as I walked into my office. I had that feeling that someone else had been there. In all the panic, I didn't even think about locking my office door. When I picked up my phone to make a call, the mouthpiece fell off. It had been untwisted from the handle, but the threads are intact. It should not have come apart that easily. Inside there was a little metal box that looked like a recording device."

"That's a serious accusation."

Sabine nodded. The elevator opened. They stepped out as people rushed in. His hand on her back guided her into a courtyard glazed with sunshine. She inhaled measured breaths.

"Any other evidence in addition to the phone?"

"Small scratch marks above a lock for my file cabinet drawer. I am not sure if it was there when I moved in, but it stuck out to me. No other drawers had them but that one. I had my keys on me. You had a key so if you needed something it wouldn't have been worth trying to break in."

George nodded and patted his front pocket. "Always keep them on me as well."

"Two thoughts. Why did it happen during the bombing? And why did it happen after I met with Madison and Duke about Karim's case?"

"Who met them while they were here?"

Her teeth caught her lip between them. "Mane. That's it."

George dropped his head back and groaned. "He wouldn't do that. He's David's right-hand man. Did fieldwork like you for years and has seen the damage done." He exhaled. "I doubt it's Mane, but no one is safe from this investigation. I have a guy I trust that I will get to sweep your office. You and I will watch the whole time so we can make sure he doesn't miss anything. How does that sound?"

"Acceptable to me."

"Meanwhile, no confidential business or phone calls are to be transacted in your office."

"Understood. And, George, may I recommend sweeping yours as well?"

"I don't think—no, you're right. It'd be the smart thing to do."

They headed inside, stopping on the second floor to enlist the help of George's trustworthy bug sweeper, Henry. As the three walked to Sabine's office, Mane strode toward them.

"Where are you three going?" Mane asked.

George patted Sabine's shoulder. "Sabine has agreed to help us with birthday gifts for our girls. Henry's daughter is born the day after my oldest."

Henry nodded. "I have no clue what to get them this year. Clothes seem so boring."

Mane's expression fell. Sabine coughed to cover her smirk. If there was one thing Mane despised, it was children.

"I initially was thinking a butterfly cake would be perfect," Sabine said. "But maybe she'll prefer a princess cake."

Mane curled his lip and headed in the opposite direction. Sabine rambled on as they stepped into her office and closed the door.

They continued discussing birthday gift ideas with Henry chiming in as he started his search at the door. When they ran out of ideas for birthday discussion, Sabine switched over to France's tennis performance. She searched for tennis videos on her computer so they had to fill the quiet with fewer words if anyone listened in.

Henry held up his hand. Her stomach clenched. He'd found something on her lamp. Sabine clicked a video in hopes the cheering and squeaky tennis shoes muffled the sound of Henry bagging the device. How long had that been there?

"Look at that," George said, his voice low.

At last, Henry unscrewed the mouthpiece and nodded at George. A listening device. The rage fired in her chest. She hated that she was right about that. Henry reached to pull it out, but George shook his head.

By the time Henry finished sweeping the room, her jaw ached from being clenched so tightly. Sabine sat back in her chair and exhaled.

"It's been a crazy day, gentlemen. Can I get anyone some water?" she said.

George nodded. "I'm parched." He motioned her out and followed behind her as did Henry.

She locked her door then moved on to George's. There they closed the door once more as Henry swept the room. Two hours of the afternoon spent watching Henry cover every inch of their offices.

Henry shook his head. No bugs. This time, they accompanied Henry to his office. With the bug safely stashed in another room, they relaxed on the couch.

"You were right, Sabine." Henry scribbled something on a piece of paper. "There was a bug in your phone. But to activate it, you have to pick up the handset. George, I recommend something more secure for her important calls. You should use the bugged phone for every day needs." The paper he handed to George had a name on it. "That guy can get you what you need."

George rested his elbows on his knees, his face covered with his hands. "This is an in-house job. It has to be." He sighed. "If you move offices, whoever did this will know we're on to him. Or her. That leaves us with you staying where you are and giving you another phone as Henry suggested. Henry, we're going to need you to analyze that bug and see where its transmissions go. Then we have to present this higher up the chain."

"What if someone higher up is in on it?" she said.

George shook his head. "Then we've been bugged for a lot longer than today. But I doubt they'd be so careless as to leave obvious clues. The work was sloppy, almost as if someone had to do a rush job. Security clears the floors during the lockdown to make sure everyone is safe, so they wouldn't have had much time."

She bit her nail. "It could have been someone on security."

"If we had cameras in our hallways, we'd know that answer in no time." George shook his head and sighed. "Stay vigilant. An inside man is the worst kind of enemy."

Chapter 18

Bamako, Mali

Random pictures decorated the note in Madison's hand. The timing of its arrival was too eerie to be a joke. The sender pasted together clippings from magazines, but the blood sealed the intentionality of it.

Madison searched the shadows covering the landscape around her. Was the sender watching her? The messenger boy was long gone. He'd appeared and disappeared like a ghost, most likely instructed not to stick around for questions. Not that she knew where to start.

A chill rippled through her body. Should she be in the light? Or should she hide in the dark?

She grabbed her kit and jogged the last few steps to the truck. The driver's door popped open. She ducked in and closed out the world. Her exhale punctuated the silence. The chaos was over, her good deeds done.

But what was left in her hand resembled a serial killer's warning.

Duke's question ran on a loop through her mind. Why was she here? She wanted to bring health and happiness to the people Dr. Cavine had loved. Yet here she was, involved in a national crisis with cross hairs marking her chest. It was her own fault. But was it too late to get out? One call to the airlines would have her stashing her bags in an overhead compartment and catching up on the latest movies.

But they'd find her, wouldn't they? Continents never stopped a loose end from being singed. Isn't that how evil worked?

She dropped her head against the headrest and allowed herself to mentally escape her panic. Cozy pillows and bright colors of her small apartment called to her. Cabinets and the refrigerator stocked with delicious foods readily available at any hour of the day. Electricity was at her whim. Bathing in clear purified water heated to perfection. The fresh crisp atmosphere of Quebec would win any day over sucking in hot dust-riddled air.

The material possessions here didn't matter. She could replace every item she'd left at Duke's. Dr. Cavine's will never said she had to serve two consecutive years to fulfill the requirements. A six-month break would do wonders for her life perspective and hopefully be long enough to clear this mess she was in.

With a twist of the key, the truck's engine roared to life. Joy bubbled within her for the first time in way too long. Going home to Canada was the only thing that made sense.

Running for the beautiful hills of Quebec.

She laughed out loud. This threat, the fear, the acid churning in her stomach, was three plane rides away from dissolving into a full night's sleep and gallons of specialty coffee. Then she'd be one of the crazy people to drop to the ground of the airport and kiss Canadian soil. Nothing sounded more wonderful.

Law enforcement barricaded RN7, the shortest route to the airport, that ran right in front of the hotel and across a bridge. Her Bamako map took her on a detour through the back roads. She crossed a bridge further down the river. In less than twenty minutes, the air traffic control tower came into sight.

There was nothing keeping her here. Not the hospital, not the will, not Duke. She let loose a string of French and English expletives.

Duke.

How could she forget him? Her breaths came in short bursts. She veered to the side of the road and popped the truck into park. The man who right now sifted through rubble looking for survivors of the blast was the one she had driven away from as if she hadn't a care in the world.

He'd been her protector and companion in some of the worst days of her life. He could have ignored her, but he didn't. Instead he opened his home to her. He could have used her as a get out of jail free card and left her, but he didn't. Instead he stuck by her.

Her heart sank. She wouldn't be blissfully free and happy knowing she'd left him to fix her problems. The disaster she'd dragged him into against his will. What was worse, she'd left him while he searched for blast survivors for no other reason than because he cared. He deserved to be treated better than that. He deserved a friend, a life partner, a woman who would stick by him with no hesitancy and no doubt.

She could be that for him until they decided it was done. But this wasn't who she was. Madison Cote didn't run from hard things. Maybe everyone else did, but that wasn't who she wanted to be.

Calm settled over her mind.

With a yank of the gear stick, she shoved her truck into drive and wheeled into a U-turn. Her heart pumped with fury. Never would she admit to this kind of insanity, especially not for a man. The stress weighed heavily on her. Fear of Karim kept her awake at night. But she had to see this through. Running was in her blood, but she controlled her actions.

No more running.

She parked close to their earlier spot. Her guilt sent her to look for Duke. The police blockades stopped her from getting very close. Duke wasn't visible from where she stood. She returned to the truck to wait for him. With the doors locked, she crossed her arms and slouched against the window. The adrenaline of the day wore off leaving her unable to fight her need for sleep. She let it claim her.

Something disturbed her sleep. An audible breath set her on alert.

Someone found me.

Why had she been so stupid to be alone?

One option was to fight, but then he might kill her. She tested her limbs to make sure everything was moving. After a silent deep breath, she opened her eyes to see a dark figure sitting next to her, then yanked the door open and rolled out of the truck. Her feet landed a split second before her knees, but she recovered and sprinted as hard as she could.

"Madi? Where are you going?"

The voice sounded like Duke's. Thank God he finally arrived. Glancing left, then right, he wasn't anywhere to be seen. She checked over her shoulder. He stood next to the truck, the street light outlining his form. Hadn't he seen the man?

Turning around she waved him over with exaggerated arm movements. "Duke, get away from there."

He jogged over to her. She stepped to the side of a building as he rounded the corner to join her. Streaks of soot covered his skin and clothing.

He grabbed her hand. "Why are you running?"

Madison pulled him toward the wall. He'd get shot any minute if he stayed out in the open. "Shh. Hide. He will see you."

"He who?" Duke flattened himself against the wall.

"The man in the truck. I woke up from a nap and he was—"

"Madi, I was in the truck with you."

She covered her face with her hands and sunk to the ground. Laugh or cry? It was a toss-up. The hilarity overwhelmed her. What a crazy person she was to drop out at a run. Duke looked mildly bewildered.

"I thought you were after me." Tears streamed down her face. Apparently, she didn't have to choose after all, but the release did feel good. "I thought you were going to kill me."

He stared down at her, then crouched next to her and touched her arm. "What is going on? Why would you think I would kill you?"

A hiccup escaped her. "Not you. I didn't know you were you. I mean, I thought you were a hitman."

A small smile cracked Duke's solemn expression. "Do I look that bad?"

Another round of laughter burst from her. No trace of his original skin color could be found. No wonder she didn't recognize him. "No, it's not that. Let's go. I'm exhausted."

Duke pulled her to her feet and draped his arm across her shoulders. "I'm sorry I scared you. I didn't want to wake you. To be truthful, I had closed my eyes for a few minutes as well. But when you jumped out, it scared the life out of me."

They laughed together and climbed into the truck. She'd made the right choice in coming back. Duke started it up and headed for the highway. Madison leaned over to grab the note from the floorboard and opened it.

"I got this while you were gone."

He craned his neck to see the note from the glow of the street lights. "What does it say?"

She shrugged. "They're pictures cut from magazines."

He drove the truck into a side street and parked. Angling the note toward the light, he studied it and gave a low whistle. "Wow. I don't mean to scare you, but it looks like something from an investigation show on TV."

"Like a serial killer?"

He shrugged. "I didn't want to say that."

"The pictures seem so eclectic. A car wreck. A follow sign. A lion standing behind a man in a uniform. A man with a gun petting a lion. A picture of a bomb flying toward a stadium filled with people. And then a streak of blood across the bottom." Madison stared out the window. "It's a riddle."

"How do you know that?"

"I don't, not for sure. I used to do something similar as a child to send secret messages to my friends. When I was a teenager, I met Dr. Cavine and Amber. For fun, we'd leave riddle pictures for each other. It became a competition to see who could solve their riddle first."

His eyebrows lifted. "You think it is from someone in your past?"

"Here? No. Plenty of kids used to do it. I wasn't the only one. In fact, kids probably still do it." Although what Malian kid had access to these kinds of magazines?

"This is a morbid note from a pint-sized terrorist?"

She shrugged. "Your guess is as good as mine."

"What is your initial interpretation?" He handed the note to her and drove the truck onto the main roads.

She played the words over in her mind.

"Car wrecks follow..." She stopped.

This was ridiculous. No matter their interpretation, she didn't have the ability to get the right answer. He said nothing while he waited.

She exhaled. "At first glance, the obvious is 'car wrecks follow when a man turns his back on a lion and a man petting a lion means destruction for a lot of people.'"

"That makes no sense. Could it be code for something?"

"Maybe it means that bad things happen when you ignore a problem."

"Like a-lion-standing-behind-you type of problem?"

She nodded. "Sure."

"What kind of problem are you ignoring?"

A snort escaped her. "I'm not ignoring any problems. Today is proof of that. If I ignored the problem, I wouldn't have gone to see the French embassy."

"Wrecks happen when someone ignores a problem, but when you address the problem, a stadium full of people die. What if it is more literal than that? What if it isn't a riddle at all?"

"Okay. If it isn't one, then a car wreck will happen. We'll see a follow sign. A lion will watch us from behind. Then we will pet the lion and a bomb will be sent to kill sports fans."

"You're right. Literal doesn't make much sense either."

Duke's fingers tapped an irregular rhythm against the steering wheel.

"What if the lion represents something?"

Madison nibbled on the inside of her cheek. "A lion might be a powerful person."

"Or a stealthy hunter. An important person is sneaking up on an unsuspecting person or someone in power is doing something behind a uniformed man."

"Wrecks happen when a powerful person is sneaking around."

"Seems like a valid interpretation." Duke rubbed the back of his neck. "But why would someone tell you about this? What can you do?"

Madison blew out a breath. "Maybe the boy got the wrong doctor."

"He called you Doctor?" Duke glanced at her, his expression concerned. "Someone who knows you are a doctor is sending you a message that there's corruption with someone powerful."

"But that powerful person could be General. Could the message be from Sabine?"

Duke grunted. "Wouldn't she pick up the phone and call you? It's obviously from someone who wants to remain anonymous. If I was ratting, I'd want to be a mystery man, too."

"Could it be from someone who doesn't speak my language, so they used pictures?"

Had one of her nurses heard her idea about pictures instead of illegible words? Her stomach sank. Whatever this note was could be an attempt at a ploy much bigger than they were prepared to deal with.

"Regardless, Duke, the end of the note is very clear. People are going to die if things don't change. And I am not about to let innocent people die because of me."

If she could help it.

Chapter 19

Dr. Thomas returned to the plane at 9:14 PM without an explanation of where he'd been for hours. He'd left them like sitting ducks ripe for an ambush with no plane key. His apology was bags of food and deodorant and a razor for Chip. The sandwiches could have contained camel tongue and Chip still would have wolfed it down. As soon as he finished eating, he got them airborne. A man couldn't fly well on an empty stomach.

From a distance, the well-lit compound beckoned in an otherwise dark terrain. Lights from the hangar tossed long shadows onto the grassy airfield. He missed the friendly air traffic controllers wishing him good night as they cleared him to land. Here there was no safety net, runway lights, or airport beacon to welcome them. Just bumpy grass that disappeared into the night.

Chip cut the engine outside the hangar where a man stood next to a golf cart.

As soon as Dr. Thomas opened the cabin door, the man called out. "Doctor, please come with me." Dr. Thomas mumbled a good night before sinking into the golf cart seat. Chip put the plane to bed while Sidi returned the keys to their top-secret location. By the time they arrived at the medical center, fatigue seeped into Chip's bones. So much so that he dropped onto his bed with his clothes still on.

A knock interrupted his fade into sleep.

"Mista Chip, Dr. Thomas needs your assistance," Sidi said.

He was wide awake now. Chip's heart raced. Scenarios requiring his assistance flashed through his mind. None of them were good. Sidi didn't accompany Chip in the golf cart with Dr. Thomas's messenger. The golf cart was moving before Chip's backside hit the seat. They stopped outside the boys' lodging and ran in. Chip lengthened his stride to keep pace with the messenger past the bunk rooms, bathrooms, common area, and house parents' rooms to a side hallway.

Sobbing disrupted the quiet. His throat went dry. Blood, torture, death—Adrienna. Chip sprinted toward the noise, flexing his hands to steady the tremors. A scream slowed his steps. He braced himself as he walked into the room. The smell of sweat and body odor overwhelmed him.

There in the corner Nafy held his stomach, screaming at Dr. Thomas who stood surrendered a few paces away.

"What happened?" Chip said.

"He won't let me examine him. He keeps screaming for you." Dr. Thomas huffed. "He's been inconsolable for almost an hour. It started right before bedtime."

"Nafy?" Chip stretched out his arms, stepping slowly toward the boy.

Nafy's breath came in gasps. Tears streaked his face. He took three steps and collapsed into Chip's arms. His whimpers vibrated through Chip's chest. Chip hugged him tight, rubbing his back like Mum used to do. Her soft words, her laugh, the sound of her beating heart had long ago been replaced by his imagination. Fifteen years later, he still wished he'd had more time with her. She was his angel which was exactly what this little boy needed.

Nafy sucked in air. His body shuddered as he relaxed. Chip sank against the wall, pulling Nafy to the ground with him. He rubbed his sleeve over the boy's stained cheeks. If only it were that easy to wipe away the pain.

"They're gone. Someone took them." Nafy whimpered the words and Dr. Thomas translated.

No. Chip's throat tightened. Nafy's last earthly possession, the proof of his mother's love and pride for her little boy. She'd sent him off to become a man in glitter shoes. And they were gone.

Chip closed his eyes against the prick of tears as he watched the replay of his drunken father shredding the matching plush elephants Mum gave them before she died. The final piece of her and her love for them ripped from seam to seam—much like their hearts—with stuffing falling like the snow.

"She didn't eat for a whole day so she could buy them for me. She said that when I saw them I would always know that I was the sparkle in her heart and the reason she was alive." Nafy inhaled a shaky breath. "I can't be here. She needs me. I have to leave, Chip. What if that monster returns and kills her, too? I must go home."

There had to be a way. Chip met Dr. Thomas's eye. The older man offered the barest shake of his head. No words of reassurance came to him. Nafy would lose his mind if he knew his training came from the man who'd slaughtered his family.

Nafy sniffed. "I have visions, usually after chapel. I pray and pray that God keeps her safe but I see soldiers going after her and my friends. God is letting me see what will happen so I will go back to protect them. Please."

"Dr. Thomas, can't you medically discharge him?"

"I cannot interfere with the process, Chip." Dr. Thomas shrugged, but fear flitted across his aged features. He was as much a puppet as the others. "The boys agreed to the training and whatever it involved."

Did they though? Did the boys really agree to knowingly become child soldiers? Or were they agreeing to the perks of an education that would "make them men"? The orphans had nothing to lose, but Nafy was losing the last person he had left.

Dr. Thomas spoke to Nafy who nodded, then to Chip. "I'm going to give him a sedative to help him sleep tonight."

Sedatives seemed like a currency Dr. Thomas spent with ease. Nafy buried his head into Chip's neck. When the needle touched his skin, he didn't move or make a sound. His hands gripped Chip's arms until his head slumped sideways. At Dr. Thomas's signal, a man retrieved Nafy and disappeared into the hall.

Chip stayed one step behind Dr. Thomas through the maze to the exit. "What about the hallucinations?"

"I don't provide cures for spiritual experiences. Whatever visions God is giving him does not involve me." Dr. Thomas coughed violently. He wiped spittle from his mouth with a monogrammed handkerchief before stepping into the night air.

He clenched his fist. "You're going to pretend it's spiritual? An educated man of medicine like you knows the difference between drug-induced terrors and spiritual encounters."

Dr. Thomas's posture straightened. His lips pressed into a thin line. "You are right, Mister Chapman. I am the most educated man on the premises, so you would do well to hear my words." He leveled a glare at Chip. "Westerners live by the adage, 'the squeaky wheel gets the oil.' But within these walls, 'the nail that sticks out gets hammered down.' Take heed. It may save your life."

The doctor walked away. Chip kicked at the gravel with a growl. Submission or death—no middle ground.

He spent the rest of the night in his bed trying to get comfortable enough to sleep, but his mind wouldn't stop. Adrienna's first real smile when he said he'd help her leave. Nafy's small hand in his and tear-stained cheeks. The somberness of the boys he'd left to be soldiers. Karim's sharp gaze taking in everything at dinner. Chip's familiarity with their fears and emotions cut holes deep into his core, yet here he sat unable to help any of them the way he wanted.

The next morning, Sidi was his wake-up call after a few hours of rest. Loris had called for him. Today having no mirror was an advantage. The man he'd see was helpless and lacking courage—a man with no viable escape and no way to save the vulnerable. He couldn't be the man who left the innocent to be ravaged by evil.

Sidi took him to the hangar and disappeared as soon as Loris greeted them. The Cessna stood ready to go. Maybe Adrienna was in the back and this would be the day.

Once again, he sat left seat so that Loris could be closest to the door. This time, they headed southwest to the border of Guinea but didn't cross over. Loris stayed unusually quiet. They landed in a field where Loris exchanged bags with people who appeared from the surrounding forests. Then they flew toward Bamako.

No Adrienna.

Along the way, Loris identified the road block checkpoints where the military troops checked cars for illegal people or substances. Loris landed the plane in a small airstrip on the west side of Bamako between two fields. He dropped a red med kit at the edge of the field, looked around, and strolled to the plane, hands in his pockets. No lights blinked in the distance. No people emerged from thin air. Loris hopped in the plane and they headed back. Odd.

When they landed, Loris motioned Chip into a room on the side of the main hangar. "Come, come. I want to show you something."

What now? Chip glanced around before entering the room. There weren't any windows, but there weren't any obvious torture devices either. He kept Loris in his peripherals and took a seat as the lights turned out. A click triggered a picture to shine on the wall opposite him. Whatever it was, he didn't want to see it.

"I have a friend who is touring Europe right now." A picture of the snow-capped mountains stretched across the wall. "He says summers in France are his favorite. I'm sure you'd disagree, because France has the French." Loris chuckled and clicked through a range of landscape photos, sunsets, wildlife, and perfectly plated food. "As you can see, he's enjoying himself immensely."

If inspiring homesickness was today's torture, Loris had accomplished his mission. The brilliantly colored photos and artistic shots dumped gasoline on his burning desire to leave this hole behind. More than that, they reminded him of Pax's art.

"Then he wandered into Switzerland. Isn't that place amazing? You lived there for a while. You could testify." The photos moved to cattle grazing on hillsides, flower boxes on windows, and goatherds dominating large portions of road. "He stopped by this quaint little church that caught his eye."

Where had he seen that church before?

"A few people were lined up to get inside, so he followed them." Loris clicked to the next picture.

An invisible fist smashed into Chip's chest, taking away the air. High pitches whistled in his ears.

His family—Pax, Opa, Oma—stood outside the church in black clothing. Father was nowhere to be seen. Black-clad friends from the village greeted each other with solemn faces. Most he didn't recognize. They'd be there for Opa and Oma, not because they mourned the loss of his life.

The photos captured Oma's pained tears and the gauntness of Opa's wrinkle-lined face with unbelievable clarity. Pax fidgeted next to them, his eyes everywhere but on the people in front of him—the behavior of one not accustomed to loss. In the next picture, Pax stared straight into the camera. Maybe he knew. Maybe Pax could feel that he wasn't gone.

"I see you understand what is happening here." Loris's smile bled into his words.

Chip's skin crawled. His teeth clamped his tongue. Loris didn't deserve any satisfaction from this.

"Look—the little church is full. For you."

A board filled with pictures of him sat on an easel in the back corner of the church. A handful of photos summarized his life, cementing the way people would remember him for years to come. A few kids huddled in front of it probably whispering about the old clothing and hairstyles and funny school costumes like he had when he was a kid. No one but Pax knew how fake the happiness in those photos was and just how much of his life was marked by pretend happiness while rotting away inside from fear and pain.

"Wasn't that nice of your brother's girlfriend to come? Sarah? Laura? Lauren, was it? Anyway, she must really care for him to be present at such a tough time for the family." The sneer in Loris's voice had Chip gripping the armrests on his chair.

The next frame was a video of Opa walking to the front of the church. He opened a paper, cleared his throat, and thanked everyone for coming.

"Baxter Charles Chapman who we knew fondly as Chip—" Opa said, his voice soft but strong. Chip leaned in and clung to the familiarity. Opa was the rock in their family. His voice soothed Chip's blistered nerves for a second.

Loris cut the video and turned on the light. "I'll spare you the pain of hearing all the things he said about you. He looked older in that video than he did in the newspaper pictures. I've heard grief accelerates the aging process in the body." Loris shrugged. "The important thing is that my friend made sure to tell them how sorry he is for their loss."

Opa did look like he'd aged. They all did. It had felt like months had passed instead of weeks. Chip focused on his fingernails, willing his temper to stay in check. He should be home with his family, not spying on their grief from another continent.

"You're lucky, you know," Loris said.

If his teeth gritted any tighter, they'd break. "How do you figure that?"

"Few get the honor of seeing their final goodbye. And there you had a whole tiny church full."

"Although I'm grateful for the chance to see them, I wouldn't call it an honor to see my family hurting."

"Yes, pain is life's worst enemy, isn't it?" Loris lifted his chin. For a second crisp enunciation replaced his normal nasally drone. A strange expression twisted his features. "We pad our lives and it still finds us."

His musings didn't interest Chip today. "Why show me this?"

The question snapped Loris from his pensive mood. His crazed grin slid into place. "I'd say it's because I'm a nice guy, but we both know that's not true."

Moving behind him, Loris placed his hands on Chip's shoulders and squeezed. He suppressed a shiver.

"Baxter Charles Chapman who we know fondly as Chip is an emotional fellow. His face broadcasts his feelings to world when he tries to hide them. And though he thinks himself smart and sly is a mere caricature of a boy, a shadow of a man locked inside a coward's body."

The drawn map of the compound and letter he'd asked Adrienna to post fell into his lap. His heart skipped into triple time. The pressure on his shoulders intensified.

"His one redeeming quality is his deep, abiding love for his family. The lengths he'll go to protect them are staggering." Loris let go of Chip's shoulders and strode to the door. "Which is why if beloved Chip creates mischief or attempts an unauthorized departure from these walls, his family will suffer immensely." He tilted his head. "Understood?"

Chip gave him a short nod. The minute Loris found him missing, a sniper's sights would find his family.

Chapter 20

Mali, Africa

The bomb. The note. Karim's project. The stress piled on and Madison felt herself buckling under its weight.

Duke swerved to avoid yet another pothole, en route to the hospital. "In the short time that I have known you, I've discovered one very important truth."

She rolled her head to look at him, her eyebrows up.

"You are not a morning person."

A laugh that sounded more like a bark came from her throat. She rubbed her eyes. "I have a stress hangover."

Duke laughed.

The sunlight made Madison's head throb. "Why are you so chipper?"

"Well, despite my lack of sleep, this is the only life I have and I'm happy to see another day." His hand rested on her arm. "Give any more thought to the note?"

Had she ever. "A little. I decided the man with the lion behind him is a game warden or park ranger. Did you figure anything out?"

"I fell asleep pretty quickly, but I thought about it this morning. There has to be more to the lion than what we think."

"Stunning progress."

He smirked at her. "I will spend more time on it today. Don't tell anyone about it yet."

They bounced down the path that led to the hospital. People hurried in the opposite direction, too eager to be leaving.

Madison twisted in her seat to watch them. "Where is everyone going?"

In front of the hospital, armored trucks blocked the entrances. Men with guns were everywhere. A giant fist clamped around her lungs. Madison jumped out before Duke put the vehicle in park. She flew past the men inside.

"What is going on?" She stormed through the halls shouting. Patient beds were in the hallways. Supplies sat next to them stacked in a haphazard manner. "Where is General Karim?"

A muscled gunslinger pointed in the direction of her office. Blood rushed to her face. Her cheeks blazed with heat. What she wouldn't give to be seven feet tall and three hundred pounds of sheer intimidation at this moment. With full speed, she threw open the door to her office and let it smash against the wall. General sat with his feet propped on her desk. This time he didn't smoke.

"What is going on?" Based on the General's smirk, her roar must have been equivalent to a bear cub's instead of the mama bear sound she'd wanted. "Why are you in my office? And why are there armed men all over my hospital while patients are running away? We had a deal."

General's smile never wavered. "Where have you been, beautiful Doctor?"

She narrowed her eyes at him.

"If you had been here, you would know what is going on."

Madison's fingers dug into her hips where her hands sat anchored. "Enlighten me, please."

General dropped his feet to the ground and stood. "You're delivering on your side of the bargain. We use your hospital to store our goods."

"We agreed that no armored vehicles or armed men would be seen. You are drawing attention to yourself and making me look like I'm in bed with you."

His smile widened. "That's what this looks like? I'm in bed with you?"

That was definitely not the picture she wanted to paint. "Not literally in bed. It's a phrase. It means that it appears to others that you and I are in a partnership with your drug trade."

He winked. She clenched her fists.

Insufferable man. "Listen. My credibility as a doctor trying to do good for these people is on the line thanks to this moving party you are having. Once is excusable. Twice, questionable. Three times is unmistakable."

"We are in a partnership."

"We are not." Her voice shrieked.

General's smile faded into pursed lips. "We are. You said the words yourself."

"I am paying a debt. This overhaul of my hospital has to stop. If the government finds out I'm doing this, I'm sent to jail or shipped to Canada or both. Then I cannot repay any of my debt to you. Nor could I save your son's life again, if need be. Are we clear?"

He edged closer to her until he stood almost nose to nose with her. "I don't like your tone. There is no respect in it. I don't tolerate disrespect from my women."

He'd taken a giant step across the line. Madison sucked in a deep breath. "The nerve—"

His finger pressed against her lips. "But you are a white Western woman who is uncultured and ignorant of how things work around here. You are visibly upset at my disruption of the hospital, as I would be if someone interfered with my trade business."

Madison's heart stopped. His look, his words—someone had told him. Was he the lion?

General continued, "I do not care who needs medical help. I only care that my business gets done. However, since this is a partnership, I will allow you to get back to your business. The closets I've claimed already are mine. Everything else can be yours."

The breath she'd been holding escaped from her lungs. Relief poured through her like ice-cold water. He didn't know. Rather, he didn't sound like he knew. She had been so rash to confront him. She was lucky he didn't slice her to pieces.

General sat on the desk. "And I want this office. I find the lock on the door and the back closet a very convenient space for my needs. As you are no longer sleeping here, I don't see that as a problem."

It wasn't a question. It wasn't a request for permission. Madison glanced around at her home away from Canada. "My things are here."

He shrugged. "But nothing personal from what I could see. You can move it out tomorrow. I believe you have patients to tend to." Then he strode out the door.

"If I have any left," she whispered.

She shut the door and locked it. Everything inside her wanted to punch something or someone. He'd snooped through her personal belongings. Of course, he had. Good thing she'd taken her important documents to the house.

Outside the hospital, voices shouted and the trucks roared to life, then rumbled into the distance. She fished the needle locators from her pocket and jammed one into each drug stack she found stashed in the hospital. When she finished, she plopped into her chair and buried her face in her hands.

Her pictures.

She rolled her chair to the stack of six heavy medical reference books against the wall. Three faded pictures and a hand-written note were pressed in between the pages of the fifth book. He must not have checked them.

One brown-haired pigtailed girl hung her arms around two tow-headed little princesses. They were her favorite foster sisters. That family had shown her more love in her short six months with them than any other family did in her eighteen years of foster care. They were the sisters she'd always wanted, but they didn't adopt her. She was moved on to a money-hungry family who bordered on abusive when the case worker wasn't around, which was most of the time.

The next picture was of Silver Bullet, her favorite horse on a farm she lived at for a few years. The family fostered as a way to bring in cheap labor. It was a house full of boys, some who belonged to the adults and others were foster boys. The wife wanted some help in the kitchen, so they'd requested a girl.

Unfortunately for them, Madison didn't come equipped with the normal domestic skills most girls knew at that age. She preferred to spend her time in the barn helping care for the animals. The wife had been determined to teach her cooking but, after three years, gave up and sent her back like an unwanted kitchen appliance.

The third picture was from her graduation from high school. Dr. Cavine and Amber stood next to her flashing a thumbs-up at the camera. Amber had died the next year of cancer. A year later, a car smashed into Dr. Cavine's on the road, leaving it torched and mangled. And his body incinerated.

A knock sounded at her door. "Madi, you in there?"

Madison stuffed the pictures in the book. Memories would have to wait. She unlocked the door for Duke and opened it.

"We need your help. I would solve it, but it isn't my decision."

Another problem. When would it stop? She nodded, grabbed her stethoscope, and jogged after Duke.

In the main patient area, two female nurses kept a man and a woman seated on separate sides of the room. A third nurse stood between them looking helpless. Duke cleared his throat.

Everyone in the room paused. Madison stepped out from behind Duke. "What is going on?"

Both spoke at the same time. Madison held up her hand. "One at a time please." She motioned to the woman. "Ladies first."

"I saw him trying to slip bandages in his pocket. He is a thief."

Madison turned her head toward the man. "Is this true?"

"It's not. I swear it."

Duke mumbled in English next to her. "He did it. See the bulges in his pockets?"

The man watched their exchange. There was no fear in his eyes. Madison rolled a seat in front of him and sat down.

"Do you need them? Is someone in your family hurt?"

The man stared at her. Then he fiddled with his shirt as he whispered. "It's my little girl. A wild dog in our village attacked her. Her wounds kept getting infected, but I can't afford to pay you for your care."

"Look at me," Madison said. He brought his gaze to hers. "You bring her in. You and I can work out an arrangement. You can mop the floors or sit guard at night while she is here. We will work it out, okay? Leave the bandages and go bring me your daughter. We can help her."

The creases on his forehead relaxed. He emptied his pockets of the bandages and ran from the room.

Duke winked and nodded. "The nurses helped me get things back in order. I will return later to get you."

He kissed her on the forehead and disappeared through the door. His calm confidence seemed so effortless.

After reassuring the staff that General Karim wasn't there to harm them, Madison spent the rest of the day talking the nurses through a steady flood of crises with bedridden patients. This kind of chaos was the reason she didn't take days away.

Five new patients came that afternoon. On a normal day, her hospital would be teeming with need. General Karim's impromptu show fixed that for her. Word had probably spread to the border about his visit this morning. She'd be lucky if anyone came for weeks.

With charts in hand, she propped herself in a chair closest to the front window. The last of her help left early because of the low attendance. She'd promised to wait around with the night nurse for a while.

A man with dark clothing limped down the path toward the clinic. She laid the charts on the floor and moved to the front door to meet him. Maybe they hadn't scared everyone off. Or was it France's undercover inspector?

She stepped out into the waning sun. "How can I help you?"

He nodded at her. "I'm here for the night watch."

Her eyebrows scrunched together. "We don't have a night watchman."

"I'm under orders from General Karim."

More surprises from General. "Are you staying outside?"

"I'd rather stay inside if you don't mind. I need to keep my eye on the merchandise."

Madison moved aside to let him in. Another surprise. He brushed past her, heading toward the office. Her office. She sighed.

Staring at her papers, she read the same sentence over and over. It was no use. Laying her forehead on her arm, she closed her eyes as the events of the day ran through her mind.

An acrid smell burned her nostrils. How long had she been asleep? Long enough for the generators to quit for the night and leave her in the dark. Coughing racked her body. She fumbled to open the slated windows.

It wasn't enough. With careful steps, she stumbled to the doorway and gasped for air. Outside was too dark to see, but the smell came from within.

She held her breath, fumbling in a drawer for a flashlight. Her fingers brushed the cool metal. The button clicked on and sent a surge of light into the room. Smoke billowed from the hall. The hospital was on fire.

Madison sprinted to the patients' room. Hawa sat in the corner weaving threads together by candlelight.

"Hawa, we have to get everyone out. Fire."

Madison grabbed the wheelchairs and dragged them to where Hawa helped the patients from their beds. They were just kids who came to her for a better quality of life, not more danger. She wheeled one outside while another held on to her scrubs and rode backward in their chair. Hawa had two more the same way. The fifth patient wheeled himself outside, not keen on waiting for rescue. With everyone safe and accounted for, Madison left Hawa in charge and ran inside.

Her feet kicked every box and chair on the floor that the smoke hid. Since General's reorganization, the flammable items were housed in a concentrated area. If she didn't do something, the whole hospital would be a fireball.

Where was General's watchman?

She pulled her scrubs top over her nose. Where did they put the buckets? She ran to grab the one from beside her desk. Smoke grew thicker in the hall leading to her office. She grabbed the door handle and twisted. A searing pain shot through her hand. The handle glowed red.

A fire hot enough to affect the door handle would claim the door next. She yanked off her scrubs top, wrapped it around her hand, and tried the handle again.

Locked.

Madison yelled as smoke flooded from under the door. Whatever General stashed inside was on fire. No one responded. There had to be something heavy enough to break down the door. She ran through the rooms, her right hand cradled against her stomach.

A metal IV rack was the sturdiest material she could find. She wheeled it to the office's side door and swung it at the handle. The rack clanked without making a dent. She swung it again. It stopped behind her and slipped from her grasp.

Madison whirled around. Duke raised the rack to the side. She could kiss him.

"Stand back."

Duke swung the metal full force into the door. It broke into pieces leaving a small dent. He stomped his boot into the dent until a hole allowed smoke to funnel through. Madison kicked at the hole beside him.

"Where are the buckets?" The smoke was getting to her.

"Stay here."

She poked her hand through the hole and twisted the knob. The door fell open.

Duke returned with three buckets and another flashlight. Madison grabbed two of the buckets and ran behind Duke to the river. It didn't matter what creatures were out tonight. They dunked the buckets and sprinted to the office, sloshing water as they went. Madison tossed hers first. Then Duke used his. It wasn't enough. After seven more trips, the water subdued the flames.

The open doors pulled smoke through them. Duke wrapped his arms around her as they huddled together in the cool night air. The warmth of his embrace soothed the heavy grief laying like a weighted blanket over her spirit. Grief for what was and what could have been.

When the smoke cleared, Duke led her inside. Her heart splintered into a thousand pieces as they surveyed the destroyed room. The flames took everything—her desk, her chair, her gifts from the young patients, her books. The closet where she'd once slept had no door.

Duke beamed the flashlight inside the closet and sucked in a quick breath. She peered over his shoulder.

Lying on top of the smoldering ashes of weed were the charred remains of General Karim's watchman.

Chapter 21

Chip sauntered to his room. Sidi's absence confirmed the reality of Loris's threat. If he could warn his family, he'd keep them inside with boarded windows. But Loris didn't promise death. He promised suffering which would likely be worse.

Inside his room, he grabbed the razor Dr. Thomas gave him and went to the bathroom. The water ran cold under his fingertips. He wet his face and began to shave by touch.

Loris had to have snooped through Adrienna's things to find his letter. She was smart enough to lie if he questioned her, right? Was that why she hadn't been around? Or maybe she had a babysitter, too. Men in Loris's position couldn't afford to let little details slide. His carefully constructed house of cards needed to avoid the slightest bump of carelessness to stay standing.

Finished, Chip dumped the clumps of hair into the toilet and tucked the razor into his pocket. Loris or his spies would search his room again, but next time they wouldn't find anything.

Thump.

"Hello?" He poked his head into the room. Nothing seemed to have been moved. The door was closed as he'd left it. He checked the hall.

No one.

A small box sat on his bed. No markings or names gave a clue as to the contents. With the box at arms' length, he cracked the lid. Nothing sprung out at him, so he opened it further.

A note sat on top of crumpled newspaper. "Three taps. Soon."

So ambiguous. The handwriting was neat but gender neutral. He moved the paper.

Inside the box laid Nafy's shoes.

His heart soared. Nafy would be so happy.

Why was the note anonymous? Who besides Dr. Thomas knew about the missing shoes? Loris meddled in everyone's business. He had to know.

Adrienna overheard happenings from Loris. Maybe it was her. Three taps would be her signal that she was in the plane with him. He ripped a corner from the paper and scribbled, "Lunch tomorrow?"

He'd ask Dr. Thomas to deliver the message if he saw him. With the box tucked under his arm, he left to meet the boys for lunch. No one hassled him that he didn't attend chapel every day. Today he waited at their usual table in the dining room, the box tucked between his feet. The minute chapel let out shouts and noise interrupted the peace. Student after student went through the line.

At last, the familiar faces appeared in the crowd, grinning at him the second they saw him at their table. Nafy's smile stopped at his lips. His tangible sadness jabbed at Chip's heart. As soon as everyone began eating, Chip started talking about England and Mali. They nodded, tracking with him. Already the boys' understanding of the language shocked him. They were dry sponges.

Nafy's mood perked when Chip described England's food, the old stone churches, and high-speed trains. While he had their attention, he talked about mountains that disappeared into the clouds and the ocean where the water met the horizon. They couldn't possibly understand everything he said, but they hung on his every word. The end-of-lunch chime interrupted his narrative. On the way out, they gave him jumping high fives, each one trying to out-jump the last.

As Nafy moved in for his turn, Chip motioned him to the side and handed him the box. Unvoiced questions flitted across Nafy's face as he examined the box. His fingers slid underneath the top crease. The glitter shoes sparkled in the sunlight. For a second everything around them stopped as Nafy stared into the open box.

With a yelp, he dove into Chip's arms. Words broken by sobs poured from his mouth into Chip's shoulder. A vice grip and sniffles replaced the stream of words. Two weeks ago, Chip would've laughed and said that girls' shoes shouldn't make a boy so happy, but he was wrong. Nafy's story changed the context. Shoes or a stuffed elephant, every child deserved a symbol of his mother's love.

Chip pulled Nafy from his shoulder. "Are you okay?"

Nafy set his warm hands on Chip's cheeks. "Tank you, Cheep."

A laugh bubbled from the ache in his chest. He'd just been the deliverer. Nafy grabbed the shoes and stuffed them in his waistband. Like a flash he ran to catch his mates. Chip didn't want to watch them learning to shoot guns bigger than themselves, so he stepped into the gym to watch the older boys learn hand-to-hand combat. Maybe he'd learn something new.

Like last time, each boy had a partner, but their attention was focused on the two men in the center demonstrating defense techniques. Abe wasn't there this time. Over and over the men did the motions slowly. On command the boys imitated them. The adults wandered through the pairs correcting form.

Class could never truly prepare someone for an attack unless they—

A thick arm wrapped around his neck, expelling the breath from his airway. The boys turned to watch. A few smirked, but no one moved to help him. He tossed his elbow into his attacker's middle, earning a grunt. The grip loosened enough for him to grab the arm, yank the body over his bent form, and slam it onto the ground in front of him. Seizing the attacker's arm, he twisted it. The man's body shook beneath him.

The boys erupted with cheering and clapping. The attacker let out a loud laugh. Chip backed off.

"Well done. You pass," the attacker said with a chuckle as he pushed himself to his feet. With a louder voice, he addressed the boys in English. "That is what you are working toward. You must always be on your guard, or you will be eliminated before you have the chance to defend yourself."

When the attention of the room returned to practicing, Chip walked out. That was a rush. Next time he'd be more prepared. He was barely out the door when one, two, three golf carts flew past him headed toward the gate. One golf cart jerked to a stop in front of him.

"Mista Chip, get in. Hurry fast." Sidi's eyes were wide and his voice strained.

Chip swung into the golf cart. Was it too much to hope he was being rescued? Sidi floored the pedal, but the cart didn't go any faster.

"Where are we going?" Chip yelled over the crunch of gravel.

"You must prepare the Pilatus. There's been an accident."

When Sidi stopped, Chip ran to the Pilatus outside the hangar. Where was Loris? A couple of guys finished fueling the plane as Chip went through the pre-flight checks. He paced in front of the stairs. What was taking so long? The guys then loaded small crates into the plane's cargo hold.

"Mates, what are you doing?" Chip said, mentally preparing his weight and balance speech.

They laughed. One said, "Loading boxes."

"Because of the accident?"

One of the guys shrugged. "Because Loris said to."

A gate banged behind them. Loris jumped out of the golf cart.

"Get in." Loris barked at Chip, then leapt up the airplane's stairs.

"What's the emergency?"

"Gunshot wound."

They worked like a well-oiled machine to crank the engines. Loris keyed their destination into the GPS. Bamako. Two men stomped up the stairs carrying a body on a stretcher followed closely by Dr. Thomas. Someone on the ground shouted something about baggage. Loris responded and slammed the cabin door shut.

True to form, Loris pulled the Pilatus airborne in no time. From Chip's spot in the cockpit, the person on the stretcher wasn't visible. Loris climbed altitude and opened up the throttle as far as it would go.

Fifteen minutes later, they landed hard on a runway in downtown Bamako. They taxied to the side and stopped. The door opened before they cut the engines. Loris grabbed the keys and shouted to the two other men who glanced at Chip. Then he joined the stretcher in the waiting ambulance with Dr. Thomas.

The form on the stretcher didn't look very long. The ambulance disappeared, leaving them to wait. Two men pulled the crates from the cargo hold and stretched out on them like they were at the beach.

"Was it one of the boys?" Chip said to one of the men.

The man nodded before turning back to his friend. Chip chewed his nails. The older boys were in hand-to-hand combat while the younger ones went to the gun range. It had to be a young one.

The oppression of the sun drove him to wait inside the Pilatus. Restless, he grabbed the rubbish bin. Tools and bloody rags littered the cabin floor. Using a clipboard as a scoop, he collected the trash. First one side then the other. Then metallic stench grew stronger. He poked at a heap, lifting one towel at a time.

So much blood.

The board clipped something hard at the bottom of the pile. He moved the final rag. His breath caught in his throat as his knees hit the floor.

No. God, please no.

Underneath a blood-soaked towel lay Nafy's glitter shoes.

Hours of pacing dragged by before Loris returned to the plane without Dr. Thomas or Nafy. Questions and guilt gnawed at Chip's patience. If only he'd stayed with the boys the rest of the day, this wouldn't have happened.

Chip met Loris halfway to the plane. "Was it Nafy? How is he?"

Loris grunted. "Dr. Thomas said the bullets damaged something important. The kid lost a lot of blood." He flicked his wrist, his nose wrinkled in disdain. "They used a string of medical terms no one had time to explain. Enough about him. Should have left the idiot to die in the field when the doctor said he couldn't fix him himself."

The words plunged a knife into his chest. Leave Nafy to die in a field? The thought made Chip firing mad. When Loris's time came, a sudden death would be too kind for true justice. Nafy was an asset to Loris, nothing more.

A black SUV with tinted windows drove onto the tarmac and stopped next to the crates. Loris walked over with a grin. The men threw the crates into the back of the vehicle as the driver handed over a bag. Loris had the plane on the runway before the SUV left airport property.

Loris's smug smile morphed into humming on the plane ride back. Chip wanted to punch him, but the consequences made Loris untouchable. Every time the annoyance threatened to boil over into words, Chip brushed his fingers over the glitter shoes stuffed in the crack between his seat and the plane.

Bargaining had replaced Chip's shock. He wanted Nafy to live more than he wanted his own escape. If Nafy lived, Chip would do anything to get that boy home. Exhaustion couldn't eliminate the accusations streaming through his mind. Why didn't he do something sooner? Anything.

The darkest night stretched into morning. The glitter shoes hid among his sparse belongings while Chip strode into the boys' bunk room in time to greet them as they rolled out of their beds. His heart hoped Nafy would be there to say someone took his shoes, to smile and put his little hand out for a high five. Tears wiped away easier than pain and death. But he wasn't.

A somber air laid heavy over the usual bunk room energy. One look at Nafy's bed untouched from the night before confirmed Chip's nightmare. The boys' faces asked the questions he wanted answers for, too. All he could do is shrug and tell them he didn't know.

Instead of high fives, Chip hugged each boy. Perhaps his hopes of comforting them were misplaced, but he would've done anything for comfort from someone he trusted after Mum passed. Instead he got slapped and kicked. The boys' teachers and house leaders might not allow "men" to grieve, but Chip did. War would have them seeing and doing worse, but Chip couldn't control that. He could only control now.

The second he released the last hug he started into silly charades for words like help, hurt, need, lost, and rescue. The boys giggled as they prepared for the day. And by the time the chime sounded as a warning to get to their first session, they used the words in short sentences. The accomplishment lifted his spirit. Throughout the morning he accompanied them to and from their sessions. The space between left him too much time alone with his thoughts—worried, pleading, sick to his stomach.

During chapel, Loris found him in the shade near the dining room.

Loris jerked his thumb at the golf cart seat next to him. "We have a flight to make."

Chip said nothing to Loris except what was absolutely necessary. His brain had no space for the usual venom Loris spewed. The takeoff was done in Loris's typical careless fashion. They landed the Skylane at the same downtown airport they'd been at yesterday.

Dr. Thomas stood alone on the tarmac. His shoulders hunched over in spasms as he brought his fist to his mouth. As they stopped the Cessna, he collapsed. Chip hopped out behind Loris and ran to where Dr. Thomas lay panting.

"We need to get him to the hospital," Chip said.

Through the gasping and wheezing, Dr. Thomas hissed, "Home."

Loris grasped Dr. Thomas's other arm and together they heaved him toward the elevated Cessna door. Eighteen minutes later, Dr. Thomas's limp form lay across the back seat undoubtedly with a few new bruises, his breathing shallow. Sweat dripped off Chip's chin. The blasted AC couldn't get cold enough.

Chip wanted to shake Dr. Thomas awake and demand answers. What happened to Nafy? Why had he left the boy alone?

Instead he bit his tongue a little harder as Loris went on about how more smart people with guns could tame the idiots running rabid in this world. Who exactly were the smart people he was giving guns to? The adolescents who had no need to shave yet?

Chip cleared his throat. "How's Adrienna?"

Loris gave him a sharp look. "Busy."

"More patients to handle?"

"Health care is not her calling. She helped Dr. Thomas for a time, but now she does more important things. No more questions. We are landing."

For the first time, Loris started the landing process miles in advance. The wheels met the ground in the smoothest landing Loris had ever executed. So he did know how to land without dropping out of the sky. When the plane stopped, Dr. Thomas stirred in the back. Loris popped the door open and yelled to someone standing nearby.

Chip crawled into the back. His eyes watered at the smell. Dr. Thomas reeked of sweat and urine.

The questions wrenched at his nerves and forced him to ignore it. "How's Nafy? Is he going to be okay?"

Dr. Thomas wheezed. Chip maneuvered the stiff seats so three of them could wrangle the doctor out the plane door. Loris and the golf cart driver left Chip alone to seat Dr. Thomas in the vehicle.

As Chip moved to leave, Dr. Thomas grabbed his arm and sucked in a big breath. "Chip, he's gone."

Chapter 22

Mali, Africa

General Karim loomed over Madison as they watched his men remove the charred body. The rancid odor of burnt flesh had faded in the night, but with the dawn came the terror. Would he blame her? She had been in the building when it happened. Would he believe her innocence or kill her too?

When he had arrived, he said nothing to her or his men. They obeyed his signals. The deep scowl etched in his features kept them on edge. Duke stayed out of sight. No need to make General more upset with her. All the same, it was nice to know he was there if she needed backup.

The men set the body on the ground. Skin remained mostly intact around the body cavity. The fire appeared to begin near his feet. They'd put the fire out in time to save most of his upper half. Madison snapped on her plastic gloves and pursed her lips. Coroner mode was more difficult when she'd seen this man alive and couldn't save him.

She glanced over at General who stared straight ahead, then she crouched over his body.

There it was, as his men had said it might be.

"Here is the bullet hole, General," she said.

General lowered his gaze, his posture rigid. With a jerk of his chin he motioned to his men. They lifted the body and struggled out the side office door, headed to the river. General followed them into the early morning light. Unsure of what he wanted from her, she shadowed him to the riverside.

He stared into the distance. "You heard nothing last night?"

Madison exhaled. This was the interrogation she had been waiting for. "No, I was asleep until I smelled smoke. I was alone until the watchman came. My patients and the night nurse stayed in their room as they do after dark."

"Your love. Did he do this?"

"Duke? He isn't my love." That was the lie she'd been telling herself for days. "He didn't arrive until I found the fire. General, that burnt body should have been me. Every night my routine is to sit at my desk after work. Maybe someone was coming after me and shot your watchman instead."

General twisted and pinned her with a fiery glare. "Do you have a gun?"

Madison drew in a breath. It didn't make her any braver. She lowered her gaze to the ground.

"I do not have a gun, although I wish I did." *To protect myself from you.*

"If you would let me take care of you, you wouldn't need a gun. Nor would you be in the same building as a killer. You are lucky he didn't hunt you down and take your life, too. It would have been simple." General straightened. "Doctor, I want you in my presence until we find that killer."

"But my hosp—"

"No one will be coming for a while. Your staff has been put on leave indefinitely. My presence has tainted your reputation, and news of the fire and the dead body will spread. Patients will find another place to go."

His words sucker-punched her in the gut. There wasn't another place nearby for them to go. Twenty-four-hour protection by General and his men. Surrender overwhelmed her. He wasn't taking no for an answer. And she didn't have the will to fight anymore. Children would die because her hospital closed. That was a failure she couldn't cope with.

"Come." He clasped his hands behind his back. "I have a task that requires your attention and then you will have dinner with me tonight. Bring that man. I need his expertise in my garden. Then he will join us for dinner."

"Let me gather my things."

Madison didn't wait for a response. She pivoted on her heel and stepped inside. The ash and ruin in her office hit her full force. The remaining memories of her life had been incinerated. Gone. Her foster sisters, her beloved horse, and Dr. Cavine's picture were banished to her mental scrapbook where they would fade in time with the rest of her past.

Defeat was the only thing she could feel. She collapsed to her knees with a groan. Tears seeped out. Her precious, few possessions fueled the fire. Why hadn't she taken them to the truck after she last looked at them? The blame ended with her.

A lifetime of suppressed tears fell onto the ash-covered cement—tears for her past locked away in recesses of her mind, for the years of never finding a place in the world, for the loss of the Cavines and the love they showed her, for the failure of not saving the ones closest to her.

Time stretched as she poured her heart out. At last, the tears stopped. She pushed to her feet, wiped her face, and brushed the ash from her clothes. General was waiting for her. She strode to the back door of the hospital where Duke kept guard.

He must have seen her in his peripherals, because he set aside the book he'd been reading and stood. His gaze searched her face. He glanced at the doorway past her, then stepped over and closed it. When he turned around, he wrapped his arms around her. His hug touched her soul. She wanted to stay in his arms until the waves of grief subsided. Whenever that was.

"What's wrong?"

The tears wet her cheeks again. What was wrong was—since knowing him—she cried twice which was more than she had ever cried in her life.

"Everything." She buried her face in his chest. "My medical books burned in the fire."

"Can you practice medicine without them? Can you replace them?" His voice was low and soothing. "Were they limited edition or signed by the author?"

She smiled into his shoulder. "The last three pictures from my past were hidden in the pages of those books."

His arms tightened. "I'm so sorry, Madi."

"I was going to grab them before I left last night, but I fell asleep and that stupid weed..." She sniffed. "General thought you or I might have shot his watchman, but I told him I didn't have a gun. Now I'm under his constant protection until they find the killer."

Duke tensed. "How constant?"

"He is insisting that I stay by his side." She wiped her cheeks with her sleeve. "The killer should have shot me. He didn't, but he may be back for me."

"No, you aren't staying with Karim. Who knows how long it will take for him to find the killer. How do we know General isn't the killer himself? This could be a big ploy to keep you under his thumb. Or worse, get you into his house."

"I don't have the authority to change his mind. And honestly, I don't have the fight in me right now." The fear bound her tight. How safe was she really if she wasn't under Karim's guard? "The closer we get, the more information we can relay. We need to go with him now. He wants your expertise for his garden and then he wants you to join us for dinner."

Duke propped his hands on his hips. "I am happy for the chance to keep an eye on you, but it doesn't feel right. I think we should let Sabine know we're under General's supervision. Anything could happen."

Madison bit her lower lip and nodded. His concern overwhelmed her. He was the closest thing to a boyfriend she'd ever known. And she wouldn't trade it for the world. What would Duke do if she told him she wanted a relationship with him? Now wasn't the time. But after this nonsense with Karim ended, then she would.

They trekked through the hospital to the front. She grabbed her purse and jacket. One of Karim's men opened the truck door for her. She slid in and Duke climbed in after her. Tinted windows and leather seats kept the interior cool. The leg room made her truck look like a sardine tin. To top it off, the vehicle still had the new-car smell.

"Thank you for joining us, Doctor," the driver said as they settled in. "Your medical expertise is required for an esteemed member of our board."

Their terrorist organization had a board of advisers? The irony was too great.

The driver cleared his throat. "He has had a lung condition since he came to us a long time ago, but his condition has declined."

Lung conditions were difficult to diagnose without the proper scans. Fluid in the lungs could be anything from bronchitis to cystic fibrosis, depending on the history.

"I didn't bring my medical bag that I use for diagnosing. Should we go back for it?"

"Everything you need is already there."

Everything I need? How does he know what I need to help this man?

279

The manholes in the road threw Madison against Duke. He smiled and interlinked his fingers with hers. The man's lips could melt an iceberg.

The driver glanced at her in his rear-view mirror. "You are privileged to be able to care for this man. He has been a champion for our cause. He has saved the lives of hundreds of our men who have been injured in action."

What would it be like to keep known terrorists alive? If he was on the brink of death, wouldn't she be doing the world a favor by letting him die?

The driver stopped at a solid gate. The walls restricted any visibility into what was going on behind them until the gate opened revealing several short buildings within the compound. Green grass and flowers lined graveled walkways. A fountain sat in the middle spewing water as if water features were normal in the bush of Mali. Solid walls keeping secrets in and the rest of the world out.

Like an oasis in the desert. "Is this General Karim's residence?"

"Yes."

"What are the other buildings?"

"Meeting places." His tone held a hint of scolding.

Meeting places must have been code for headquarters. They stopped.

The driver got out and opened the door. "Sir, please come with me."

As Duke unlaced his fingers from Madison's, he leaned in for a kiss. His lips brushed hers with an electrified touch.

"Please be safe. See you for dinner." He murmured in her ear before exiting and taking her bravery with him.

She caught the door before it closed. "Duke."

As soon as he turned to her, the rest of the words wouldn't come out. It was silly and way too fast. But he knew. He must have, because he paused with a grin lighting his face.

She scrunched her nose. "I'll see you soon."

The door closed. Why couldn't she have just said it? If he didn't feel the same, he wouldn't be stringing her along. Duke wasn't into games. Next time she had the chance, those words would be the first thing she said. The driver cleared his throat as he held the door open for her. She'd missed the rest of their drive.

With a mumbled apology, she slid from the vehicle. They entered a small building. Darkness shrouded the L-shaped hallway they occupied.

The man knocked on a solid wood door which opened to a room bright with daylight. Near the window, a half-dozen pillows propped up a sleeping man. Thrown over the lower portion of the bed was a quilted navy blanket. Her training and the oaths she took boiled down to caring for a man who regarded others' lives with so little value.

Inside the door, a table held boxes of face masks and gloves. She donned both before entering. His condition was more serious than she'd assumed. The room smelled of wintergreen ointment and fresh-cut pine as if it was permanently Christmas here. Her spirits lifted. She could do this.

The doctor's companion who answered the door assessed her. "He asked to be awakened for the examination and that we leave the room." He scowled, raising himself to his full height. "We will be outside the door should you decide to act out of regulation. And if you do, General has ordered us to be sure the consequences for your actions will be swift and irreversible."

Alone with this man? Her pulse quickened. The damage he could do to her if his illness was a reason to get her alone set her on edge. She blinked against the prick of tears behind her eyes. An overwhelming desire to go home washed over her so hard she fought to keep her feet in place. First this man needed care. Then she'd convince Duke to leave the country with her. Away—where General couldn't touch them.

She stepped to the side of his bed and touched his arm with her gloved hands. "Doctor, I'm here for your examination."

His eyes opened at the sound of her voice. A smile spread across his face. Madison turned to the bedside table and grabbed the stethoscope. The back of it had a faded yellow smiley face sticker that bore the proof of age. She smiled and pushed the ear buds into her ears.

"Doctor, my name is Dr. Madison Cote. Would you lean forward for me, so I can listen to your lungs?"

The doctor grabbed her hand. Madison froze staring at the hand that gripped her. Panic built in her chest.

"Thank you for coming. It is so good to see you." His voice wavered and cracked.

He had to be aware that it hadn't been her choice. "You are welcome."

His grip eased as he straightened, so she slipped her hand from his and swung the stethoscope into place. She pressed it against his chest.

"Take a deep breath for me." She repeated the process three more times. His lungs were full of liquid, his breathing understandably labored.

He wheezed. "Can you listen to my heart, Doctor?"

She pressed it against his chest once again. The beat was regular. Pulling the buds from her ear, she smiled at the old doctor.

"Sounds fine to me."

"Do you know what you hear?"

Did he doubt her medical assessment? Heat rushed to her face. "Yes, it's regular and strong."

"No, you hear the sound of regret and sorrow mixed into one lonely cry."

"That's very poetic."

"It's my heart begging for forgiveness, Madiloo."

Madison froze. Ice blitzed down her spine. One man had called her that in her lifetime. And he had been pronounced dead eight years ago.

Chapter 23

Mali, Africa

The next morning, Sidi waited for Chip after breakfast. "Adrienna waits for you."

They rode to the airstrip in silence. What if this was the fulfillment of the note—their chance to leave? He should have been excited, thrilled even, but he didn't care anymore. His freedom wasn't worth the cost. He didn't want to have to disappoint her, but he would if she pushed him.

Adrienna stood next to the Cessna in a colorful flowing gown and a head wrap. An armed muscleman stood next to her, dwarfing her slight frame. Her greeting lacked warmth and her tight-lipped expression masked her usual energy.

"Kone is coming with us."

Kone crawled to the back, folding his large frame into the seat. The gun packed as much firepower as the man. What exactly were they getting into that required Kone's presence?

Whatever it was, Chip would bet his life Loris put her up to it.

"How have you been?" Chip asked.

A hint of sadness flickered across her face.

"Keeping well."

"I got your gift and note. It meant a lot to me." And Nafy.

Her frown deepened. She didn't meet his eye, but then she hummed and nodded. What the heck? She lifted her chin and read the destination's coordinates. It was nowhere near Bamako. He relaxed in his seat.

As they flew, he sneaked glances at her as she watched out the window. Twenty-five minutes later, he landed at Segou Airport. Adrienna twisted around to face him. Her expression held a hint of anxiety.

"Stay in the plane while we meet with the buyers. We're doing a simple exchange. They take the goods and hand me the money."

Sounded simple until they shot at you.

She pushed on his shoulder. "Slouch in your seat so they don't see you."

Cars stopped nearby on the tarmac.

"That's our cue. I'll be back." Adrienna pinned him with a look. "Stay here."

She spoke to Kone in French and exited. He pulled a bag from the luggage compartment then tagged along carrying the bag. Three men met her halfway. Their heads were wrapped in the traditional Muslim headdress. They talked, gesturing largely. Kone set the bag at their feet as Adrienna motioned at the plane. A man who wasn't talking slapped her across the face. Her head recoiled.

Kone jumped in between them, dropping the guy with one punch. The next second Kone sank to the ground, limp with blood pooling around his prostrate form. Adrienna ran toward the plane, but the two men grabbed her from behind and threw her to the ground. She curled into a ball as they stomped and kicked at her torso. Chip leapt from the plane, fury burning in his chest. He shoved Kone's body off the gun and twisted it in the attackers' direction.

The trigger stuck.

Both men had their handguns pointed at Chip's head. He dropped the gun and raised his hands. Behind them, Adrienna didn't move. Her flowy dress bunched around her knees as she lay sprawled on the ground. This was for her.

He charged the man closest to him. The man was lightweight. Chip had the upper hand—

Chip blinked five times to clear the fog from his eyes. Light from an opening in the ceiling added to the agony ricocheting in his skull. One foot had no shoe while the other foot had a shoe only covering his toes as if stuck on by afterthought. He straightened his back against the solid, cold pole behind him. No wiggle room. Where was Adrienna?

The room was empty.

A creak echoed through the space. The flowy dress came into view from beside him. Adrienna squatted in front of him, setting a plate and drink beyond his feet. Her movements were slow and deliberate.

He swallowed hard against the desert in his throat. "Adrienna, are you okay? What have they done to you?"

She stared at him without answering, her eyes searching his for a moment before gazing at something behind him. Her bruised face was cleaned from the cuts.

"Will you untie my hands so I can eat and take a drink?"

Again, she stared at him. Was she hypnotized?

His tongue was thick and his mouth felt as if it was stuffed with cotton. His whole body ached.

"If you can't untie me, will you bring the cup to my lips?"

She stood. Her eyes flicked back and forth watching something behind him.

He heard nothing. "Please? A sip?"

With a jerk of her hand, she grabbed the cup and bent beside him. She had wanted him to beg before she helped him? As she brought the cup closer to his mouth, he parted his lips. Instead of pouring the liquid into his mouth, she drained the cup down the front of his shirt. Then with a grimace on her face, she crumbled the food from his plate around him.

His heart sank. The opportunity for relief from his parched throat soaked through his t-shirt and trousers.

"Adrienna?" He moaned as she stalked away. "Adrienna. Adrienna!" The words left his lips as a scream.

There was no answer. The betrayal hurt worse than his body did.

Pain squeezed his chest in a vice grip. Tilting his body to the side, he slumped to the floor. The cool concrete eased the throbbing of his head. Her innocence, her plea for help escaping was a huge farce. He cursed his foolishness. How had he missed the signs?

She wasn't victim to Loris's cruelty. She was part. Loris hadn't taken Chip's letter. Adrienna had handed it to him, probably laughing that he'd trusted so easily. Her tears had moved Chip right into place so she could join Loris's schemes. Shame slipped over him. She'd played him while asking him to be her hero.

His moans were the last thing he heard before the black intervened.

Something smashed against his cheek and stung. Words he couldn't understand flew around him. If he was the words' intended mark, they missed by a wide margin. Three men stood in front of him. One babbled something and motioned up.

The two others clutched Chip's arms and yanked him off the floor. His hands had been released. Lights swirled. His mind ushered him from the light, but a jolt of electricity zipped through his back, startling him into consciousness once more. His legs gave out.

They shoved him forward. Every few steps the electric shock paralyzed his back muscles. His plodding pace infuriated his escorts. He was in no rush to arrive at his destination. Visions of a stark brown room, a camera, and angry terrorists hovering over him with torture devices escalated the fight within him to stay calm.

Betrayal and death—none of it mattered anymore.

"Please. Just end this now," Chip said.

They kept moving. Chip shuffled through an open door into the sunlight to another hangar that smelled like fish. Shade brought relief. They stopped at a small, well-lit room. His body screamed in agony. Put him out of his misery.

Finally, they led him into the larger version of the room on the opposite side of the wall.

When he lifted his head, seven men stared at him from their seats. General Karim looked like a general today with his posse surrounding him. No one from his camp moved a muscle and General's face was stone, offering no insight or comfort. He spoke in a quiet, controlled manner to counter the heated words spouting from the turban-clad captors. If death was the sole vote on the docket, he'd pick anything that made it quick.

No one glanced in his direction, regardless of his conspicuous location in the center of the room. Adrienna limped into the room and took a seat beside General. She kept her chin lifted, watching the men between swollen eyelids. General whispered to her. She leaned in next to his ear, probably trading Chip for crates of drugs or telling General how to kill him slowly.

No one uttered a word.

General nodded at the men. With a shout and a flick of the wrist, Chip's escorts hauled him out the door and plopped him in front of a different pole. Chip didn't fight them, as they pinned his arms behind him cinching the rope tightly. Every sensation registered.

His last moments.

A deep breath steadied his frantic heart rate. They glared at him for an agonizingly long time, cradling their guns in their hands.

"Don't I get a mercy hood? You know, one of those black hoods that keep me from seeing exactly when you shoot me and you from seeing my face when I die. Don't they sell those in Terrorist Weekly?"

One of the men lifted the butt of his gun above Chip's head and jerked toward him. Chip flinched. The strike never landed. The men laughed and disappeared behind him. They were going to shoot him in the back.

Cowards.

He craned his neck but couldn't see. Using his feet, he spun himself around the pole so his body faced the door. Not one person remained in the hangar.

A measure of satisfaction followed by disappointment coursed through him. He closed his eyes. Imagined conversations with his family, even Mum who'd been buried for years, assaulted his sleep—closure before death.

"Chip, wake up. Wake up." Warm hands gripped his shoulders and straightened him into a sitting position.

Chip hissed.

"No, stay awake. Wake. We take you home," the voice said.

Home? Someone had found him and would take him away from the pain reverberating through every inch of his body and soul? He didn't want to leave his family tucked inside his dreams. He wanted to be there with them. Chip opened his eyes.

The dark face in front of Chip smiled. He sucked in air. The pressure on his shoulders increased. "Remember me? I'm Sidi."

Then he wasn't going home. Something ripped behind him, loosening the pressure on his wrists. His hands fell limply to his side.

Sidi slid his arms around Chip's chest. "Stand."

Chip pushed with his feet, but his assistance did little compared to Sidi's strength. Sidi said nothing as he carried Chip from the hangar.

Outside, Sidi stopped to rest. "How do you feel?"

Atrocious was the word that came to mind. Chip rolled his head to the side to look at Sidi. "Better."

"We go home."

There was that word again. Home. Sidi knew nothing of what home felt like to him.

"Is General going to kill me?"

Sidi squinted at Chip. He didn't understand.

"You know, kill." Chip pointed his finger gun at his head and pulled the trigger. "Am I a dead man?"

Sidi shook his head with quick jerks and placed his hand on Chip's shoulders. "Why die? You are a hero."

Chip stopped, his eyebrows raised. "I'm a hero?"

"You risked your life for Adrienna."

Because Loris had sent them on an impossible mission and nearly had his daughter killed like her bodyguard.

"General is happy."

Chip swayed into the sunlight. In his mind's eye, he could almost envision himself in Switzerland with Pax and Opa herding the cattle and tending the garden for Oma. He'd give anything to get back what he'd lost. His screwed-up relationship with his delinquent father. His overbearing university class schedule. Staying fit for Air Force basic training. Scraping together money for flight lessons. The crisp air. The mountains. The cozy pubs with his mates on a Friday night. Hiking with Pax.

But that wasn't his reality.

On the ramp, the Pilatus waited with the door open. Sidi helped him up the stairs and lowered him to the floor. His shoes were gone and his t-shirt stained. A cup touched his lips. Chip gulped huge mouthfuls at a time. The liquid had a strange aftertaste. Minutes later a numbness spread to his limbs.

Drugged.

Sweet relief.

Karim and his men filed in without a word. Chip relaxed when the door closed behind them. No Adrienna. The wall next to Chip still bore a blood stain from Nafy's accident. The difference was that Chip deserved his wounds.

A stranger poked his head out of the cockpit for takeoff approval. Someone else knew how to fly this thing? Karim was smart not to fly with his brother. But Loris dragged him through those flights and threats. For what?

None of it made sense.

The familiar rumble of the engines lulled him into rest. The flight was too short. After they landed, Sidi loaded him into one of the ever-present golf carts.

"You are very fortunate. General is very happy with you." Sidi drove in the opposite direction of Chip's room. "He had your things sent to a nice room where the honored people stay."

If he had the energy, he would have laughed. "Like who?"

"Dr. Thomas, Charlie his favorite cook, and special visitors. You get a shower and window in your room." Sidi almost sounded jealous. "And I heard General will be hosting a celebration banquet tonight, and you're a guest of honor."

Food sounded amazing, but so did a bed. "A big banquet?"

"No one will want to miss it."

The thought of seeing Adrienna again stressed him out. "Even Karim's family? And the students?"

Sidi shook his head. "No, children do not celebrate with adults."

He pushed Chip's wheelchair inside. His room was down the right-hand hallway. The open bedroom door revealed plush carpet, a bed of fluffy blankets and lots of pillows, a chest of drawers, and an en suite bathroom. It was decorated like a quaint bed and breakfast in the UK. The contrast to his room in the medical center was laughable.

"I will send the doctor to see you as soon as possible." Sidi patted Chip's back. "You should get a shower. You will need to look presentable for tonight."

He'd been asking for a shower for weeks. Chip opened a drawer. His extra set of clothes had been transferred. The glitter shoes sat next to his shirt and trousers.

"Is what I have acceptable attire?"

The look on Sidi's face said no. "I will bring you something better to wear." He walked into the hall.

Chip paused in the bathroom doorway. "Will you bring me sleeping pills? I don't think I'm going to be able to sleep tonight without help."

Sidi nodded and left.

Warm water from the shower steamed the entire room. He peeled off his sweat-caked clothes and walked into the heat. The needles of water stung his skin. Streams washed the layers of filth and blood but didn't purge the ache in his soul. The day's events played through his mind on repeat. He'd felt this kind of pain before. Only then he'd attempted to end the misery by slipping crushed sleeping pills into Father's alcohol.

That wouldn't work now.

Chip froze.

Or would it?

Chapter 24

Mali, Africa

Madison backed away from the bed. "I'm sorry. I don't know who you are. I don't know your name or anything about you, but that you've been a champion for General's cause. If you need forgiveness, you need it from someone else. Not me."

Her hand gripped the door knob. She'd tell the guards that the doctor had lost his mind.

The doctor cleared his throat. "Amber wouldn't have wanted it this way. She never approved of my involvement with General Karim." His voice was raspy and the pronunciation of each word was a struggle.

Amber? Madi-loo? "Dr. Cavine died eight years ago. I saw the wreck that took his life. He was kind, caring, and concerned with bringing life to his patients. He wasn't involved with terrorists or hurting innocent people like you were...are. And Amber, his Amber, was an angel on earth."

A tear slid down his leathery cheek. "I staged the wreck. I loved that Mercedes, but it was the best way."

It was him. A chill swept over Madison as she sank to the floor. Her mouth hung open in anticipation of a response, but no words came out. It was Dr. Cavine.

Alive.

She repeated it to herself, yet her mind refused to believe it. She couldn't. He had died. She'd given the eulogy at his funeral. Each year she'd placed fresh flowers at his headstone to mark his passing.

"Why?" It was the only word to make it to her lips from her brain.

"A bookkeeper spotted irregularities in my records. He did some digging. Somehow, he found out that I was involved with Karim. He confronted me to get a confession, but I accused him of lying. He lost his mind when I denied it. He was headed to the papers and the police with the story the next day." Dr. Cavine wheezed and coughed violently for a few minutes.

Madison made no move to assist him. That man, whoever he was, was not the Dr. Cavine she knew. Shock locked her emotions.

"The summer after Amber died, Karim offered me money, a lot of money, for doctoring his family. At first it was a sick child or pregnant wife, but eventually it wandered into illegal territory. For a few months, I told him it was the last time, but with each request the payment grew more significant. I quit resisting. Each month, money is sent from an anonymous donor into my foundation which helps the charity hospital stay afloat and paid for you to get through med school without debt."

Just when she thought things couldn't get worse. Her schooling had been funded by a terrorist. The good she thought she was doing at the hospital, the difference she was making was all aided by drug money. She buried her face in her hands as Dr. Cavine continued talking.

"I knew you would be sad about my passing, but selfishly I couldn't bear to watch everything I worked for be destroyed." He adjusted in his bed with a hiss. "But it wasn't just about me. It was about Amber's name and the work we had put into teaching our students and the effort to help the people of Mali."

"You planned for me to come to the hospital. Why? To aid in the drug running? To become Karim's latest conquest?"

Dr. Cavine wheezed some more. The fluid in his lungs would kill him sooner rather than later. "I wanted to secure a way to see you again if I lived that long. To make amends. I wanted the hospital to have a good doctor caring for them and making wise choices, because I couldn't any longer. I knew you would resist General's charm. Your heart is too pure to fall prey to what ended me."

Charm. It was as if he knew the forwardness that General had approached her with on their first meeting when...

Madison's jaw went slack. "It was you who told General his son needed a kidney transplant, knowing full well we weren't equipped. You sent him to my doorstep."

Dr. Cavine didn't look at her. "I knew Roger would be around to assist. And I had to see you again. The only option was to have Karim bring you to my bedside. Literally." Another huff of air escaped him. "COPD is taking over my body. It's been getting more aggressive lately. My time left is limited."

She squeezed her eyes shut. They burned but she wouldn't shed tears for this man. "Amber nagged you for years to quit smoking. Years."

He coughed. "And this is my reward for not heeding her advice. I figured I should get my lungs used to smoke since I'll be inhaling it for eternity." A wheeze replaced his usually contagious chuckle.

"I wish you wouldn't say stuff like that. It isn't funny."

"Madi-loo, I want you to remember how much you are loved."

Madison leapt to her feet and yanked open the door. The guards stared at her with raised eyebrows. She closed the door quietly behind her, leaving Cavine to tell his lies to the walls. "He needed a moment of privacy, so I thought I'd step outside for some fresh air."

She power-walked through the hallway and burst through the door into the daylight. This is what her life had amounted to. The shock had simmered into white-hot rage that threatened to erupt at any moment. The last eight years of her life came into question. No, nine years. Or was it ten? Had the man who had been a sort of father-figure to her through her most critical years of life been nothing but a liar? The values he and Amber taught her meant nothing to him.

The Cavines had lived well. But was it because he was a doctor or because of Karim's dirty money? Their large estate sat on thirty acres overlooking the river outside Quebec City. Their marriage had seemed filled with genuine love. When they housed her for two years before the foster system released her, the value of truth and honesty had been core in their household. No lie would go unpunished. Vulnerability was praised and rewarded with affirmation and love.

Had it been too good to be true? Her heart had been destroyed first with Amber's passing and then with his. The years of treasuring their memory amounted to a farce enacted to prevent justice from taking its course. She sucked in air. She was a pawn used in his scheme to reconcile for all the bad he'd done. Today was nothing but a Hail Mary for the past. The wounds mended from long ago ripped open once more. The Dr. Cavine she met in that bright but dismal room was not worth revisiting the piercing agony of abandonment. She straightened her posture and marched inside. She kept her chin high but avoided eye contact with the guards who no doubt wondered by now what had taken so long. Their job was to guard Cavine and her, so they'd take the day at her pace.

She knocked on the door, feigning courtesy, and slipped into the room. The door clicked shut behind her and she stepped into the room, her eyes on the window.

"I'm glad you returned, Madi-loo. I thought you'd left without saying goodbye." His voice was pathetic.

"I thought you two were different. Life was everything it was supposed to be in those years. It was what I thought normal looked like." Her lip twitched. "My parents left me. And in the end, you did exactly what they did. You and Amber showed me love and taught me to turn away from bitterness.

But then, you left me." She stopped, listening to his labored breathing. "You are just like them."

She wheeled around.

"Wait." His commanding voice had returned. "I sent you the riddle."

She bit the inside of her cheek. He was toying with her to make her stay longer. She inched toward the door.

"Wreckage happens where the lion treads, yet the game warden doesn't know. And when the lion is friends with the hunter, the spectator has the most to lose." Dr. Cavine held out a paper to her.

She took it from his hand. It was a black and white copy of her note. "I thought it was saying that something bad would happen to a lot of people."

"It was the best I could do with what I had."

"What does it mean?"

"Sit down first and listen closely," Dr. Cavine said. Everything inside her wanted to run out the door covering her ears. Instead Madison perched on the edge of the chair beside his bed. "In short, there is a leak in the French embassy. I believe the person is on the drug investigation team, but I'm not sure."

"Do you have a name?"

"I have suspicions."

"I can't take suspicions to the embassy. Obviously, you were watching me closely enough to know I went to the French. Who do you suspect?"

Dr. Cavine coughed. "Mane Komot."

Madison grunted. "That slimy man with greased hair?"

He laughed. "He does look a little like a well-greased pig, doesn't he?"

That he did. "He drooled all over my hand when he said hello. I should have known he was more than a creepy French diplomat." She shook her head. "How have you been keeping tabs on me in your condition?"

"I have resources that report directly to me. They are not on Karim's team, so he cannot interfere. The resources tell me what you do, where you go, but they know nothing of what is in the past."

"Were these resources spying on me when I bathed in the river?"

"I hated that you stayed in that hospital unprotected. It was too open and vulnerable to anything."

That was a yes. "There were people there overnight when we needed them to be. I wasn't alone."

"I'm much happier with your arrangement now. He seems like a nice young man with a good head on his shoulders. He cares about you."

The compliment made the hair on the back of her neck bristle. "Don't you touch Duke. Don't bring him into any of your schemes. I may be a pawn, but he has had nothing but tragedy in his life for the last year. He doesn't need more messes to clean up."

"Then why did he let you take him out of that jail cell?"

The truth of his words kicked her feet from under her. Knowing he was involved in trying to help her and knowing he could tangle with the wrong people without being aware made her physically hurt. She swallowed the fear squeezing her throat. Duke was the last and maybe the only good thing to happen in her life. She jumped up and pushed Dr. Cavine's chest with her fist.

"You make sure that Duke stays out of whatever it is that Karim has planned. I don't want a hair on his head harmed."

Dr. Cavine sputtered and wheezed. She eased the pressure and dropped into the chair shaking. What had come over her?

"I promise he won't be harmed."

Madison stood. "I don't want your promises any more. They aren't worth anything to me. I spent eight years mourning you. And for nothing. Everything good in my life came from the hand of a terrorist and his sidekick doctor. Forgive me if I'm reluctant to believe what you say."

Her heart had to be made of stone to say words like that, but she wasn't sorry. Not yet at least. He said nothing in return to her as she strode to the door.

"Goodbye, Dr. Cavine. Today has been a day I will never forget." She twisted the knob and stepped into the hall. "My assessment is finished. I need to stop by a restroom."

Her escorts nodded and accompanied her down the hall. Almost a decade of living in a lie. She brushed the hair from her face to make herself look more authoritative. Her hands shook, so she balled them into fists.

There would be no more mourning the past. No more wishing the past hadn't happened the way it did. Dr. Cavine never should have contacted her. The memory of him had been untainted, free of flaws and imperfections.

She'd called him a deserter and a liar. Maybe he had found peace with seeing her or he felt atoned by telling her of what really happened. Could she walk away from a decade of her life with no hint of remorse?

In the restroom, Madison fished her phone from the interior pocket of her scrubs and opened a text to Sabine.

Mane Komot works for Karim. Respond that you received.

She tucked the phone back into its hiding place and walked out.

"Dr. Cote, we have another patient for you to see," the guard said.

He ushered her through the halls. Outside the door where he knocked a black bag sat against the wall. He handed it to her and entered the room which rivaled a hotel room in the West.

"Chip, this is Dr. Madison Cote. She'll be assessing you today." The guard spoke in English. Interesting.

Madison hadn't had time to think about what to expect, but a twenty-something white male wasn't it. The guard walked out of the room but left the door cracked open. She sat on the end of the bed.

"Pardon my rudeness, but where's Dr. Thomas?" Chip said.

"Who?"

"The older doctor that coughs all the time."

Dr. Cavine. "Oh, he's not well at the moment so I'm here." She edged closer to the bed. His face was bruised and his arms red with burns. He survived the fight, at least. "Can you tell me what is going on?"

"I'm not sure you have enough time in your day to hear my story, Dr. Cote."

"Please call me Madison."

Chip pushed the blankets to his waist, exposing a colored torso.

She gasped and leaned closer. "Who did this to you?"

"A handful of guys who aren't my biggest fans." Chip chuckled. "I'm sure you know the kind."

Did she ever. She pulled her exam tools from the bag. "What brings you here, Chip?"

"I thought most of the compound knew my story already. You must not be part of the gossip mill."

Madison withdrew her stethoscope from his chest. "That is correct. I work in a nearby a charity hospital."

"You aren't on the general's payroll?"

"I owe him a favor." Two hundred thousand favors to be precise. She flashed a light in his eyes. "You never told me your story."

The guard popped his head in. "Almost done, Doctor?"

Madison pressed her fingers into his abdomen to buy them more time. "We're wrapping up."

Chip glanced at the door and whispered. "Madison, my name is Chip Chapman and I'm not here willingly. If there is anyone you can tell, please send help."

Her heart tripped a few beats. "Consider it done."

Chip's eyes widened as she dug into her pocket for her phone. No verification text from Sabine yet. Why wasn't she answering? She texted again. *Chip Chapman held against will with General. Send help.*

The guard walked back in as she returned her phone to her pocket.

"All right, Chip. Looks like you have a concussion. I would know more if I had the ability to do advanced testing on you. And I wouldn't be surprised if you have a couple of broken ribs."

Chip squirmed in his bed. "Do you have any sleeping pills and pain pills to take the edge off?"

Madison glanced at the guard. He nodded and led her to a room across from Dr. Cavine's room. The closet contained a mini-pharmacy with everything labeled and in alphabetical order by the problem it solved. On each shelf was a binder detailing the medications, side effects, and conflicts. She grabbed one bottle of sleeping pills and one bottle of medium-strength painkiller.

In Chip's room, she plopped the bottles on his bedside table. "The instructions are on the label. I'm trusting you not to take them all at once." Then she opened her swatch with her sleeping herbs and scraped a heap out. "I'd recommend a more natural route. Try this mixed with water. A little goes a long way, so use it sparingly."

He threw her a sharp salute. "I promise to use them wisely."

"It'll be better soon." She hoped she wasn't wrong.

The guard led her to a third room and opened the door. He motioned into a gorgeous room stocked with amenities she hadn't seen for years. In addition to a luxury bath suite, her room had a foot bath, a back-massage pad, and a well-lit cosmetics station complete with make-up and brushes. Someone had thought of everything.

"This room is for you. General wants you to rest before dinner. Your outfit is hanging in the bathroom. Someone will come get you at six o'clock this evening."

The clock read 3:12 PM when the guard left her by herself. After she showered and rinsed the ash from her skin, she soaked her feet. Then as her nail polish dried, she laid on the massager until she twitched in her sleep. The bed could have been a cloud with its soft pillows and fluffy comforter. No wonder Cavine had been so easily bought.

As she nestled into the bed, her phone chimed with a text from Sabine.

Noted. Stay tuned and watch your back.

Chapter 25

Sabine flipped through the papers one more time. It wasn't possible. Maybe the dim lighting in her office played tricks on her. The data they'd collected from General Karim's drug runs had disappeared.

All of it: inconclusive.

She'd watched the live tracking data go from in the middle of nowhere to land at Segou Airport with her own eyes. When she printed out the results, the recorded destinations were mysteriously gone.

It couldn't have been more obvious that someone on the inside was working against them. The evidence of that left her glancing over her shoulders and changing her passwords every couple of days. As promised, George took the problem to the big wigs. Hallway cameras were installed, and Henry's team swept the offices for listening devices regularly. Yet she still played along with whoever listened to her conversations. Their earlier sloppiness hadn't been repeated.

Her cell phone trilled. She jumped. Too loud. The text was from Madison. She called George on her secure line while she read it.

"George, it's Sabine." She pinched the bridge of her nose. He hated having his evenings interrupted for work.

"What can I do for you?" At least he wasn't yelling.

"Our contact with Karim's team texted that Mane is the inside man."

George whispered a curse. "All right. I'm calling a team to bring him in right now. Get to his house and see if he's run already. I'll be there soon."

"You got it."

She ended the call, grabbed her things, and locked her office. Mane could still be in the building waiting for her. Bring it on. Her security was tucked safely in her purse. If Mane so much as touched her, she'd put more holes in him than Swiss cheese.

When the car door clicked shut behind her, she let out the breath she'd been holding. Easing her car out of the embassy parking lot, she weaved through the streets at a rational speed for someone trying to catch a traitor. He lived a few blocks away from her, thanks to the regulated embassy housing. She turned onto his street. A black surveillance-type van sat within watching range of Mane's house.

Already? She glanced at her watch. How had someone beaten her here when it took her eight minutes to get from her office to his house? His house was dark as she passed it. If they were lucky, he'd be watching television in his room or sleeping instead of headed out of town. She parked along the street and walked casually to the van.

The door opened as she approached. "Sabine?"

How did he know her name? "That's right."

"Our team is two minutes away and George is three. Come on in."

"Thanks." She stepped in and walked a few steps. The guy monitoring the computers turned.

Her eyes widened. God's hand-crafted perfection and the man she couldn't have—Burke.

A heart-stopping smile spread across his face. "Sabine, how do you get more beautiful every time I see you?"

Don't punch him. It's not worth it.

She plastered a carefree grin on her face. "Why, Burke, what brings you to our lowly part of town at this time of day?"

Burke motioned at the monitors. "We're hunting a weasel and we hear this is a good place to catch one."

"Any movement?"

He shook his head. "None since we arrived two minutes ago. Is there any possible way he knows we're coming?"

Sabine shrugged. "I wouldn't put it past him. How did you get here so quickly?"

Burke grinned and returned his gaze to the monitors. "My team is here for a briefing before we head south. George called me, and we were in the area so it worked perfectly."

"That is perfect." Too perfect. Since when did ops teams have briefings in Bamako? The team's arrival on Mane's property stopped her from asking. Six men moved in from the perimeter.

"On your word, Cam," Burke said into the microphone.

The lead whispered the signal and three surged into the house while the other three stayed outside to watch for any quick exits. A thrill coursed through her. The nerves and the adrenaline clashed as the team did its job.

"Do you miss this?" Burke's whisper was so close to her ear she jerked back. She'd been closer than she thought. She placed her hands on the table to watch the screens.

"I do. The hunt is the best part."

"Agreed," Burke murmured.

The helmet cameras showed nothing of use in the house. No drawers were disturbed. No food had been left half-eaten. It was almost as if he'd never been home. Or he was waiting for them. He'd be reckless to try to ambush a professional team. The van door opened and George introduced himself.

"Any sign of him?" George checked the screens.

"None." Burke didn't spare a glance. He was too into the game.

George sighed. "He knew we were coming. We were afraid of that."

"All clear, Commander," Cam said over the radio. "No sign of him in the house."

"Head to our meeting point. We'll see you there." Burke's commands were void of a tell.

The van's engine roared to life.

"I'll follow you in my car." Sabine opened the doors and jumped out before it moved. Once in her car, she trailed them to the meeting place which was an abandoned parking lot. They circled their vehicles and met in the middle.

George spoke first. "Our target must have had phone lines tapped to know we were coming for him. My guess is he's headed south to near Amdalay. That's a couple hours, but we have no idea what kind of lead he has on us. I've called in a request for two more teams to be mobilized, but that will take until noon tomorrow to be ready. We need to pack up and get down there. The last thing we need is General Karim's operation moving out before we have a chance to strike."

"We have everything we need in our truck. We're ready to go," Cam said.

"Good. Karim has three locations that we know of that we will target. We'll need to take all the vehicles we can so we can have eyes on all three places before the rest of the team arrives." George looked at her. "Sabine, you okay to drive down in your car tonight?"

She nodded. "No problem."

"Great. Get on the road as soon as possible." George turned and talked to the drivers. "We'll pinpoint a meet-up location as we get close."

Burke strode over to her. "Mind if I ride with you? I'm not one for sitting in the back of a windowless van for longer than necessary."

Sabine swallowed. Of course, he would do this to her. She was a toy to play with, a little ball on a string. His smile was so confident it almost seemed arrogant.

"Sure, if your team doesn't need you with them. I need to stop by my place to change and grab a few things. Then I'll be ready."

Burke nodded. "No problem. Let me get my bag."

He disappeared around the truck. He was coming with her to her house. That was not at all what she had planned. What would they talk about for the hour and a half drive? Did he plan on sleeping in her car while she drove? This much closeness was not a good thing for the mission.

Keep your head screwed on straight. A traitor is out to kill you. This is no time for love games.

Burke stood at the passenger door. "I put my bag in your backseat. Is that a good place for it?"

Why couldn't he be more of a jerk? Sabine nodded and swung into the driver's seat. As he closed himself in beside her, she cranked up the engine. The car seemed smaller with him in it.

"There will be no criticizing my driving, understand? I know how you men work with your judgmental thoughts about women drivers."

Burke grinned and lifted his hands in surrender. "You won't hear any from me. I promise."

She backed out of the circle and onto the street. When she was going fast enough, she hit the brake lightly jerking them forward and back. Burke's head came dangerously close to the windshield, his seatbelt doing nothing to help. He held out his hands to catch himself on the dash.

When they stopped, he stared at her with wide eyes. "What was that?"

"A test to see if you could keep your promises. I have it on good authority that you might not always, so I wanted to see if you've changed."

Burke let out a breath. "No criticism from me, but I beg you to keep my head from going through the windshield at any speed."

Sabine let out a laugh. The next two hours might be more enjoyable than she thought. At her place, she hurried inside. The sound of a second car door closing had her cursing to herself silently as she unlocked her front door and went inside.

"Cute place you have."

She nodded. "Compliments of the French government. Decorated like the Palace of Versailles."

She flicked on the light and ducked into her bedroom. In truth, the walls were bright white with very few decorations around. She hadn't had time to care and living out of suitcases didn't merit toting around a home for years on end.

"Need me to grab anything?" Burke's voice sounded too close to her closed and locked bedroom door. She yanked a shirt over her head with lightning speed.

"My vest and gun should be in the corner if you can get those into the car."

When the front door banged closed, she switched into her black pants and sturdy mission boots. After tossing a few more things into a bag, she met him in her living area. She had to admit—it was nice to see him again.

She dropped her bag and headed into her kitchen. "Snacks? Water?"

"I'll take whatever you have. Have you eaten dinner yet?"

"Nope. I left the office after I called George."

Burke grunted his disapproval. Her refrigerator had a few things she could eat on the go. It never hurt to have fresh fruit from the market and packaged snacks imported from France to the embassy. She plopped a full food bag into Burke's arms, so she wouldn't be tempted to walk into them.

She grabbed her bag and headed for the door. He filed out behind her and she locked it. They were on the road again, and none too soon in her estimation. The trip to RN7 was done with little conversation. When they hit the open road, Burke shifted to face her.

"I owe you an apology."

Her heart melted a little. *Stay strong.* "For what?"

"I promised you a going-away spar and dinner before you left, and I couldn't deliver on either."

He remembered. Sabine shrugged. "Albert gave me a good workout in your place." More like she laid into him, pretending he was Burke.

"Yeah, he said you were a spitfire. He told me he'd go easy on you, but I said that he should just try to not lose his dignity. He scoffed, but when I talked to him the next day he admitted I was right." Burke laughed. "I've seen you in the gym. You don't take it easy on anyone."

Sabine straightened. His flattery would not crack her resolve. She took a deep breath. "Unfortunately, he had to pay for your sins. Nice guy though."

Burke cleared his throat. "I will make it up to you. I promise."

She flicked her wrist at him. "There you go again with the promises. How will you keep your word from Timbuktu?"

"I won't." Burke glanced out the window. "I've been reassigned to Bamako. At my request."

Her head snapped to the right. "Since when?"

"Yesterday. Finding Mane is our first op. I wanted in on the Karim case." Ah, his real motive for the transfer.

Disappointment replaced her surprise.

Get it together, Roux. Burke's world doesn't revolve around you. You aren't even in his solar system.

"He's a hard man to trap. Leaves his fingerprints on nothing. He used a plane to bypass our checkpoints on the highways." Elusive men were her bread and butter. Thank God she was better at catching criminals than she was boyfriends.

"Sabine, do you know why I'm here?"

She laughed. "You just told me."

Burke stared at her with a serious expression. "I didn't tell you. Ask me why I really moved."

This was ridiculous. "Okay, Burke. Why did you really come to Bamako?"

"So I could be closer to you."

Sabine bit her lip. Here she was getting her hopes up again, but this wasn't like the envelope Colonel Catre had placed in her hands weeks ago. This time, she'd rip open the flap to find some terrible joke. As if a guy like Burke would pursue her. She opened her mouth to say something clever, but nothing came.

"Aren't you going to say anything?" Burke said.

"Honestly, Burke, I'm not sure what to say. Do you blame me for being surprised?"

Burke snorted. "And women say men are obtuse. I have been dropping hints since you left."

Sabine stared at him. What was he talking about?

"The congratulatory flowers I sent you?"

She raised an eyebrow. "The flowers were from you? There was no note, but thank you. They were beautiful."

"The note was lost? Why do these things happen to me?" He slumped in his seat. "What about the email I sent?"

Sabine shook her head. "Spam filter?"

"The wine and chocolate for your birthday?"

This was getting out of hand. Sabine laughed out loud. "Minks, one of the old guys on security, brought them to me and told me they were from him. He'd signed the happy birthday note that came with it."

"Minks is a rat." Burke growled in frustration, and then broke out into laughter. "I thought you were giving me the cold shoulder."

All those little things had been to show her he cared. For her. Years of hope and admiration finally realized.

"Let's start this conversation over." Burke set his hand on her arm. "Sabine, I've missed you since you left. I really enjoyed our connection. I hope that we will continue it now that I'm headquartered in Bamako."

He was beautiful and adorable at the same time, an irresistible combination in her book. "Yes, Burke. I'd love that. And thank you for the flowers, the note, and the chocolate and wine for my birthday. That is very kind." She took her eyes off the road and pecked Burke on the cheek. "That was what I gave Minks for the gift, so you get the same since it was from you."

Burke grinned. "I'll take whatever I can get. So now that I know where we stand, let's talk about your driving—"

Sabine pointed her finger at him in mock disgust. "Don't even start."

Chapter 26

Mali, Africa

True to his word, Sidi brought Chip an outfit for the party—a collared shirt, sharp-looking trousers, socks, undershirt, and shoes. Then he fished two pills from his pocket. Chip grunted. Enough for one night. No more.

That was okay because Madison left him everything he needed. Now the pill bottle rested in his pocket. Once he dressed for the banquet, Sidi drove him to General's house. He guided him through the maze, but this time Chip knew where he was. On the left was the kitchen. Three doors past that was the gentlemen's room. Sidi opened the door.

Chip stopped. "I'll meet you in there. I need to use the restroom. One moment."

Sidi nodded and pointed to the restroom across from the kitchen. Chip went in and waited. When the hall was quiet, he cracked the door open. Sidi wasn't in the hall, so Chip ducked into the kitchen.

Two women banged around and both had their backs to him.

The closest pot to him was full of steaming rice. Small enough to be effective, big enough to not overdose. He dug the ground pills and herbs from his pocket and poured them in, then grabbed the wooden spoon and stirred it in. No one would notice it with a mouthful of other food. The spoon clanked the side of the metal pan.

He dropped it and jumped out of the kitchen as one of the women turned around. He tiptoed to the gentlemen's room. His pulse raced on super-speed. Avoiding the rice would be no problem. Everyone would be drowsy and leave him the freedom to waltz out the door. If he couldn't steal a plane, he'd take a car. In an hour, he'd be at the UK embassy in Bamako and his family would be warned.

No one had to die. Everyone would feel really good and he got a free pass home. The simplicity of the plan had scared him, but now he had nothing to lose and all the right tools.

Sidi acknowledged him with a nod as he walked into the gentlemen's room. Men he'd never seen packed the room from wall to wall. In a wheelchair off to the side, Dr. Thomas sat with oxygen tubes wrapped around his face and stuffed in his nose. Chip weaved through the crowd to get to him, ready to question him more about Nafy. However, a chime sounded and the crowd of men surging to the door carried him with them.

He was ready for the party to start. And end.

A stream of ladies filtered in from a door on the other side. He did a double-take when Madison walked through the door dressed in traditional Malian garb. Her hair fell in waves around her face. He didn't give her enough credit. She was beautiful. Any man could see that. What they didn't know was that she'd helped him.

A host pointed each person to their seat. One long table sat on a raised block, clearly visible to the round tables that occupied the rest of the room. Chip's seat was at a table near the front. Madison walked over to him with a nervous look.

"Hi, Chip. We meet again." Madison ducked her head. "I hadn't expected dinner to include this many people."

When she offered her hand, he went in for a hug. "Doc, don't eat the rice."

She tentatively patted him on the back. "What?"

"Trust me. Don't eat it."

She probably thought he was crazy. So be it.

"Does it taste—" Her lips parted as she saw something over his shoulder.

Chip turned. A tall European-looking guy took his seat at a table near the back. His eyes scanned the room. The moment the man found Madison he smiled.

"A friend of yours?" Chip said.

Madison beamed. "Duke. Yes, hopefully soon to be more than a friend."

A blush crept over her cheeks. Their connection sizzled like a live wire. No question there that Duke felt the same way about Madison. General and Loris stood behind the table, facing everyone. A hush fell over the room.

"Ladies and gentlemen, please have a seat and enjoy the first course."

Boys dressed in uniforms brought in bowls of soup. Chip relaxed when he didn't recognize any of them. His boys weren't forced to serve. His boys. Somewhere along the line, he began caring deeply how they viewed him. If he had a guess, it was between Nafy dancing onto the plane with glitter shoes and being whisked away in an ambulance to the hospital.

After the bowls were cleared away, General stood.

"Welcome to my house. I hope you enjoyed the first course." The guests thumped the table in approval. General raised his hands for quiet. "As the chefs plate the next course, I want to recognize someone new to our ranks but who has become a valuable contributor to our cause. In fact, right now he bears the marks of having tried to protect my niece, Adrienna."

Chip froze. Sidi warned him this was coming.

"Protecting one of ours is as if he protected me personally. To honor his sacrifice, commitment, and cooperation I have decided to name Chip Chapman the new Chief of Flight, an esteemed position that Loris and I have decided together would suit him well."

What? Chip stared at the smirk on Loris's face. What just happened? The tables thundered under the guests' fists.

Madison turned to him, the accusation clear in her eyes. "I thought you said you weren't here willingly."

"I'm not," he said with a hiss.

Hands pushed Chip from his seat. He lifted his hand to acknowledge the General and sat again. The joke was on them because this was only going to last until the effects of the rice took hold. Then he was out of there.

Once the applause died down, the next course arrived at the table—a perfectly plated vegetable dish. Everyone lingered, relishing the luxury cuisine of General's top chef. Chip eyed the exits. This was taking too long.

Once again, General stood after the boys cleared the plates. What now?

"I'd like to honor fallen heroes, Kone and Moussa, who died in the line of duty. I'm proud to say that Kone's killers suffered and Moussa's killer will also die when we finish with the investigation."

Another course appeared. The aroma enticed a sigh from him. Meat slices lay on a pillow of rice all drenched in a light sauce. He dipped his finger into the sauce for a taste. Of course, the forbidden rice accompanied the most delicious course. He raised his eyebrows at Madison. She didn't have to believe him. And if she didn't, she'd get a good nap out of the deal. She picked around it like he did and left the rice scattered on the plate.

Already General was on his feet before the plates disappeared, eager to get on with it. About time.

"As many of you know, our esteemed Dr. Thomas has been in ill health for the past few months. Recently his situation escalated to interfere with his duties. We are privileged to have him with us and help provide for his health needs as he has cared for so many of us in our times of need. Please stand with me to celebrate the service of the great doctor."

The guests rose to their feet as one. The roar of appreciation deafened Chip. From a table opposite theirs, Dr. Thomas's grey pallor and oxygen lines gave him a dire appearance. Chip gave a slow clap.

The sleeping pills could affect him for the worst. Nothing he could do now.

A fruit plate with a sweet cream appeared in front of them. When was this banquet going to end? The nerves gnawed at his stomach. Anytime now, he'd need to be ready to make his move.

General stood again. "Since our honorable Doctor will be stepping down from his duties, I'm delighted to tell you that our new doctor will be Dr. Madison Cote."

He motioned for her to stand. Madison didn't move. Her blanched face was a mixture of shock and sheer panic. Dr. Thomas's spoon halted halfway to his mouth. General was full of surprises tonight. Slowly Madison stood, her hands clutching her stomach. She swayed as she acknowledged the noise of approval. General stepped off the perch and offered Madison his hand to help her onto the platform. She stood beside him clasping and unclasping her hands.

"The last person I'd like to honor is my brother Loris who has been steadfast in his devotion to me." General placed his hand on Loris's shoulder. "Brother, for many long years you have been faithful."

Loris beamed, his posture obnoxious and smug.

"Your wellbeing is very important to me. You have been without a wife for much of that time and have still been a caring father to Adrienna." Chip barely restrained his snort. "The support of a wife strengthens you as a man. You know I am a very strong man." Everyone laughed with General. "I have found someone who would strengthen you. Brother, to you, I give lovely Dr. Madison Cote."

Loris's face fell a fraction. General Abdou Karim gifted his brother a wife. A Western doctor. And no one looked more shocked than Madison, the gift herself. Everyone clapped, but the enthusiasm lacked any vigor. When the clapping stopped, Dr. Thomas stood from his wheelchair. His complexion turned grayer if that was possible.

Dr. Thomas beckoned to the General. "General, may I have a word with you please?"

Loris tsked. "Doctor, anything you have to say you can say in front of our friends."

"General, please?"

General squinted at Dr. Thomas, then motioned for him to speak.

Dr. Thomas looked ready to claim he forgot what he was going to say and sit back down, but instead he cleared his throat. "General, I have reason to believe Dr. Cote has not been faithful to the cause and thus would make a very poor match for your esteemed brother."

Madison's mouth dropped open. She was a deer in the headlights. No one dared to breathe. General lowered his head, his eyes dagger blades.

"That is an ill-timed accusation you make at a time of celebration. Do you mean to embarrass me and dishonor my brother by saying this? Or are you willing to risk your life that Dr. Cote has betrayed us?"

Dr. Thomas fell into his chair, his shoulders hunched in exhaustion. "General, my breath is precious these days. Please, a word."

General nodded at one of his minions to grab Madison as he stalked to the door leading to the gentlemen's room with Loris on his heels. Someone wheeled the wheezing Dr. Thomas across the room.

General stopped at the door, scanning the room with a furrowed brow. "Where did the agriculture man go? Someone find Dr. Cote's lover."

The room dissolved into chaos. A handful of men sprinted from the room in pursuit of Duke. Some staggered out as if drunk. Madison stumbled as a guard led her in the opposite direction of General. Chip shadowed their movements at a distance.

Treason meant death.

She'd helped him when he needed a favor. Karim wasn't known for being merciful. And time was not on her side. His escape would have to wait.

Chapter 27

Mali, Africa

Her escort led Madison into a room occupied by two plastic chairs and motioned for her to sit. Then he disappeared without a word. Her shock morphed into full-blown terror. How would she get out of this one?

She'd been mad at Cavine before, but now he'd blown every chance at reconciliation. Who was he to contact her after eight years of being dead and apologize, then to accuse her of treason to the most lethal man they both knew? The satellite phone tucked in her waistband taunted her. What if they caught her with it?

She didn't care. Madison dialed Sabine.

"Come on. Come on." Her hands shook violently as her hope sank with each ring. When she needed someone most, there was no one. It was the story of her whole life in one soul-crushing picture.

Madison hung up and opened her texts. To Sabine:

Karim knows. Need rescue STAT.

Next, she texted Duke.

Cavine squealed. They're coming for you. Get out of here.

The minute General announced her as Karim's new doctor, Duke disappeared out the door. Maybe it was foresight on his part or a really well-timed bathroom break. He had to know that she had no part in General's decisions. A shudder shook her shoulders. She'd choose the loneliness of being single every time if it meant not having to wake up to Loris's face every day.

What was General thinking? There would be no mutual love or respect in that relationship. She didn't know him or his daughter. It'd be a prison. Or worse. To think she'd dismissed Duke's warning so carelessly. She returned the phone to her hiding place. And paced and paced.

She needed an escape and Cavine certainly wouldn't do it for her.

The door banged open. She jumped.

A guard strode in. "Come with me, Doctor."

Pacing did nothing to steady her racing heart. Black spots blotted her vision. She should have eaten the rice—whatever was in it. The guard opened a door to a room with one-way mirrors covering each wall—an interrogation room on steroids.

She stood, paced, then sat again. The process was stuck on repeat. Time crawled by. Had it been hours or mere minutes?

Sitting against the wall in the corner gave her a small measure of calm. At last, the door opened to General Karim. His eyes landed on her like he spotted his prey. She could have sworn a smile played at his lips.

"Madison." The way he said her name made her heart leap, a small burst of hope. He lent her his hand and pulled her to her feet. She sat in the chair he motioned to. Couldn't he get to the point? "A beautiful, intelligent doctor like you must laugh at men like me who take their time making decisions."

Flattery. Was that a good thing or bad thing?

Madison stared at her lap. "I don't laugh at you, General."

"Doctor, let's not waste time. Tell me. Do you know a man by the name of Mane Komot?"

The slime ball. "I may have heard the name before, General, but I am better with faces than I am with names. It's how I knew I would be a good doctor." An awkward laugh escaped her lips.

General stared at her. "Very well."

He motioned at the glass. The door opened and in walked Mane Komot in all his slimy, greasy glory.

"This is Mane. Do you recognize him?"

Her breathing came in beats. The sweat trickled down her back in a free flow. No way to lie herself out of this one.

"Yes, I do recognize Monsieur Komot."

General bared his teeth, as he patted Mane's shoulder. "Monsieur Komot was sure you would." General circled the room. "He seems to think that you told the French Embassy he worked for me." General laughed. Mane joined in. It was bait. She didn't bite.

Instead, she faced Mane. "Why would you think I did that, Monsieur?"

Mane stopped laughing. His face dropped into a scowl and turned a light shade of red. No one spoke. Madison stared at Mane. She wouldn't lie, but if she was going to be accused, he'd better step up and tell her the transgression.

"How would I possibly know if you and General were working together? From my understanding, you were..." She stopped. What if he was undercover and she was about to blow his cover wide open?

"He was what, Doctor?" General stepped toward her.

Madison glanced at General then at Mane. No going back now. If he was undercover, he'd better have a backup plan because she was going to shove him in front of the bus.

"From my understanding, you were a loyal French diplomat committed to leading the drug investigation team."

Mane curled his lips upward. "Trafficking of Illegal Substances Investigation Team or as I so fondly call it, TISIT."

He cackled. A glance from General silenced him.

Madison plugged on. "If you are, as I understand it, committed to TISIT, then how would I report you to the French as working with General if I had no idea if the accusation is true or not? No one has said one word either way."

Mane growled. "Someone must have told you or you overheard them talking. Regardless, the point is that I was ratted out by someone and I have come to warn General that his shipments have been tracked by the French Embassy thanks to you."

Madison glanced at General. His face didn't move. It could not have been new information to him if it garnered no reaction. She said nothing. He'd made his accusation. What would General do with the information? She was seconds away from kicking the sneer off of Mane's ugly face.

General flicked his wrist. "Thank you, Mane. You have had your say here. You may go."

Mane's smug exterior faltered, but he gave a half bow and walked out. This was not going to end well for her. No matter how much General liked her. He covered the space between them in two large strides. He swung the back of his hand, striking her across the face. She fell backward.

"Tell me the truth. Were you helping the French track my shipments? The shipments that helped me pay for your freedom from that jail cell?" General didn't yell. He hissed.

Her mind searched for any technicality that would allow her to say no. There was no escaping without implicating Duke as well. As Dr. Cavine put it, he had already been brought into her messes. She would keep him out of this to the end. She owed him that much.

"I was."

General grabbed her by the front of her dress and rammed her into the wall. "Why would you cross me like that?"

Madison gasped to recover the wind forced from her lungs. When she could breathe, she spoke.

"I am a twenty-seven-year-old Canadian doctor for a non-profit. I came to Mali to serve the patients of that hospital so that this region could enjoy good health and prosper as everyone deserves a chance to do."

"Answer my question." Drops of spittle landed on her cheek.

In a second, she knocked his hands off her as adrenaline swept through her.

"If you were caught by the French storing illegal drugs in my hospital, my life would be over. If I wasn't sentenced and fined here in Mali, I would be extradited to Canada to face the consequences. Years of my life would be lost in prison for nothing. When I finally got out, no one would allow me to practice pediatric medicine because who would take their child to visit an international criminal?" She was screeching. It didn't matter. If this was going to be the end for her, she might as well drive her point home. "I didn't want you ruining my life as you have destroyed so many others. The people of this area are innocent and deserve a chance at a good life. You take that from them. You are selfish, unkind, and a disgusting human being."

General grabbed her by her throat. With a shout, he shoved her into the glass. Her head cracked against it. And again. And again. She thrashed. No air.

Fight for air. No, let go.

She relaxed and he dropped her to the ground. She sputtered. The air refused to enter her lungs fast enough.

General screamed words she didn't understand and stormed from the room. He hadn't killed her yet. Someone picked her up as if she weighed nothing and dropped her into a chair. Her body roared with pain. Regrets and guilt overwhelmed her.

She should've never come to Mali.

A warm stream trickled down her neck. Her fingers touched it and came back bloody. The guard cinched her legs against the chair and roped her wrists to her knees. Her head sagged forward. She didn't have the strength to fight. Ready or not, death would take her soon.

No one was coming for her.

Except God.

Chip ducked into a side hallway when the guard returned. Another two guards joined the first. Holstered handguns hung on their belts. One guy he could take, but not three. The room had no windows, only one door, and a solid ceiling. He needed more help.

Where was Du—

A hand slapped across his mouth and dragged him backward. The door closed him into the dark with someone.

"Tell me what you know about Madison." The low voice whispered to his ear.

"Duke?" Chip said.

"What have they done with her?"

"She's in the room with three armed men at the door. Clock's ticking."

Duke cracked the door open. A stream of light landed on a desk. When he closed the door again, Chip clicked a lamp on. Duke jumped toward him.

"Easy." Chip extended his hands. "I need to see if there's anything in here we can use."

"There's no 'we.' You are one of Karim's."

Chip snorted as he rummaged through the near-empty desk drawers. Stray pens and scraps of paper slid around the space.

"Don't waste your time on distrust. If I were truly one of Karim's I would have shot you, not told you how I plan to rescue the woman who loves you."

Duke blinked. "What?"

"I'm not Karim's henchman."

"Never mind. If we create a diversion…"

"Like if they think they can grab you?"

Duke tilted his chin. "I was thinking of starting a fire."

Fire. The man was genius.

"Stay here." Chip stuffed a handful of paper into his pockets.

The hall was empty, so he jogged to the corner. Two more turns. The place was a ghost town with everyone presumably out looking for Duke. He tiptoed into the kitchen.

The ladies occupied the far end near the sinks with their backs facing him. They sang and giggled with so much gusto they couldn't possibly hear him. A platter of sharp knives sat on the counter as did a steel pot filled with water. Chip grinned. Tools of destruction waited for him.

In the corner, embers from the meat pit glowed a hazy orange-red. He lit one corner of a paper on fire and he was out of there, hauling his goods with him. Two guys passed him in the hall, but they nodded and carried on as if knives, a pot, and burning paper was completely normal.

Sidi was right. Being on General's good side lifted him from the pile of suspicious hostage scum he'd been in.

Before he turned the final corner, a guy thrashed and fell backwards across from the room Madison had been put in. Then Duke's head popped into sight and waved Chip over. Brash move. He couldn't have waited?

Chip hurried after him into a storage room.

"They moved Madison. She's not in there." Duke took the paper torch from Chip's hand and set it on a stack of towels lighting them instantly.

"Did you ask the bloke you incapacitated where they took her?"

Duke shrugged. "He didn't answer fast enough."

"All we have are knives and water. We need to get moving."

Chip tucked three knives between his belt and trousers while Duke slid the rest of the knives blade-down into his pockets. Only true love would make that seem like a good idea. Hugging the steel pot to his chest as a shield, Chip led the way. They stopped at the corner and peeked around.

Karim, Dr. Thomas, Loris, a guy in a suit, and a guard stood outside a door halfway down the hall.

Duke muttered a curse. "That's Mane Komot, an official from the embassy. Look—the doctor is holding a tray. What's the plan?"

They needed to even the numbers. A shout came from the other end of the hall. Loris answered and jogged away. One down. Karim and Dr. Thomas marched into the room, leaving the guard and Mane.

Duke nudged Chip's back. "I get Mane. You disable the guard."

With a deep breath, Chip left the safety of the corner. The guard and Mane watched through the window, missing their approach. He set the pot on the ground, making a clank. The guard turned. Chip kicked the side of the guard's knee and wrapped an arm around his thick neck as Duke attacked Mane. The thrashing nearly swept Chip's feet from under him. Duke dropped Mane's limp frame and reached for the guard's jaw. In seconds the guard quit struggling.

"Next time try the pressure points first," Duke said.

Chip made a face and grabbed the gun from the guard as Duke tossed the water in front of the doorways. Inside the room Karim moved, offering a clear view through the window. Dr. Thomas hovered over Madison with his needle poised.

"Duke, we're too late."

Chapter 28

The door opened. General stomped in, come to finish the job. Behind him, Dr. Cavine limped in with a tray in his hands.

Snake.

The man who'd taught Madison to do anything to sustain life—hers or others—was ending hers. The betrayer set to perform the ultimate betrayal. Next to her chair, two needles sat side by side on the tray. Death by lethal injection was fitting.

She tested her ropes again but found them firm. Duke was gone, as was her hope. A tear slid down her cheek tracing a similar path as the blood. No good deed went unpunished.

In front of her, General stood with his legs in a wide stance. His arms crossed over his chest, the picture of authority over life, her life. Dr. Cavine flicked the tube as if an air bubble in poison mattered. Habit. He didn't look at her face as he bent over her arm. The sound of his stridor would be the last she heard. Anger washed over her, then defeat.

He didn't ask if she was ready. Like he didn't ask if she wanted to be involved in Karim's scheme. He just pricked her skin.

The first injection was a sedative. Who didn't want to die calm? The warmth spread across her chest, the pounding in her ears hollowed out.

"I'm sorry I failed. I tried." Her whispered words weren't meant for either of the men in the room, but for everyone in her life and no one at the same time.

Dr. Cavine uncapped the lethal dosage. He covered his violent cough with his sleeve, leaving a trace of blood behind. He'd be gone in months, if not weeks. He leaned over her slowly but said nothing. If he wanted forgiveness from her or a release from his part of this, he'd be disappointed.

"Tell Duke I love him." Duke—the hope of love, family, and everything she'd ever wanted for herself. He was the sole reason she regretted death. She clamped her eyes shut. This was the end.

The prick.

The ice.

The darkness.

An explosion rocked the building.

Chip ducked. Bits of the ceiling rained on them. Whatever that was wasn't promising.

Loris led the charge of a group of men around the corner, his gun aimed straight at Chip and Duke. They didn't count on him being armed. Chip fired a spray of bullets in their direction, sending the men scattering. Duke flung the knives with astonishing accuracy.

In front of them, the door crashed open. General Karim ran onto the wet concrete and his feet whisked from underneath him. A roaring Duke dove onto him, his fists flying as General attempted to dislodge him. A bullet smashed into the wall next to Chip. He dodged into a doorway.

General knocked Duke off and scrambled to his feet with Duke right behind him. He pulled a gun from his boot and fired at Duke before Chip could get him in his sights. As Duke's body recoiled and slumped to the ground, General disappeared around the corner.

Karim wasn't going to kill everyone he liked. Chip held the trigger, raining bullets on the shooters while he grabbed Duke's arm. With one firm yank, they fell into the room where Dr. Thomas sat patting Madison's limp hand as she lay prone, her face covered with a coat. Tears dripped from Dr. Thomas's cheeks. Chip slammed the door behind him and propped a chair under the handle.

Blood oozed from Duke's left side.

"Madi." Duke clawed at the ground to get to her.

Dr. Thomas moved toward Duke. "You're bleeding badly."

"No." Duke gasped, struggling to sit. "Let me die. You killed Madi."

His screams shredded Chip's heart. Losing Nafy was still fresh.

"Either I injected her, or Karim put a bullet in her head. I loved Madison. She didn't deserve to die by Karim's gun. Now let me help you before Karim kills you, too." Dr. Thomas lifted Duke's shirt over his head and pressed it into the wound.

A long burst of gunfire in the hall laid them flat on the floor until everything went quiet.

BAM!

Chip jumped out of his skin. The door tossed the chair across the room like a toy. Armed men in black flooded in, their guns leading the way. Chip sucked in a breath and lifted his hands in surrender. Someone said something, and Duke responded with a few labored words.

One man stayed with them. The rest of the team vanished like ninjas.

"My name is Burke. We're going to get you out of here." Burke jabbed his thumb over his shoulder. "The team is looking for Karim, but we're going to need some help identifying bodies and people while we clear the compound."

A woman jogged into the room. Her eyes widened as her gaze landed on Madison. "Oh, Duke—"

Burke lifted Duke with little effort. Not surprising given Burke's size. Chip trailed them into the hall but stopped. Sightless eyes and twisted forms lay strewn where the French interrupted the assault on the interrogation room. Loris's body lay closest to the door with a knife lodged near his sternum.

A lump tightened in his chest. The happiness he thought he'd feel didn't come. Instead sadness and pity took its place. Abuse, exploitation, and greed defined Loris. Who wanted to remember a man with that kind of life?

His heart plummeted when Adrienna came into view. Her flowy pink dress accented her dark hair. She stopped at the corner, her shoulders back and her chin high. The soldier spoke and she nodded. As she stepped over bodies, she scanned the faces.

Chip met her halfway. "Adrienna, this isn't something you need to see."

She tucked a stray strand of hair behind her ear, her gaze on the floor. Bruises still colored her face. "I've been asked to identify his body."

"I can do that."

Her chin quivered. Raw pain and hurt radiated from her. "I need to do this. Do you know where he is?"

He nodded and led her to where Loris lay. She stopped when Chip did but didn't look down. Her eyes were closed. The blister of her betrayal soothed as her lips moved. He knew intimately the twisted emotions—the agony of losing a parent, the freedom from her captor. At last, she lowered her gaze.

"This is my father, Loris." Her voice cracked. She knelt beside him and placed her hand over his heart. "You cared for me in your own way after Mama died. I never went without things because you provided, but I wanted so much more from you as a father. I resented your control so much. Dad, every day I will mourn what we could have had. I forgive you and I will never forget you. Be at rest."

She opened her arms with her head back and mumbled words Chip couldn't understand. Her lips touched Loris's cheek. Chip helped her to her feet. She stood, her hand in his and walked him from the scene. When she turned to him, her beautiful brown eyes searched his. What was there to say in this moment?

"Chip, thank you." Tears welled in her eyes. "You risked your life for me."

"I—"

She held her finger to his lips. "The water and food were poisoned. They didn't know I knew, but I could smell it on the plate." Her hands shook. "They wouldn't have tolerated disobedience. Insulting you as I did was the only solution I could think to keep us both alive until Uncle Abdou arrived." Her fingers stroked his cheek. "Please forgive me."

He caught her hand. "Did you really intend for us to leave? Or was that a ploy for your father?"

Adrienna sighed. "It was foolish, but I truly believed we could leave this life behind. I didn't understand the depths of Dad's control until I tried to find a way out. Now we can do as we wish." Her shoulders hunched as she folded her arms, as if protecting herself from the battery of regret. "Promise you won't ruin the rest of your life by holding on to the prison of bitterness."

Who was she to lecture him about holding on? Yet she was right. It was time to let go of so many unforgiven hurts.

"I promise." How could she so easily forgive her father? Her innocence attracted and frustrated him at the same time. "I forgive you, Adrienna. And I'll forgive your family, too. Maybe not in this moment, but it will come."

She wrapped her arms around his waist and tucked her face into his neck. The touch calmed his questions. She'd lost everything she'd ever known in the past hour, and yet forgiveness and peace were her first responses. Remarkable.

With a final squeeze, she wiped the tears from her cheeks. "I wish things turned out differently for us. But I hope we meet again when things are more at peace."

A smile crept through the deep ache. "I'd like that."

Adrienna left his side and didn't look back. With her went the pain and bitterness he'd clung to like a weapon he brandished at the world. A weapon that paralyzed him for wielding it. There was a lightness to her step he wanted—needed—for his own.

A hand rubbed his shoulder. He twitched.

"Chip, right? I'm Sabine from the French Drug Investigation Team. Madison texted me about you. We're going to get you home."

Home. She'd said he was going home. He hoped she meant his real home. Chip studied her bronze skin and curly hair. Creases made her eyes smile when her lips didn't. She was an angel. Relief buckled his knees. He pulled Sabine into a hug. Laughter welled inside of him. Never had he heard such beautiful words. All this time flying and working with the boys—

His throat tightened. "As much as I want to get home, I can't leave until my boys are okay."

A strange expression crossed Sabine's face. "Karim's been apprehended. The compound is surrounded, and I've got men guarding the airstrip. Let's take a walk."

Sabine spoke into her two-way radio then led him from the hall into the cool night air.

"I've been waiting for freedom for what feels like a lifetime." Chip grunted. "It's surprising that there are so many more emotions involved than just happiness."

Sabine pulled a recording device from her pocket. "Why don't you tell me your story?"

As they strolled across the compound grounds in the stillness, Sabine asked specific questions until she fell silent to listen. Chip told her everything in as much detail as he could remember. He paused when they stood outside the dining room filled with boys. Inside armed soldiers kept the peace. The fear on the boys' faces transmitted loud and clear.

He couldn't look away. "What happens to them now?"

"Rehabilitation. Trying to undo the training they've been given." Sabine sighed and rubbed her forehead. "They'll never get their innocence back."

"How do you convince them to give up their need for control?"

"We redirect it. We won't succeed with all of them. Sometimes people don't want help, but we leave it to local law enforcement to help prevent collateral damage."

Turning away help was a familiar sentiment.

"And if law enforcement is unsuccessful?"

Sabine lifted her hands. "We're not here to force our justice on Mali. We're here to help Mali enforce their own justice on the drug trade. In turn, we help stop the tidal wave of illegal drugs that are ruining Europe. We'll have a tough time making sure Karim gets to trial. His pockets are deep and there are probably more like Mane Komot who don't want to see him stopped."

"If he makes it to trial, I'm on the hit list because I'm a witness."

"It's in the world's best interest that you testify. We'll find a way to keep the target off your back."

If not, he was a dead man walking.

Chapter 29

Sunlight streamed in through the sheer curtains rustling in the warm breeze. Bright colors gave the room a Spanish flair. Was this heaven? Madison turned her head to the side. Duke lay propped up on a couch a few feet away, watching her.

This was definitely heaven.

"Are we dead?"

Duke grinned and lifted the hem of his shirt. A large, white bandage wrapped around the middle of his torso. "Does God use bandages when he heals people?"

"I didn't die?" She checked her pulse. It was steady. She felt okay. "What happened?"

"Dr. Cavine injected you with a drug that shrunk your veins, so Karim wouldn't find a pulse. The second injection knocked you unconscious. Then the French invaded General's house and hauled everyone in."

"And Dr. Cavine?"

"Alive. He sent this letter for you."

Duke grabbed an envelope off the end table next to him and handed it to her. Dishes and medication bottles cluttered the glass-topped wicker table between them. And she was taking up the bed when he needed healing, not her.

Madison slipped the papers from the envelope. Dr. Cavine's neat print filled two pages, front and back. She used to tease him about not having the doctor's illegible writing. He called it his perfectionist curse.

Dearest Madi-loo,

I wish I could be with you when you wake up to ease your fears and apologize in person. That was not possible so I'm writing this, knowing full well that it is a feeble grasp at a slippery straw. Sabine is working on a plea deal for me, but this is likely my goodbye.

I'm an old man with a couple months at best. You know that better than anyone. What I told you before about my reasons for being in Mali was true. But I also fell into a trap that was laid carefully for me. Although I recognized the trap, I still walked into it.

I missed Amber so much. She was the center of my universe. After she died, Karim caught me at my weakest—when I was looking for a distraction from my pain and sorrow. Predators sense these things. I was too weak to say no and the money was too much to refuse.

Don't be like me, Madi-girl. Don't let someone entice you into believing the moral black area they stand in is actually gray. The payoff isn't worth the guilt. I am ashamed of myself.

What brought you to Mali was not actually a will. They were conditions you needed to fulfill for receiving money from my trust. I knew you'd fall in love with the kids and they with you. I figured if you were in Mali and I didn't get to see you or talk to you, then you'd receive the final sum and always believe I was dead. But when I found out Karim's plans for you, I couldn't stand by and watch.

I have done a lot of unforgivable things—things that I can't forgive myself for. But I hope to make it up to you in a small way by helping you start the rest of your life off well.

The house you are in is yours, in addition to the trust money if you'll accept it. This is the home Amber and I always told you about. I'm sure you'll recall it is my favorite—Las Palmas de Gran Canaria.

One last thing before I say goodbye. When you came to live with us those many years ago, you were a brilliant and lovely girl, but you were hurting inside. Amber and I really loved you as our own. You were especially the light of Amber's life—

a joy. At the time, you had so many questions we had no answers to. One day you will understand the lengths you will go to for love. So, I intruded where I was not invited, and I found your birth parents.

If you ever want to contact them, their address is in an envelope on the office desk. They asked the agency not to be contacted, but who am I to stand in the way of reconciliation? Age has granted me some clarity despite my many failings. Meeting them may be helpful in your quest of putting the past behind you. And because I know you'll ask—you have sisters.

Once Duke heals, I'd love for you to come visit me. Sabine knows all the details. But if that is too much, a note from you would make my heart glad.

To intrude once more—of all the men you've dated, I like Duke the best.

My words aren't sufficient, but they are sincere. I love you, Madi-loo. Please forgive me for betraying your trust. You have a thrilling future ahead. Don't doubt yourself out of the life you've always wanted.

Love Always,

Dr. Thomas Cavine

Where words escaped her, her heart filled in the gaps. His actions still hurt, but she loved him and always would. And what was love if it didn't forgive completely?

Duke held his arm out to her as she wiped the tears from her cheeks. She left her bed and snuggled next to him on the couch. Dr. Cavine was right. Duke was the best.

She laid her hand over his bandage. "Tell me what happened."

"The French breached the door after Dr. Cavine injected you. General made a run for it, so like the fool that I am, I tackled him and he shot me," Duke said.

"I could have lost you."

He cupped her face in his hands. Madison leaned into his embrace. A lifetime of this wouldn't be enough.

His thumb stroked her cheek. "I couldn't see straight. Karim killed you and I could do nothing about it. Just like Anna Grace, I couldn't save you. But this time, I preferred to die with you. I'm tired of being the one left behind."

Duke brought her face closer to his as his eyes watched her lips. Her breath caught in her throat. More than anything she wanted this relationship. The closeness. The ownership. His lips brushed hers. He was everything she never knew she needed. Best of all, he felt like home.

"Madi, will you marry me?"

Dying was so worth it. "A thousand times, yes. I can't think of anything I want more. Is tomorrow too soon?"

He laughed. "Whenever it happens, I think we need to settle into a lifestyle that isn't so…"

"Illegal?"

"I was thinking life-threatening and dangerous."

She rested her forehead against his. "I can't wait. Where should we live?"

Duke looked around. "Well, this house is an option."

"You read my letter?" She poked his chest.

He rubbed her back. "I had to make sure he wasn't going to tear you to pieces again. I already thought he'd killed you."

She let the silence linger, as she mustered her bravery for her next words. "Tell me what happened to Anna Grace."

He sighed, his hand tracing lazy circles on her back. "The reason I ran the roadblock was because I was trying to get her to a hospital for help. But whatever the poison was in her body took her too quickly. Her body was cremated, and the ashes were waiting for me at the embassy before we left Mali."

She hugged him tighter as if she could take the pain from his heart that way.

He cleared his throat. "But back to a home country. How about Austria?"

"Would that put us too close to the in-laws?" He hadn't talked about his family much, but she desperately wanted to live near loved ones, to be accepted and experience what a real family was like.

"It might, but I'm game for anywhere but Mali. We can still visit on occasion, but full-time isn't going to work for me anymore."

"I need one more visit to Mali to see Dr. Cavine and wrap up a few final things with the hospital, but I can practice medicine anywhere. Besides, I would love to meet your family. I think aside from marrying you, being with your family might be the best thing in the whole world."

"My family is going to love you."

Those were words she had wanted to hear for twenty-seven years. It was the best gift she'd ever received.

Chapter 30

Somewhere over Algeria, Chip had reached the end of his travel tolerance. Bamako's British embassy worked an overnight miracle to get him home today. And time could not go fast enough. This morning, newspapers across the world exploded with the story of the drug bust. Chip's picture and name remained confidential for the time being, but that timer would soon run out. And Chip feared his private life wouldn't be the same.

Frosted sliding doors separating the baggage claim from the atrium opened in front of him. A small crowd looked past him trying to catch a glimpse of their loved ones. He scanned the faces.

There.

To his right, Opa and Oma flagged him down. He burst into a big grin as he jogged the last few feet. Their arms wrapped around him and squeezed him hard. Oma smothered him with kisses, murmuring words he couldn't understand. The lump in his throat tightened with the free-flowing tears. Every day he'd imagined this moment.

Home. Opa wiped his wrinkle-lined cheeks. "Your Oma hasn't stopped crying since we received the call hours ago that you were alive and coming home. Welcome home, son."

"I've missed you both so much." Chip checked behind Opa. "Where's Pax? I thought he'd be here for proof that he's not an only child anymore."

Opa and Oma's smiles faded.

Oma tucked Chip's arm under hers and walked toward the exit. "We didn't tell him about your return yet. He's at home healing..."

"From?"

"Chip, this will come as no surprise, but your father has liver disease. He needed a transplant and Pax was a match, so he donated part of his liver," Oma said.

Chip's jaw dropped. Pax could barely sit still for an hour before he needed to move. The mention of bed rest made him break out in hives. To voluntarily do it for Father must have been an olive branch.

"How many months before he's fully healed?"

"Six," Oma said, blinking. Her tears returned. "He's such a brave boy. We brought him home from the hospital last week."

"What if Father's body rejects it?"

Opa sighed. "If this doesn't work, then your father is—well—he's not going to try again. He's still at the hospital recovering. So far, his body is accepting it."

It was so like Father to put his parents through that. Chip swallowed his response. Back from the dead for five minutes and he already was angry at Father. This wasn't what he wanted.

As they loaded into the car, Oma changed the subject. She talked nonstop for the hour's trip home to Emmental. The lush green hills contrasted with the sharp crags of the mountains. Snow and warmth in the same view.

Heaven on earth.

The car bumped along the drive, but it took too long. Chip jumped out before Opa stopped in front of the house. He sprinted to the front door. The breeze carried the aroma of freshly baked bread and stew. The aroma made him close his eyes for a split second.

"Pax might be asleep." Oma called after him.

He eased the door open and took the stairs two at a time. In the hall he zigzagged to miss the creaky spots. The door to his room was closed, but Pax's stood open a fraction. Chip pushed the door open wide. Pax sat in his bed hunched over his computer, wearing his glasses. He only wore them when he really needed to focus on something.

Chip grinned. It felt so good to see him again. "I hear you're poorly, mate."

Pax's head shot up. He stared with his mouth hanging open. "Opa. Oma. Can someone come to my room for a moment, please? Quickly."

A laugh threatened to escape Chip's mouth, but he suppressed it. Pax hated being laughed at. Oma and Opa both walked in a few seconds later. Chip moved toward the window so Oma could sit on the edge of the bed.

But Pax didn't take his eyes off Chip. "Do you see him this time? Or is it another hallucination?"

Opa smiled. "He's real. He's home to stay."

Oma hiccuped as the tears started again in earnest.

The moment a huge smile spread across Pax's face Chip grabbed him in a gentle hug. "I missed you so much, man."

When Pax released Chip, he chucked his glasses on to the quilt and wiped his cheeks. "You guys didn't tell me? I'm not that weak. I should have gone with you to get him."

Oma patted Pax's hand. "You're terrible at bed rest, love. The doctor barely let you come home from the hospital because you wore them out. We thought it best Chip see you here."

Pax turned to Chip. "How did you survive that?"

Adrienna's smile flashed through his mind. "An angel of sorts, but you're not going to believe me."

The hospital stank of bleach and burnt toast. Opa drove Chip to see Father but settled into a corner of the cafe to wait. Voices mixed with rattling carts and beeping machines created a chaotic level of noise. Nothing like the Karim's medical center. Sleep evaded him last night as he played through the scenarios of today.

In truth, he didn't do this for Father. He did this for himself. It was time to be rid of his chains.

Inside Father's room, flowers decorated the window sill behind the bed. Good thing Father couldn't see them. He hated flowers. They reminded him of funerals. Particularly Mum's. Chip took a fortifying breath and stepped inside.

Father lay motionless, pale and aged ten years since Chip saw him months ago. Tubes and cords crisscrossed to their linked machines like electrical wires under a dashboard. Chip was a grown man, but he still double-checked that Father wasn't able to move. Once long ago, Father's seeming frailty had lured Chip close enough to get knocked over by a strong backhand to the face. Chip never made that mistake again.

As soon as Chip's bum met the chair, Father's green eyes flicked open and searched the room.

Like a crocodile. Maybe he shouldn't have come. So many things could go wrong. Father's expression didn't change when his gaze landed on Chip.

After a few moments, Chip broke the silence. "Opa said your body is accepting the new liver so far."

Father blinked.

No response. A knot of annoyance twisted in his chest, but he pushed it aside. That was the old Chip.

"How long have you known about the liver disease?"

"For four months."

No wonder Father didn't show up at graduation.

"That was kind of Pax to be your donor." Especially considering the depth of loathing that Father inspired in them.

"Should've let me die." Father's rasp was soft but firm.

"That's the easy way out. Pax offered you a second chance at life, something you'd never ask for yourself." Heck, Father didn't even want the first chance. "You should grab it with both hands and never look back."

Father looked tired and vulnerable. "Is that why you came back from the dead? To tell me I should make good use of a second chance?"

Sadness barreled into him with the force of a high-speed train. Chip pinched the bridge of his nose. His promise to Adrienna was never far from his thoughts.

"I came here to tell you that I forgive you. I wasted loads of time and energy wishing you loved me and then hating you for what you did to me, to us. But I'm not letting that weight crush me anymore. This is my second chance, too, and I'm not going to waste it waiting on people to complete me."

Father said nothing.

That was his cue. He blew out a breath and strode to the door. Liver disease hadn't changed Father's ability to end a conversation whenever he didn't like it.

"I have regrets, too." Father's voice shook slightly, a weakness he'd never allowed before.

Chip glanced over his shoulder with a small smile and nodded. Mangled relationships didn't heal overnight. And Father's admission wasn't much of a bridge, but it was a start.

Months later, Chip wiped his palms on his trousers for the ninth time in two minutes. This was a long time coming. He dreaded this meeting to the bottom of his soul, but it was important. His therapist called the trip "learning to let go of the past in order to embrace the future." In a word, closure which was vital for healing.

He shifted the box in his hands to knock on the door. These London flats were in a decent area of town which set his mind at ease. He shook out the nerves and knocked.

Muffled voices spoke behind the door and then it opened.

"Leila?" Chip asked to the dark face that peered through the crack.

"Yes? Who are you?"

"Chip Chapman. I knew—"

"Who is it, Mama?" The door swung wider.

Frozen in place, Chip gaped. Chills rippled through his body. No way.

There in the doorway stood Nafy.

Alive.

Relief weakened his legs. The box fell from his hands as he grabbed Nafy into a hug, touching his back and face in disbelief. Nafy giggled and hugged Chip back. Not in a thousand years had he expected this. Tears blurred Chip's vision and they wouldn't blink away.

"You're dead. Dr. Thomas told me you're dead. You were shot. I saw the blood and they came back without you." Chip sniffed and swiped at his cheeks. This was his dream come true. "Nafy, I'm so sorry that happened."

Leila grinned. "Would you like to come in, Mr. Chapman?"

He was making a scene in the hall, but he didn't care. Chip retrieved the box and stepped inside. The apartment was sparsely furnished but warm and overlooking a small park. Chip sat on a wooden chair across from the couch where Nafy sat.

"Cheep, the roads and buildings are just as you said. I listened and understood. When I woke up, Dr. Thomas asked where Mama and I wanted to live. I knew I wanted to see where you described." Nafy tapped his head, proud to have remembered. "It is so big. We never see all of the places. That is how big London is."

"Dr. Thomas sent you here?"

Leila brought him a cup of tea. He thanked her and smirked into his mug. They were already remarkably well adjusted.

"Dr. Thomas paid for us to come to England as refugees. Then his friends help Nafy go to school— a real school, teach us English every day, and gave me a job at an office," Leila said.

He hadn't seen that one coming. Dr. Thomas was a decent fellow after all. Sabine gave Nafy's mum's address to him as an under-the-table favor. He never expected her to be in London and certainly not funded by Dr. Thomas.

Chip handed the box to Nafy. "I was going to give these to you, Leila, but Nafy might want them instead."

Nafy tossed off the lid and gasped. His sparkly shoes glittered in the early afternoon light. They fell from his lap as he launched into Chip's arms. Leila covered her mouth as the tears streamed down her cheeks.

Chip cleared his throat. "They won't fit you anymore since you've grown so much since I last saw you."

They laughed through the tears. Nafy knelt in front of Leila and offered her the box of shoes.

She kissed his cheeks. "My sweet boy."

"Nafy-mate, I need to tell you something else that is going to make you upset." Nafy's trusting brown eyes propelled him onward. "The man who ran the school was the man who killed your father and sisters and brothers. You should know he was caught and is in prison, paying for what he did."

Leila reached for Nafy's hand as his happiness faltered. Anger crossed his features before he settled into a smile that didn't reach his eyes.

Nafy lifted his chin. "We live here now with big roads and schools. We are happy, right Mama?"

Leila nodded, her pride for her son undeniable. "A new life in a new world."

An hour later Chip left their apartment with promises to visit again soon. For the first time in his life he was truly and completely free, his heart the lightest it'd ever been. Never had he imagined that the pain, abuse, and heartache would lead him here.

His path to freedom started on the wings of an avalanche.

Sign Up for C.D. Gill's Newsletter!

Get new release updates and event alerts delivered right to your inbox so you don't miss one! www.cdgill.com

---

Review ☆☆☆☆☆

If you enjoyed this book, would you leave a review on your favorite retailer site?

You can find me on:
Facebook: www.facebook.com/cdgillauthor
Twitter: www.twitter.com/cd_gill
Website: www.cdgill.com

More from C.D. Gill

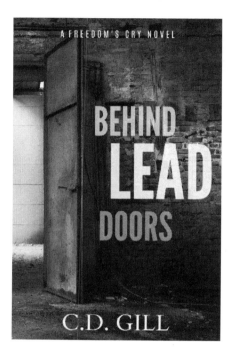

Twenty-one-year-old Taddeo Pravo joins the Freedom Fighters and volunteers to go undercover inside Italy's most prominent human trafficking ring to bring the ring's leaders to justice. His urgency escalates exponentially when he discovers his seventeen-year-old sister Fiamma held captive, waiting to be sold into prostitution. Although frantic to free her before she disappears forever, he can't compromise the mission. His dilemma: watch his sister be sold to the highest bidder to save hundreds, or put hundreds of women and children's lives on the line to save one.

Acknowledgments

Originally, I wrote this story in 2013. Since then, it's taken many different forms and been seen by more people than can remember they saw it. Of course, I don't remember everyone who has seen it either, but I owe massive thanks to many who I will mention here.

Throughout the writing of the story, I leaned heavily on my pilot husband for all things aircraft-related and on my father-in-law, Peter Gill and twin Cindy McVey for medical instruction. These three tolerated ridiculous questions and often laughed at the unlikely scenarios I had imagined. Thank you from the bottom of my heart for always being so accessible for my random inquiries and taking the time to explain things I didn't understand and likely still don't.

To my early and final beta readers—authors: Shenandoah Valley Critique Group, Regina Rushing, Connie Kuykendall, Brandy Heineman, Sherri Wilson Johnson and family: Dave Griffith, Isla Gill, Joan White, Charla Sindelar, and Cindy McVey. Your insights, encouragement, and friendship put steel in my resolve to see this through even when the process was painful. To you, I'm indebted.

A huge thank you to my editor Sally Bradley for giving this story the boost it needed. You gave me the final assurance that this could and would be awesome.

Sherri—one of my masterminds, you are my go-to expert on publishing, formatting, and asking big things of God. Thanks for your constant encouragement, answering my questions, and showing this newbie the ropes. You are a true treasure.

Brandy, my writing partner-in-crime, you have been walking through this wild journey with me since we carpooled as complete strangers. The workday chats, deserted house explorations, B1G1 wisdom, late-night joke sessions, passage approval, and hours of brainstorming with you have enriched me and my writing one hundred-fold. I couldn't have done this without you. Your friendship is such a gift.

To the rest of my family and friends who have encouraged me along the way, thank you isn't sufficient. Your support has meant so much to me.

From the day I announced I wanted to start writing fiction to now, my husband Matt has encouraged chasing this crazy dream. His real-life events inspired parts of both Madison and Chip's stories. Because of him, this book came into publication. He celebrated and cheered me on my way with each new step towards my goals. Thanks, babe, for always adventuring with me, introducing me to Africa, and for quitting your job so I could finish this book—that's true commitment. (wink) I thank God for you every day.

And to you, the reader, thank you for picking up this book and spending your valuable time with Madison and Chip. I hope this story has touched you in some way and taught you more about a world you didn't know. I sure learned a lot by writing it!

Hope you chase another adventure with me soon!

C.D. Gill

Made in the USA
Columbia, SC
12 February 2018